REVENGE
ON THE FLY

MICHAEL CAVENDER

This book is a work of fiction. Characters, incidents and dialogue are not real, and any resemblance to actual events or persons, living or dead, is coincidental.

To Paulette,

My first reader and editor,

And most importantly,

My dearest love.

CHAPTER 1

The Soque River's cold water made Ben's muscles ache as never before, and his knees felt like they were packed in sand. He didn't know when he would finally fall, humiliated.

The dry September air brushed his cheek as he forced himself to smile. He watched the faulty execution and wondered if any of his repeated instructions had penetrated the man's bald head. "Always know your surroundings and be aware of every obstacle that could interfere with zapping your target."

"They never listen," Ben hissed as he watched the Atlanta banker Wiley Blount snag another dry Adams on an overhanging rhododendron branch.

Ben's cell phone vibrated beneath his frayed vest stuffed with fly boxes, leaders, floatant, nippers, clippers and forceps. He reached for it, welcoming a distraction that might be an editor offering good money for a real fishing story. The name "Phelps, Inc." glowed on the display screen. An older brother he had shunned for forty years owned a company by that name. Their last conversation had ended badly.

The middle of a stream was no place for a discreet phone conversation because Blount might reward any lack of attention with a miserly tip. Ben let the phone vibrate unanswered and wondered why one of the richest real estate developers in the South wanted to talk to him. After all, Watt and their sister Reggie got their parents' money.

"That's okay, I got it," Ben said as he began slogging through the hip-deep stream.

Carefully wading over mossy rocks to the fly piercing the leaf, Ben berated himself for never making enough money to have any left over to save, knowing it could have been different.

He squinted through his reading glasses to extract the tiny dry fly, then let it drop to the stream. "Okay, try again," Ben said. "Look where you're gonna back cast. Remember I'm here." He mumbled to himself, "Hook me in the nose and I'll sue your ass."

Ben had accepted this assignment to write about Walton Lodge for *Garden & Gun* magazine. The luxury fly-fishing resort eagerly agreed to host the group if Ben helped guide. He reckoned the lodge owners and their guests had an inflated sense of themselves because the magazine appealed to affluent readers and high-end advertisers. The magazine paid just enough for him to overlook having to guide as well.

A fresh breeze snatched a few leaves from early-turning dogwoods and scattered them across the stream where they skimmed the surface like primitive purple sailboats. He'll catch at least one of them, Ben thought.

Blount began to cast but didn't give the line enough time to bend the rod back before pushing it forward. The line lost energy and collapsed next to Blount and began drifting downstream. Ben knew the man was a spin caster who found the transition to a fly rod unnatural.

"Bait chucker," Ben muttered, as he smiled and nodded.

He watched Blount flail the rod wildly, trying to get the fly line airborne. By luck, a cast finally shot forward and placed the small Adams at the edge of an over-hanging rock. A small ruffling of the water's surface was the only indication a trout had sipped in the fly. The line tightened and the rod quivered as it bent into a broad arc.

"Fish on," Ben said as the banker began moving backward. "Just a little tension. Keep the rod tip up."

Blount jerked the rod back. The line went slack and began drifting downstream. A large rainbow trout shot out of the water and shook its head violently as it tried to dislodge the tiny hook from its mouth. It crashed to the surface, made another leap and disappeared.

"Nice try," Ben said walking toward the man reeling in the limp line. "Seemed like a good size." He resisted the urge to grab the rod and give the client one last lesson in fly casting. He knew some guides liked to humiliate their clients, but that behavior only discouraged tips. "Keep at it. You'll get the hang of it," Ben said.

"Orvis has a new graphite rod. Really light, but strong," Blount said as he held out his handmade bamboo rod and flexed it back and forth. "That might get me a better presentation, right?" A half-smoked cigar wagged in his mouth.

The man's new Gore-Tex waders showed no trace of scum, dirt or algae. A starched Ex-Officio shirt was covered by his spotless Patagonia fishing vest. Ben calculated the man had easily spent thousands of dollars on his equipment and clothing, all to catch a fish he would toss back after the trophy photo. Ben was having an increasingly hard time taking this business seriously.

The purchase would help the economy of Vermont where Orvis was headquartered and certainly wouldn't threaten the trout, Ben thought. "Could help," he said. "Couldn't hurt."

Ben looked at the sun overhead. "Close to noon," he said. "Time to pack it in." He took the rod and finished reeling in the line and leader. "Just remember to work less and fish more," he said. "Then you'll really terrorize the trout. You're getting better."

How he would write the article baffled him. The previous night, Ben had begun his story in a way he knew an editor would slash and trash:

Walton Lodge, modeled in an elegant Craftsman style and furnished with new Stickley furnishings, knows how to nourish the myth of the gentleman angler.

They have restructured their stretch of Georgia's Soque River to encourage the most inept fisherman's delusion he's smarter than a pea-brained trout. Overhanging trees and shrubbery have been trimmed back to lessen the chance a careless caster will snag an intrusive branch. Thoughtfully placed rocks and boulders create falls, pools and riffles creating comfortable holding stations for the bloated trout overfed by concealed feeders dispensing food pellets at sunset. Disney couldn't have fabricated a better wilderness experience.

After a rugged day fighting behemoth browns, the anglers relax at linen-covered tables brimming with fine wines and gourmet meals described in menus hand written in French and English.

Over late-night cognac, the angling bankers regale each other with tales of women they hope their wives never discover or, even dearer to their hearts, exploits of packaging mortgages and credit-card debt into complex securities they sell around the world. *"I want to be long gone when they wise up,"* one banker said as he sniffed his Courvoisier.

The cathartic words disappeared after he had punched the delete key.

On the way back to the lodge, Blount bragged about his upcoming fishing trip to Patagonia. "There are more huge trout than you can imagine," he said, with the certainty of a well-read armchair sportsman. Ben said his good-byes at the lodge and accepted a modest tip. They have all the money and they're still so cheap, Ben groused.

Returning to his cabin to pack, Ben retrieved the message on his phone. Hearing a ghost almost made him stumble.

"Hey, little brother, I bet ya never thought you'd hear this voice again. It's me, Watt." A silence followed in which Ben plunged back decades to the last time he had heard his brother's voice. "I guess you're out with some babe, or on a fishing trip. Anyway, I need to talk to you pronto. It's about money, a lot of money that could be yours if you call me." Another pause, then the final words, "If you never want to have to work again, call me at this number."

Ben almost reached for a pen before he realized the number was recorded, along with the promise of money.

He could have accepted the possibility of a lot of things happening that day, but hearing from his brother wasn't one of them. Fifteen years ago, Ben received a token payment from his parents' estate. He felt cheated, and lately wondered if he hadn't cheated himself. Living without a family had taken years of adjustment. Ben worked hard at forgetting through various mixtures of cheap booze and lust masquerading as love. And now, because of words recorded in a cell phone, all that effort was shattered by a voice that was as fresh and familiar as if they had seen each other last night.

Why in hell would Watt be calling now, Ben wondered. Their parents' estate had been settled long ago, so nothing should be coming from that. What big pile of money was Watt talking about? Ben didn't have anything Watt wanted. He didn't even have much of anything *he* wanted. His studio apartment in Atlanta contained plenty of fly-fishing gear, a computer, thrift-store furniture and cheap clothes — a paltry legacy for years of work. He did have abundant independence. That's how he described his world, where only editors made occasional demands on his time. But the words "a lot of money" and "never have to work again" seized his attention.

Suppressing his curiosity, he decided to let Watt stew a while, and headed for the shower. He squinted at his reflection in the bathroom mirror. Everything was slightly out of focus without his reading glasses, but not enough to hide his thinning hair and a belly that demanded ever more sit-ups to defy gravity and beer. The top half of his face was pallid compared to the deeply tanned bottom half. Always wearing a ball cap and sunglasses outside made his face look as if it lived in two different worlds. Given the neglect and abuse, Ben decided that he didn't look as bad as many of his fellow beer-guzzling outdoor writers. Curious about how Watt had held up, he hoped the years had taken an especially gruesome toll, that gravity had been severe and unrelenting.

Hot water filled the shower with steam as Ben lathered his face. He swiped one side, then the other. As he dragged the razor along his upper lip, he realized his shaving sequence was out of order. He always moved methodically from his right side, to the middle, and finally shaved the left side of his face. He finished up, worried about forgetting his shaving pattern, as if he were an old man tottering on the brink of dementia. Lately, he noticed he could walk into a room and briefly forget why he was standing there. He usually remembered, but worried about what else was escaping his mind like dandelion seeds lifting in a light breeze. Letting the hot water pummel his scalp, he closed his eyes.

He remembered that night in Charlottesville when he last saw his older brother. Ben had been studying in his dorm room at the University of Virginia when someone knocked at his door. Watt filled the doorway with his mammoth body, the one that had smashed so many runners when he was an All-American defensive end at the University of Tennessee. Runners rarely scored a touchdown charging in his direction. A decade off the field hadn't softened Watt's appearance. A smug grin, filled with expensive dental work, spread across Watt's face.

"What's up little brother?" he said, ambling into the small room.

"Is something wrong at home?" Ben said.

"I love to see that puzzled look on your cute face," Watt said as he flopped on the bed. "You look like someone just said you sired a bastard."

Ben stood awkwardly. "What are you doing here?"

"It's your fiancée," Watt said. "She's flown the coop."

Ben had shocked his parents a few weeks earlier by telling them he had proposed to Maggie, a nurse at the medical college, and she had said yes. They went into extreme protective mode, warning their son she only wanted to get her claws into their family money. His father said, "If it's just the sex, you can have that without marrying her. She's not pregnant, is she?" His mother said, "There are so many fine girls out there. Please give yourself time to find someone really special."

"For ten thousand dollars and a good job in some L.A. hospital, she dumped you like a bad habit," Watt said, shaking his head. "We thought she'd put up a fight, but being an older woman, she knows a good deal when she sees it." He added she was warned that refusing the family offer would have serious consequences for her career. Phelps family connections were marshaled to make the arrangements.

"She left so fast she didn't even turn out the lights," Watt said.

"You're a goddamn liar," Ben said and quickly dialed her phone number. Her roommate, after some stammering, confirmed Maggie had suddenly quit her job and headed west.

"She got a really good offer," she said.

Ben threw the phone and stormed from the room, with Watt yelling after him to come back. Ben remembered entering a bar in downtown Charlottesville on a mission of drunken oblivion. That worked until he woke up on a Trailways bus somewhere in Ohio with a ticket for Los Angeles and a fifth of Early Times. He smelled of damp cigarettes and stale beer, and felt as if his head had bounced along behind the bus for most of the trip. That was the last time he saw Watt. Now, forty years later money was being offered again, this time to him.

The shower began turning cold. Ben got out and dried off, thinking about the money Watt mentioned. There weren't retirement plans for freelance writers. He didn't have any children he was aware of to care for him in his golden years. Writing assignments were getting harder to land because younger writers with a looser style and social networking skills were gaining popularity with readers and advertisers. Of course, Ben knew he was working in a dying business where too many magazines had gone belly-up as advertisers stampeded to cable TV and cyberspace. Attempts to work in front of a camera never panned out. He couldn't overcome his apprehension as the lens stared at him, as if it discerned his darkest thoughts.

Ben replayed the message and saved the number.

CHAPTER 2

Ben stared at his phone for a long time. His finger hovered above the buttons as he remembered when his parents died. A bank trust officer who said he had Watt's help, tracked him and sent a letter enclosed with a ten thousand dollar check. The man said Ben's parents believed Watt, Reggie and several charities would better appreciate their wealth, which was in the vague millions. "They were deeply hurt you never contacted them," he wrote. Ben thought the sympathy was misplaced.

A lawyer had advised Ben that he could always challenge the will, but success was unlikely unless he could prove his parents were crazy. Mean and cruel, Ben said, but probably not crazy. Now, suddenly, money was perhaps coming his way from . . . where? What scheme did his brother have in mind? Ben thought about the tease and decided there wasn't much to lose by taking the bait. He punched "reply" on his phone and listened to the ringing, wondering what this call across the distant past was going to cost.

A few rings were answered by a voice Ben didn't recognize. He asked for Watt and was told to wait. In a moment his brother answered.

"You told me to call," Ben said and regretted not saying something with edgy wit.

"Hey, Ben," Watt bellowed. "I wasn't sure I'd get through to you. Could have been out of pocket on some fishing story, right?"

Ben let the silence settle between them.

"Listen, too much time's gone by. I have some good news. At least you should think it's good news. I know the folks didn't treat you right, but I think I can make it up to you. Some compensation. You still there? Talk to me, little brother."

"Why don't you just tell me why you called," Ben finally said. "You said something about a lot of money. Tell me about that." He heard Watt slowly exhale.

"Not much for the niceties, huh? I can appreciate that. To the point, then. Some stuff needs to be settled that never was dealt with when the folks died. A careless mistake, really. But the result is that you could be due some money. In the millions. I need you to come up to Mossback. That's where I am now. Reggie's here, too. She really wants to see you. We have a lawyer on standby who can be here quickly, get papers signed and a check in your hand in a couple of days. Am I getting your prick hard yet?"

"Tell me about the money," Ben said.

"It's a little too complicated to go into on the phone. Just that you have a share of something nobody was really aware of until recently. Once you were poor. Now you're rich, sort of. You've got your life. I'm not trying to drag you back into anything. This ain't any family reunion with lots of tears and hugs unless you want it that way. Just some business. But I'd sure like to see you again. No sense dying strangers, huh?"

What did he mean by the dying strangers remark? Ben wondered. Was Watt sick and this was some grand departing gesture to make amends? "This isn't some perverse trick?" Ben said. "The last time didn't turn out so well for me."

"You were the one . . ." Watt hesitated, and then said, "Nothing sinister, I promise. You don't even have to shake hands when we meet. Just come up and get what should have been yours a long time ago. No tricks or bullshit. My word."

The promises were wasted, but Ben was curious. The chance to see what had become of Watt and his sister Reggie tugged at him. And the money grabbed his attention. Ben asked for directions to his parents' summer home in the Blue Ridge Mountains. "I haven't been there since I was twelve," Ben explained when Watt said he surely remembered Mossback. "I wasn't driving then." He hadn't thought about Mossback for years, but it was one place in his past that didn't make him grind his teeth when he recalled it.

He scribbled some directions to Kelsey, North Carolina, in his notebook, then remembered he had a G.P.S., and said, "I've got to see if I can rearrange my schedule so I can come this weekend. I'll call you if there's a snag." He enjoyed the idea of Watt waiting impatiently.

Ben made instant coffee, and was puzzled why there could be anything in his parents' estate that might involve him. Fifteen years should have been plenty of time for any executor to discover loose ends, especially very valuable ones. Watt must be in some kind of a bind to call me now, Ben thought, intrigued by what it could be.

As he sipped the weak coffee, he wished he hadn't quit smoking. He leaned back in a chair and watched dusty sunbeams piercing the window blinds. Propping his feet on the kitchen table, Ben recalled fragments of the years: making a new life where his talents, luck and cunning were the only tools he had; discovering that an over-sexed drinking buddy didn't make a good wife;

and learning things he never imagined when he sat in American history classes.

Whatever else happened, he knew Watt would quiz him about his life, and the answers would be trifling compared to the accomplishments of the Phelps brother with the Midas touch. Nothing demanded Ben explain his life. He certainly hadn't lived it to impress anyone, especially his brother. It wasn't remarkable, but it wasn't something to be ashamed of, either. Only one part he remembered with lingering discomfort.

No amount of mental exertion could reconstruct why a drunken bus trip to Los Angeles ended off course in West Yellowstone, Wyoming. That memory was drowned forever. Only fragments existed of that arrival: wandering in an alley among garbage cans and feral cats, hearing something about Martin Luther King being killed, sitting in a bar watching on TV as enraged people burned his home town Memphis in revenge.

"Now there's people who know how to throw a barbeque," someone yelled to cheers.

The next clear memory he had was being in a jail cell, told he was charged with stealing a car and driving it into the Madison River. The judge said Ben was lucky it hadn't happened in Yellowstone Park, because he would be facing federal charges. The old man in black robes was surprised when Ben declined volunteering for the army so he could avoid jail and a record.

"You're not some commie sympathizer?" the judge said. Ben shook his head.

He had watched the news about Vietnam and chose six months in the county jail rather than volunteer to face angry Asians who certainly wanted to kill him. He paid for the court costs and damages to the car with what was left of his college money. Robert Kennedy was murdered while Ben served his time. When he was allowed to watch television, he saw a country at war with itself in flaming riots, student revolts and rampant black power. Ben felt safe in his concrete and steel home among the other petty criminals.

"Women's nothing more than money-grubbing whores," his cellmate Marvin said when Ben confided part of the reason for his drunken exodus from Virginia. "Don't trust nobody who can steal something from you." Ben nodded in agreement.

During those weeks, Ben often stared at the cell's bars and wondered how this could be explained to his parents. He looked at his shaved head and numbered denim shirt and tried to recognize the stranger inside the wrinkled uniform.

Some of the inmates laughed at Ben's driving a car into the Madison River. "Stupid college kid trying to herd buffalo with a Chevy. Shoulda used a Ford 250 with mud grips. Good thing you didn't drown anyone."

Although he had a vaporous memory of someone in the car with him, Ben was the only person the police arrested. He never mentioned another person because he was unsure. In his dim cell he imagined a body floating unnoticed down the Madison. He also imagined the disappointment in his mother's eyes and a father turning away in disgust. His shame grew like a tumor he couldn't excise even when he reminded himself who had initiated Watt's treachery in Charlottesville.

"Is it hard changing your name?" Ben asked Marvin one night. "You know, start fresh when you get out?"

"Done all the time," Marvin said. "Most people don't check that stuff too close. If they do, just move on. It's no big crime."

He liked the idea of walking out of jail and abandoning Ben Phelps, the jilted criminal. A lot of names were tried on and discarded. He thought about the men he admired who were murdered that summer.

"Ask for Bobby King, if you look for me," Ben told his cellmate one day. Anyone from before his incarceration could trace Ben to the county jail, but they wouldn't find the man who walked out after six months.

He remembered leaving the West Yellowstone jail not knowing what he would do the next minute, much less the next week, month, year or the rest of his life. With the few dollars he had left, he got the cheapest motel room he could find and began exploring the main road, looking at the windows for help-wanted notices and hoping a desperate employer wouldn't be too particular about his recent whereabouts.

After a few days of wandering and being rejected for menial jobs, he ducked into the newspaper office to get a free look at the classified section. He saw a notice on a bulletin board for a reporter: "someone who can write, show up on time, meet deadlines, and stay sober on the job." I can do most of that, he decided. He was hired that day by a boozy sports editor and started covering local sports. Soon he started writing a regular column about fly fishing on the best rivers in the West. Assignments from national magazines eventually followed, and Ben got enough work to quit the paper and make a modest living as a freelance writer. Years later, when he learned of his parents' death, he took back his given name because the demons haunting him were gone.

Compared to his brother, Ben felt he'd lived a lot but accomplished little. He remembered Watt once adorned the cover of *Time* magazine as the real estate developer reshaping the South. Mention the name Watt Phelps and people were envious of his wealth, political connections and wives, not always in that order.

His fame and business celebrity were just behind Ted Turner's, the article claimed.

Ben resisted a creeping inferiority complex because, he insisted to himself, there was nothing wrong with being a freelance writer. Few people he knew could survive writing about fly fishing. You had to be able to tell essentially the same story in a hundred different ways. Lately, though, Ben worried his writing was getting stale. How many ways could you describe the weather, the geography, the accommodations, the guides, the gear, the river, the fish, the casts, the strikes and misses? All the parts were essentially the same, just in different orders and locations.

The trout were either at the head of a pool or at the tail of the pool, unless they were in the middle of it. They were in a riffle or below a riffle. They were in the flats or in a run. They were rising or resting, sipping dries, spinners, or emergers. They were full or hungry. They were biting or they were down. The moon was full, or it was new, or it was blue. Some of the above, or none of the above.

He found he could take note of the weather, time of day, time of year and write just about anything he wanted because if it sounded true, it could have been true. The stories became as predictable as the photo of a grinning angler holding a trout on the cover of a fishing magazine. Only the locations changed. And nobody seemed to care or notice. All he had to do was remember that some poor guy in a hermetically sealed office wanted to experience what Ben was doing.

But lately, Ben dreaded he was going to end up an old man repeating stories in a cheap saloon out West near a trout stream where the office class came to have real experiences. He could tell them stories about how it was in the old days, and they would buy him beers and listen for a while. He was beginning to worry about that old man.

He had not seen his family in more than forty years, and even more time had passed since he was at their summer place. His recollection of Kelsey allowed a few clear glimpses: a shooting gallery on a side street where he fired his first rifle, an open air grocery market, antique stores with the smell of lemon and brass polish, a movie theater with hard seats and sticky floors, a soda fountain where he lingered over brown cows. The town was just a village with a few streets and trees lining the sidewalks.

A vision of hewn logs and the sensation of wet wool stirred his memory of the mountain house they called Mossback. It was rambling place full of whimsical spaces, unlike their formal Georgian house in Memphis. The log home had a kitchen with open pine shelves stacked with jars, cans, and white plates, bowls and mugs. A cast-iron cook stove with white porcelain sides stood to one side of the room and chased morning chills. He hadn't thought about that stove in a long time and wondered if it still warmed the kitchen, and if mice still dashed along the baseboards to hidden sanctuaries.

Ben remembered a vast, forbidding forest surrounding the log home — a shadowy place, broken occasionally by flickering sunlight. In all the years he traveled doing fishing stories, the closest he had come to Kelsey was the time he fished in the Great Smoky Mountains Park for native brook trout. He'd thought about making a side trip to see Mossback, but he wasn't sure it was still in the family. The few pleasant memories weren't strong enough to draw him back, anyway.

He drove his van east of Helen, Georgia, then connected with the newly expanded four-lane Highway 441 that funneled tourists and second-home owners north to their escapes in the ancient mountains of North Carolina. The traffic was heavy with fall leaf-lookers.

Ben groaned as the traffic edged forward slightly, then stopped for no visible reason. An angry horn blaring behind jolted Ben to the present, and he caught up with the traffic now moving at a faster pace. There was nothing he could do or say that was going to relieve his anxiety except meditate on the money Watt said would be enough to retire on.

As he gazed absently at the back of a dusty U-Haul truck a few yards ahead, an image seeped into his mind of a young Reggie, radiant in the bright summer sun. The sunlight reflected off her white tennis dress that shimmered against her summer tan. Streaks of pale yellow highlighted her shoulder-length hair, pulled tightly in a ponytail that whipped around with her slashing strokes. She dashed and slid across the court, the wooden racquet an obedient extension of her sinewy arm. Sweat dampened her thin cotton dress. Her green eyes were hooded by thick dark brows that shaded her raptor's glare. She was small, explosive, and not more than a teenager, hardly old enough to drive legally.

The memory of his little sister made him relax his death grip on the steering wheel. Everyone said she could easily get a scholarship to any college that wanted a winning tennis team. He wondered if she had fulfilled everyone's expectations, or had she simply gone to college, joined a sorority, got married, had children and joined the Junior League? Did she miss him? She probably had when he disappeared, but she was very tough and certainly had gone on with her life.

A double trailer truck roaring past Ben pushed air against his van and jolted him from his reverie. The clogged highway traffic thinned a little as travelers gradually veered away toward their destinations. The highway rose to an overlook, from which Ben could see an umber haze over Atlanta's horizon. To the north, fat lazy clouds snagged on the highest mountaintops, reflecting yellow light from the afternoon sun. The van's engine struggled as he drove higher into the Blue Ridge Mountains toward Mossback

CHAPTER 3

Rounding a curve, Ben saw what had always signaled the final approach into Kelsey, a small waterfall spraying across the road chiseled into the cliff wall. A short bypass now spanned the stream below the falls so traffic avoided the cramped cutout road.

He remembered fighting Watt and Reggie to thrust his sweaty fingers from the station wagon window to catch the cool spray sparkling across the outside lane. Now families gathered on foot to photograph each other on the unused roadbed beneath the water cascading like a bridal veil. Sadness seeped through him as he saw billboards and signs promising golfing among the eagles, world-class spas, utterly unique shopping and tranquility.

As the traffic moved faster beyond the waterfall, Ben wondered what else had changed since his childhood vacations. His parents had packed him off to boarding school after his last summer in Kelsey when he was twelve. He never saw Mossback again, and he didn't know if his family ever returned. Ben struggled to recapture some defining memory, but only incomplete images teased his effort. He realized things changed over time, but he had never lived in one place long enough to experience the emotions change provoked. He rarely returned to familiar places because his readers wanted new adventures, not recycled ones. As he approached the town, he resigned himself to disappointment. Better to expect the worst, he decided, despite a small part of him wanting to believe a sweet fragment from his past would emerge.

Ben knew he was near high civilization when he drove past the Whiteside Country Club. A tall, closely clipped hemlock hedge isolated the clubhouse from public scrutiny. On the other side of the road, fairways and large homes bordered a lake where white swans glided across the water. He saw golfers putting on one green near the road while caddies in white shirts and trousers quietly held bulging golf bags.

Watt's directions were to drive through town and follow the old road to Mossback. Ben hadn't asked for clarification because he didn't want to appear dependent. Now, as he gazed down the main street, he couldn't find the road. Kelsey wasn't the small village he remembered. He wondered if he had changed as much as the town had. Traffic moved slowly as drivers searched for parking places or at least brake lights signaling the possibility that someone might be backing out from a parking space.

Shops selling anything from art to toys, from fine cashmere to hiking gear, from antiques to collectibles, from books to bagels lined the streets. People wandered in and out of the open doors, while others stood before the window display and pressed their noses to see if entering was worth their effort. Weary children tugged and cried.

Ben heard bits of amplified bluegrass drifting over the slowly moving cars. As he watched the traffic and looked at the parked cars, he realized that only in Aspen had he ever seen so many expensive automobiles in one place. BMWs, Mercedes-Benzs, Range Rovers, Infinities, Cadillacs and a couple of Bentleys dominated the streets. He felt righteous in his utilitarian old van.

Ben knew he would never find the way to Mossback. Directions were what he needed, and he decided the local newspaper would be the most logical place to start. After cruising a few streets, he saw a sign advertising "*The Kelsey Gazette:* The Pulse of Mountain Living." He could learn the way to Mossback, plus anything else he might want to know. Of course, a reporter could be just as curious about Ben and ask him why he wanted to know. He didn't want to explain that his family owned

Mossback, but he didn't have anything to do with the place now. He wanted to remain anonymous until he had a better understanding of what was happening. He felt certain if Watt were involved in anything local, it would incite controversy and passionate feelings. What developer didn't?

He found a place to park a few blocks away. Inside the newspaper office, a large woman sat behind the counter typing classified ads.

"Can I help you?" she said, as she continued to type without looking up.

"Some directions, if you don't mind," Ben said.

"Chamber of commerce's down the street on the right," she said, nodding in the general direction.

Ben leaned on the counter and waited for her to stop typing and look at him. He realized the wait could be very long.

"Is the editor here?" he said. He had conned more than one gatekeeper in his years of freelance writing. "I'm doing a story for *Sporting Life* and need some information."

She turned and smiled sweetly. "I'd be very happy to help you. No need to bother Mr. Holt." The mention of the outdoor sporting equivalent of *Town & Country* made her more attentive.

"The editor . . . Mr. Holt? . . . he'll do just fine," Ben said, as he smiled just as sweetly and watched her smile melt.

She mumbled into a telephone, and then said, "Mr. Holt will be here, just a minute." She returned to her computer screen.

The room reminded Ben of the newspaper in West Yellowstone where he first began working after getting out of jail. Stacks of special advertising supplements and unsold newspapers cluttered desks. Now computer screens, glowing with screen savers, replaced clacking typewriters. And he didn't smell the stale tobacco odor from overflowing ashtrays.

From the rear of the room a short, slight man walked through swinging doors, carefully letting the doors close behind him. His precisely brushed white hair just covered the collar of his blue shirt. A perfectly knotted bowtie bound the collar close to his wattled throat. He stood erect in his black tasseled loafers. Thick, red-framed glasses drew attention to his pale blue eyes. As he approached the counter, the woman jerked her head in Ben's direction and said, "Him."

"Yes, I'm Ralph Holt. You needed to see me about a story?" He held out a spotted hand with slender fingers. Ben felt his weak grip as they shook hands.

"Ben Phelps. Thanks for your help. I'm doing some research for a story on private fishing clubs. Who owns them, what's their lifestyle, how they spend their time here. I was hoping you might be able to guide me in the right direction. Local editors know everything, right?" Ben tilted his head, grinned and hoped his line flattered enough to get the old man talking. The elaborate ruse amused Ben.

Holt took off his glasses and used a white handkerchief to clean the lenses. Without them, his eyes looked tiny and receding.

"I'm not really a fisherman," he said, replacing his glasses and blinking rapidly to refocus his gaze upon Ben. "There are a few large places here, perhaps big enough for a good-sized stream. There is one private club on the Chattooga headwaters, and another on the Nantahala. Both very exclusive and expensive, I hear."

"Yes, I've heard of them," Ben said. "My editor wants the most spectacular. I heard about one place around here, supposed to be enormous, big enough to be a private club or preserve."

Holt frowned in thought while Ben leaned on the counter and waited, hoping the bait was sufficient.

"Oh, yes. You mean Mossback. The old Phelps place. But the owners are dead. Drove off a cliff or something. Anyway, the place has been closed up since then. It's really too bad because it's the grandest place I've ever heard of around here. Several thousand acres of virgin forest and a spectacular home made of chestnut logs. All tucked in a valley surrounded by high cliffs. It brings to mind the old Tarzan movies. Anyway, as I said, the place is all locked up. Funny, no one knows who owns it . . . some corporate registration. We haven't heard from the children. I believe there were some, but no one here's ever seen them since . . . well, I don't know when. A long time," he said, as he gazed out the window toward the street. "You said your name is Phelps? You'd be lucky to be part of that family."

Ben laughed, "I don't think I'm part of that family tree."

"No? Too bad. Anyway, a caretaker watches after the place. There'd be a story, I suppose. What will happen to such a grand place? I'm surprised some developer hasn't chopped it up already."

Don't be too sure a developer isn't doing that already, Ben thought.

"Nobody's got any permits or zoning requests for the place?" Ben said.

"Not that I know of. But, we usually wait for such things to come to us. I'd hate to reveal someone's business plans prematurely. We need to help each other, you know."

"I'd like to see this place," said Ben. "How do I find it?"

The old man drew him directions on the back of a news release. "But the gate is locked. You can't get in."

"Maybe I can find a way. Thanks for your time," Ben said as he walked out the doorway.

He wasn't in any hurry to face Watt, even if there was a lot of money at stake, and began strolling along the sidewalk like any other tourist. He tripped on a buckled sidewalk and almost stumbled into a woman pushing an empty stroller as her little girl walked beside her. As he recovered, he realized he had walked past his van into the middle of town.

While he tried to get his bearings, he noticed he was standing beside an old three-story clapboard building that dominated its end of the block. A dusty sign above the entrance said "Kelsey Inn," but no one was walking in or out of the decrepit building that appeared vacant. He peered through a dirty window and saw the structure was empty from the roof to the ground. The floors and interior walls were gone, and he could see dark roof rafters. He peered closer and saw a series of thick chains stretching from one side to the other and bolted through the walls, keeping them from buckling under the weight of the roof. A sign by the door explained that the owners were restoring the old inn so it would be ready for another century of hospitality.

As Ben gazed into the cavern of taut chains, his memory flickered on a dining room filled with people smiling at each other and speaking in soft, friendly voices. He remembered sitting in a straight wooden chair at a long table filled with platters of mashed potatoes, fried chicken, green beans and corn bread. He could almost smell the odors as he closed his eyes. He wondered if the recollection originated in this building. Sometimes, chasing childhood memories was like trying to catch a nighthawk.

Turning back toward his van, he saw three men coming out of a shop ahead. One man carried two large boxes with Orvis stamped on the outside, and under his arm was a long slender tube covered in dark green canvas. His two friends lugged bulging shopping bags.

"Now you have to catch a whole lotta fish," one of the men said through a cigar clenched in his teeth. " Your first one cost several hundred bucks, but the more you catch, the more you average your cost down. Someday your trout might be cheaper than the grocery store . . . if you ignore the cost of your fishing trips."

He laughed, slapped the newly outfitted fisherman on the back, and the trio swaggered down the sidewalk trailing gray-blue smoke.

Ben looked through the window of the fly-fishing shop the men had just left. He had been in dozens of similar shops, and after a while their differences seemed to fade. How many ways could you package the same fantasy? He thought about Watt waiting impatiently for Ben's arrival and decided to let him stew awhile.

A bell jingled as he opened the door. Several men huddled near a rack of fly rods on the far wall. One man poked through the display of trout flies. Another man helped his wife try on fishing vests and explained the purpose of each pocket. Behind the counter, near the entrance, sat a very fat man wearing a tight red flannel shirt. His moon-shaped face was bisected by a long, flowing handlebar moustache, and a ball cap with the shop's logo covered his head. He was putting the finishing touches on a streamer clamped in a vise attached to the counter. After he wrapped the thread a few last times and tied off the knot, he looked up and nodded at Ben, who nodded back.

"Your shop?" Ben asked.

"Mine and my banker's," he laughed, which caused his body to quiver.

"Hope he likes fishing," Ben said.

"He's a fanatic, thank God," he said. "And he owns the bank, so everyone's happy. Need any help?"

Ben looked around and said, "Just browsing."

The man loosened the vise, removed the streamer and clamped another hook into the vise. He wrapped a layer of fine black thread around the straight shank and began tying in feathers and chenille to make another streamer.

"You fish?" the man asked, as he built up layers on the hook without looking up.

Ben had engaged in hundreds of conversations in fly shops and they always followed the same pattern of question and answer. Establish the level of interest, then the level of skill, and the finer aspects such as stream, rod and fish preference. Then comes the display of one's particular knowledge. The nuances could take hours to explore, especially if nourished with beer. Ben had to decide how far he wanted to carry this budding relationship. If it ended by the man learning Ben was a fly-fishing writer, the man would never leave him alone. He knew some people regarded writers with undeserved reverence. Probably had something to do with combinations of envy of their imagined lives and the illusion of fame by association. Whatever the motivations, Ben decided this wasn't the best time for any complications. He reminded himself why he drove to Kelsey.

"Talk about it more than do it," Ben said, and it wasn't too far from the truth.

"Don't we all," the man said as he looked up and grinned beneath his moustache. "About everything. We've got anything you need," the man added, remembering why he sat behind the counter all day. "The best gear. And good guides if you want the best chance of catching something. They know spots most folks never see."

Despite his resolutions, Ben's curiosity prevailed. Patterns of familiar conversations were so easy to repeat.

"Who's your best guide? The one you'd spend your own money on?" he asked.

The fat man stopped tying his fly and twirled one end of his moustache and then the other as he regarded Ben.

"The best's not available very much, especially on short notice. Works a day job pretty regular. But we got plenty of sharp ones who could put you on some fish."

"How can some guy be the best if he fishes the least?" Ben asked, thumbing through a book about irresistible Appalachian fly patterns.

"Oh, he fishes a lot. Just not always for hire. But I can set you up with someone who really knows where the fish are and what they're hitting."

"Why is this guy so great if he doesn't guide that much?" Ben said.

The fat man resumed tying his streamer. "Grew up in the Eden of trout waters," he said, as he twisted a grizzly hackle feather about the increasingly thick streamer.

"A big area that nobody gets to fish, at least that they'll admit. Zeke has the run of the place 'cause he's the caretaker. Has been for years. He's seen wild brookies nobody else has, or ever will, I reckon. Big as your arm, I hear. Zeke don't talk about it much. Says he don't want to get poachers all lathered up and have to end up shooting 'em." He carefully tied off the feather and dabbed glue on the knot.

"Never heard of brookies that big in these mountains. Canada maybe," Ben said, as he put the book down and picked up another one. "You ever see one that big?" Ben began smelling a story possibility. He couldn't help himself, like a hungry trout chasing an emerging mayfly.

"Nope, but Zeke's not a bullshitter. He says something, you can pretty well count on it. He don't say much, though. Unusual for a fisherman, huh?"

"Where's this place he guards so carefully?" Ben said. "Any chance of getting to see it?"

The fat man snorted at the notion this stranger could just saunter into this fishing Nirvana.

"You'd have to be somebody really special to get on that place. It's near town but only Zeke gets to see it. Some family from Memphis owned it, but they died and it's been locked up ever since. Thousands of acres just sitting there."

The man's comment about the dead owners from Memphis surprised Ben. He might get to meet this famous fishing guide without the fat man's help, but it probably wouldn't have much to do with fishing. Ben was irritated hearing about a guy prancing around Ben's land, catching mythical brook trout and getting a reputation for something Ben could have been doing just as easily. Slowly he remembered that *he* left his family and this fishing Eden. His emerging resentment dissolved.

"This fishing paradise, where is it exactly?" Ben said.

The fat man's directions matched the newspaper editor's instructions. Ben thanked him and said he wouldn't be in town long enough to go fishing. He thought about the directions. Both men said finding Mossback's easy—just look for a locked wooden gate in front of the biggest forest you've ever seen.

CHAPTER 4

Ben felt light-headed and excited as he made a right turn at the intersection near the entrance to Mossback. Cracked pavement and potholes from years of spring thaws slowed his approach. Limbs littered the roadside and wildflowers sprouted through the disintegrating asphalt. With the gate closed all these years, Ben figured nature was reclaiming the road, but the clutter of beer cans and bottles showed that others also made a temporary claim on the road.

Dodging potholes and bottles, he arrived at the gate, which stood wide open. The brush, saplings and vegetation at the entrance were recently cut back well past the stone gateposts. Inside the gate to one side, a small hut, no more than six by six, faced the approaching road. Ben watched a man leave the hut and walk to the middle of the road. Dressed in khaki pants and shirt and military boots, he had a closely cropped Van Dyke beard flecked with gray on his weathered face. A ball cap, like the one worn by the fat man in the fly shop, covered his shaved head. Ben noted the heavy revolver strapped to the man's waist, what appeared to be a .44 magnum pistol, not a weapon to be dismissed lightly. *Why the hell would an armed guard be checking me?* The guard signaled Ben to pull over and stop. As he walked to the van, Ben rolled down the window.

"Can I help you?" the guard said. Silver wraparound sunglasses concealed his eyes.

"Here to see Watt Phelps," Ben said.

"He's expecting you?"

"He asked me to come."

"May I see some I.D.?"

Ben's resentment at being challenged was tempered by what was definitely a .44 magnum pistol, probably loaded.

"Sure," he said and handed the guard his driver's license.

As he scanned the license, a grin emerged. "Well, hell, why didn't you speak up," he said, handing back the license. "Go on in." He stepped back from the van.

"Enjoy your work," Ben heard him say as the van chugged through the gate.

The comment bewildered Ben. Was that an order telling him to enjoy something, or was he saying he enjoyed something of Ben's? He preferred to believe the guard was telling him he liked his fly-fishing stories. The hat from a fly-fishing shop indicated he likely had some interest in the sport. But, a lot of men walked around in outdoor clothing with exposed labels proclaiming their refined judgment in gear, while they didn't know a trout from a tuna. As Ben glanced into the rearview mirror, he decided the guard wasn't a pretender.

Nothing about the road into Mossback seemed familiar. Ben hadn't thought about whether or not he would recognize the natural world of his childhood. Impressions of thick green forests stretching forever drifted in his mind. He remembered combing the forest litter for the secret creatures hiding beneath rotting damp leaves.

Most of his adult life had been spent in forests of some kind – in the West with evergreen forests that yielded to bottomland meadows, or the eastern forests, dense with second growth struggling for dominance. As the road descended from Kelsey's wide plateau, Ben noticed openness within the forest, bathed in light that was one moment pale green and the next a flash of yellow or red or orange. Beneath the forest's high canopy, the distance between trees was expansive and very little undergrowth obstructed his view through the woods. He downshifted through switchback curves sharply descending along the steep mountain slope. A few springs and creeks nourished old thickets of mountain laurel and rhododendron, with branches as thick as a line-backer's arm.

The road finally leveled out, turned to gravel and followed a stream along a flat stretch. Vast expanses of ferns, native azaleas and buckberry spread across the woodland floor. Once he thought he glimpsed some movement, but when he turned for a clearer look, he saw only tall swaying ferns. He couldn't stare too long because the enormous trees anchored along the narrow road could turn a distraction into a fatality. Now the road straightened, and he could sometimes see almost a hundred yards ahead before the road again curved out of sight.

Around one turn that led to a long straight stretch, a rabbit dashed across the road. Ben smashed the brake pedal and slid to a grinding stop in the gravel. At the edge of the woods he saw a bobcat staring at him from where the rabbit emerged. The predator sniffed the air, twitched its short tail and sauntered across the road after the rabbit.

Speeding up, he saw the forest thin out into a clearing where the light was brighter. Trees gave way to a recently mowed meadow. Heavy piles of clippings matted the meadow like drying hay waiting to be bailed. The road turned sharply to the right into a driveway with an allée of white pines whose branches interlocked over the road. Light strobed through the high boughs. He saw the house of his childhood summers at the end of the tunnel.

The two-story house was built of large hewn logs chinked with mortar that had crumbled out in places. Along the front spread a wide porch overlooking the lawn. An unpainted clapboard addition with tall windows extended from the rear. Old boxwoods screened the lower part of the house from the driveway as it curved to the right behind the house to a parking area. Ben thought the house looked like an old friend he'd been out of touch with too long.

He pulled into the gravel parking area where three men stood next to a large black Mercedes sedan. Their conversation interrupted, they looked up and watched Ben park his van. Killing the engine, he studied the three men. One was very tall and heavyset. The other two men wore dark buttoned suits. Ben watched the large man say something that made the others laugh. The suited men were strangers, but the other man, despite the decades, still resembled the University of Tennessee defensive end who often motivated quarterbacks to run bootleg patterns in the opposite direction. Ben saw Watt's physical presence still had a hint of danger. Although he welcomed the notion of unexpected wealth, Ben was apprehensive about what deal he would have to make.

As Watt walked toward him, Ben noticed a slight limp in his brother's gait. He wondered who had been so lucky to mark the beast for life and envied the unknown man. Ben looked at Watt, who smiled as he peered directly into Ben's eyes. Ben thought this must be what trapped prey felt like just before the predator pounced.

"I thought some old hippie was driving up in this van," Watt said, as he reached for the door handle. "Didn't know these old death traps were still popular."

Ben held on to the door latch. The door suddenly jerked open, almost pulling him with it.

"Come on outta there and let me look at you. What's a famous writer look like? Hey, guys," Watt bellowed to the two men. "This is my little brother, the famous writer."

Ben slid out of the seat and was engulfed by Watt's embrace. His brother wore faded khaki pants and a wrinkled white oxford cloth shirt that smelled musty. He imagined what Watt's gridiron opponents must have dreaded and why they preferred the opposite side of the field. Who could escape these arms? Watt pushed his brother to arms length and examined him.

"You look great!" he said. "How did you keep from going to pot like me? Chasing fish must keep you trim."

"More like chasing a salary," Ben said. "You look like you could still own your side of the field."

Watt laughed and slapped Ben's shoulder with a heavy hand. "It's the whole field now." He dragged Ben in the direction of the suited men. "Want you to meet someone. Could be useful to you someday."

The two men straightened up and smiled while their eyes remained wary.

"Boys, this is my little brother, Ben, a great outdoor writer. Knows more about catching trout than anybody. Ben, this is Billy Forrest, local congressman. He's a great friend."

Watt guided Ben to the shorter man while the other shuffled into the background.

"Watt moves in powerful company. Good to meet you," Ben said. He was puzzled why a congressman hung around the parking lot like a supplicant.

They exchanged small talk that never broached the brothers' decades of separation. Ben had heard of the congressman. Many outdoor publications mentioned him as the most powerful man in the House of Representatives on federal land and resource issues. Ben couldn't remember any specifics other than conservationists vilified him, while timber and mining executives praised him.

"Well, boys, we've got some catching up to do. Talk to you later." Watt steered Ben to his van with the suggestion he bring his bag to the house. "You've got some ghosts to get reacquainted with," he said.

Ben heard the Mercedes' fat tires on the gravel as it pulled away.

"You and me and Reggie. You wouldn't believe how excited she got when I said you were coming. Insisted on being here to see you again. Be nice for her sake. It'll mean a lot. She hasn't had it easy. Been kinda sick. She could use a little cheering up."

Watt slapped Ben on the shoulder and said, "Let's get you settled and have a drink. I bet you could use one after that snaky drive up these mountains in that thing."

They walked to the house, Ben thinking about Reggie. She was barely a teenager when he fled west. He wondered why the tiger on the tennis court needed cheering up from him.

"Does she still play tennis?" Ben asked. Watt looked puzzled at the question. "Tennis. She used to be pretty good."

"Oh, that," Watt said dismissively. "Nah. Got distracted by other things. Couldn't stay focused."

Ben knew his brother could focus like a demon, turning dollars into oceans of money. He wondered if anything ever distracted Watt.

"Reggie's taking a nap right now. She said she wanted to be her best at dinner. You should have heard the questions. Told her I didn't know any more about you than she did." Watt led Ben into a room filled with books on every wall. The shelves of old books emitted a pungent mildew smell that stung Ben's nose. In front of a window sat a tray of liquor bottles, glasses and a bucket of ice.

"She knows you write about fishing. We have a clipping service for the business. They check the fish magazines for your stories. She saves the stuff in a folder. She's your biggest fan."

Watt laughed at his assessment as he poured two drinks. He took a sip of his, then handed one to Ben. The last time Ben and Watt were together, Ben ended up drunk and headed for the unknown West. He looked at the amber liquid. "Just a Coke for me, thanks."

If the refusal bothered Watt, he didn't reveal it. "Whatever you want, you got. Coke it is."

While Watt made another drink, Ben examined the books on one wall, some bound in leather, dark and cracked from age and neglect, others in dust jackets spotted with mildew and ragged from hungry silverfish. He looked closely and noticed dense dust along the tops of the books and spider webs connecting the dust layer and the shelf above.

"You much of a reader?" Watt asked, as he handed Ben the Coke. "Never did much for me. Can't match the intrigue of a complex financial statement or partnership agreement. Keep up on sports. Everybody wants to talk about sports. Even fishing sometimes. You read any of this stuff?"

Watt waved his drink along the wall. Ben noticed a heavy gold Rolex watch adorning Watt's left wrist. He wasn't wearing a wedding ring.

"Doesn't look too familiar," he said, as he pulled a dark red leather book from the shelf. The gold letters said *North American Indians* and George Catlin. He blew dust from the top and flipped through the pages. Ben stopped occasionally to look at the engravings of Plains Indians in the 1840s. The pictures stirred a vague feeling of recognition. "I don't remember reading much when I was here. Just playing outside." He carefully wedged the book back in its space.

"I don't recall reading much around here, either. But there was one summer I sneaked in a *Playboy*. Me and those ladies got real intimate that summer." Watt chuckled at the memory and took a big swallow of his drink.

Appearing to study the dusty books, Ben sidled along the bookshelves. He didn't want to engage in any conversation such as asking how Watt had been doing all these years. The answer was well documented. But he realized that he didn't know anything about Watt's family. The stories he read praised Watt's business acumen and mostly ignored his family. Any inquiry into Watt's life probably would invite similar inquiry into Ben's, and he wasn't eager to explain why he had never successfully married or had children. The best magazines still bought his stories, usually for good money. At least I did it without any family influence, Ben thought, as he continued perusing the books. He turned toward Watt and glared.

"Speaking of money, when are we going to talk about the money you said I'd be getting? That's the whole point of my coming here. I don't want to stay here any longer than necessary. I've got some assignments to finish."

Watt was freshening his drink and spoke over his broad shoulder. "You're about to get a huge amount of money and you're thinking about doing menial work for somebody else. Can't you function without somebody pulling your strings? I'm going to help you cut those strings. Of course, some people like strings. Feel lost and helpless, adrift without somebody pulling them in some direction. Are you like that?"

Of course he wasn't. Ben glared at the hulking man standing next to him. He should talk about manipulation. *What about that night in Charlottesville? That was the last time you manipulated me. Nobody manipulates me. I chose to do what I'm doing. And I'll keep doing what I want to do tomorrow.*

"Where's this great wealth you talk about coming from?" Ben said evenly. "You feeling guilty about getting so much and me so little?"

"Guilt and me are strangers, little brother." Watt beamed. "Nothing that simple. My lawyer's coming tomorrow to explain all the details. He's prepared to answer all your questions and has documents and checks ready. I hate to spout legal stuff. It gets me in trouble. But the bottom line is that you are going to be paid for your interest in Mossback. Without going into all the lurid details, the place was put into a corporation that was managed by a trustee. Now the corporation is restructuring and I want to buy your interest. You can sell only to me. I've already got controlling interest, and I'm going to make you rich in exchange for your share."

Ben was puzzled by the explanation. "How was this" he waved his hands expansively, "kept from me all these years?"

"Nothing malicious, I assure you. It just became a corporate stock that got lost in the paperwork of a very large estate with a hell of a lot of other paperwork. Sort of became dormant stock that collected dust in a drawer. But look at it as a good long-term investment on your behalf, a stealth 401-K. The place has increased in value and now you can have enough money to do whatever you want. No more people pulling your strings."

Ben's mind swirled with memories of times when he had to beg money from friends and co-workers. He even pawned a priceless bamboo fly rod to cover a bar tab when the owner threatened to extract payment pound by pound. Ben wondered what happened to the rod. His ex-wife would have loved to have this good fortune. She only got half the thrift store furniture and their savings account. Ben was warming to the message of the money, if not to the messenger.

"What makes you think I'll sell," Ben said and wondered what made him ask a question that was ridiculous on its face. "Maybe I'd like to live here. Maybe I have different ideas." The provocation of his hollow threat astonished him.

"The corporation owns the place," Watt said. "You just have some of the stock, so don't get sentimental, or possessive. I think my idea will be real good for your future."

"I remember the last time you came to me with a story about doing something for my own good," Ben said and immediately wished he didn't sound like a whining ass. He didn't want Watt to think the pain of that last meeting lingered and smoldered. After years of forgetting, Ben was at the mercy of his family again. The lure of a large payoff hobbled him. He plunked his pride down on the auction block, and didn't run. The years can mellow a person, he reasoned.

"So this isn't a home place, just a corporate asset," Ben said.

He put his drink on a table stained with the interlocking rings from a hundred sweating drinks and walked to the window. The library occupied an end of the house overlooking an expansive lawn. Beyond the lawn rough rock terraces rippled like a dangling accordion, then abruptly ended in a sheer cliff. A weathered split-rail fence separated the green lawn from the rocks. A few of the rails had lost their grip and rested on the ground. Beyond the rocks, deep forests covered rows of mountain ranges, each a paler blue-green and less distinct than the previous one.

"Do you remember much about this place?" Ben asked. "There's little detail to my memory."

"You didn't spend much time here," Watt said. "The folks kept this place for themselves. We were off at camp or school most of the time. I hated coming here, the most boring spot in the universe. No girls, sports, friends – nothing. What's to remember?" Watt poured another drink, stronger than the previous one. He took a long sip and seemed satisfied.

"Came here once during college. The folks never knew about it. After the first game my senior year. On a Sunday after we beat Clemson in an easy opener. No one was here and we had the place to ourselves. We were so drunk we cut Monday classes. But it was worth it," he said with a soft smile.

Scanning the horizon, Ben said, "I liked it here. I turned over rocks and logs to see what lived under them. It was always a surprise to find a hidden snake or salamander. Did you ever do anything like that?"

"I usually just shot snakes," Watt said and laughed. "Thought every snake was going to bite me, and I'd get it first. I was deadly with a .22 rifle."

Ben turned from the window and looked around the room. He longed for vivid memories about a childhood spent in joy, but came up empty, like peering into fog.

"I'm going to take my bag to my room and rest. I was up late and woke up earlier than expected," Ben said. "Which one's my room? Upstairs I guess, but I don't remember."

Watt drained his drink and lumbered out the door. "Follow me," he said, walking up the hallway to the stairs. Ben noticed Watt's shoulders almost brushed against the pictures on the walls and compared the ample clearance of his own shoulders. Despite the years since his glorious gridiron days and his limp, Watt took the stairs nimbly. Ben hurried after him, but breathed heavily at the top of the stairs and felt the sand in his knees.

"Try not to wake up Reggie," Watt said softly. "She's a little under the weather."

"How'd she get sick," Ben asked.

"Self-inflicted, as usual," he said, quietly walking past Reggie's closed door.

At the end of the hall, Watt stopped by a bedroom on the right, opposite a small bathroom. Ben saw a claw-footed tub in the middle of the bathroom. He didn't see a shower. Watt led him into the bedroom.

"It's simple but comfortable, and the view's not bad." He looked out the window at the same view Ben had seen from the library. "This was my old room. Not that there's anything special. Reggie's in the room you used to have. I'm in the folk's room at the other end of the hall. Clean sheets on the bed."

Ben could see the view from the bed where he sat down. "I was wondering how much land is here. I have no idea. I don't see another house anywhere. It's like I crossed a foreign border when I came through the gate."

Watt glanced sideways out the window. "Enough," he said. "Have a good rest. We'll eat around seven, so you can get a couple hours sleep if you want." He turned and softly pulled the door closed.

Ben listened to the floorboards in the hall creak under Watt as he walked back to the stairs. Despite his determination to resist any friendly feeling toward his brother, Ben was surprised his anger was not boiling over as he had expected. There was only an intense curiosity about why Watt had summoned him and what his sister might be like now. He had no idea what she looked like — certainly not like a teenager. And what was her life like? Was she married? Did she have any children? How had the family afflicted her?

He remembered the last time he had briefly seen her, the time he had come closest to visiting the family. After a weekend of duck hunting at Horse Shoe Lake, Arkansas, Ben headed across the Mississippi River for Key West to write some stories about fly fishing for tarpon. Irresistible curiosity overtook him as he crossed the bridge into Memphis.

Christmas lights and decorations brightened the city. In his old Central Gardens neighborhood, winter-naked oaks and maples sheltered the grand old houses. When he drove onto Harbert Avenue, he stopped a couple of houses down from his old home. Streetlights were coming on as dusk settled in. Gradually, cars began parking along the street, and well-dressed visitors walked up the driveway to the house. He pulled his car a little closer, hoping to catch a peek inside. Holiday lights sparkled around the porch columns and across the roof. Single imitation candles flickered in each window facing the street.

"They're not shining for me," he said, slinking down in the seat to avoid being seen.

He heard fragments of music and laughter as the front door opened for each guest. After a couple of hours most of the guests departed. Then the door opened once more, and Ben saw his mother saying goodbye to more guests. She was too far away to observe clearly, but she appeared to be thicker and her hair had turned gray. She hugged and kissed a man and woman. As the couple walked down the driveway, he couldn't see the woman's face, partly covered by a scarf. In the shadows, Ben stopped breathing when he realized the man was Watt. At the bottom of the driveway, before they turned toward their car, Watt stopped and briefly stared in Ben's direction, then walked on to his own car. Ben didn't see any sign of recognition from Watt. The woman argued with Watt as he tried to push her toward his car. She broke away and stumbled as she tried to return to the house. When Watt pulled her up, Ben saw her face. It was puffy, but he recognized Reggie. Watt growled something he couldn't hear, and she quit resisting and staggered to the car. Ben was relieved when the car drove off.

He looked back at the house and watched the lights go out in each room. Only the light in his parents' bedroom shone behind the pulled shade, where shadows passed behind it. Finally, all the lights were out except for the candles in the downstairs windows.

Years of smoldering hatred roiled as Ben sought some way to demonstrate contempt for his parents. Looking around his car he saw a McDonald's bag containing his half eaten supper. He lobbed it out the window onto his parents' tidy lawn.

"Enjoy," he had said as he started the car and drove away.

Now Ben stretched out on the bed, the rusty springs squeaking under his weight. He settled comfortably on the old mattress and heard through the open window a slight wind teasing the leaves. A few birds calling each other were out-shouted by an alarmed crow cawing high in a pine tree. The house's old logs popped and creaked from the sun's heat as it moved toward the western horizon. He closed his eyes and tried to retrieve a happy memory from his Mossback childhood.

He was about to drift into sleep when he heard a moan from the next room, then what sounded like vomiting. Watt said Reggie wasn't well. What were his words? "Self-inflicted, as usual." Alcohol, the old family friend, he thought. Maybe this reunion upset her to the point of seeking refuge in a bottle. But Watt had said "as usual." His tone of voice had an edge of disgust and impatience, tinged with martyrdom.

After the retching subsided, Ben listened to occasional soft moaning followed by what sounded like crying. He wondered if he should go to her room and ask if he could help. It would be a lousy reintroduction after so many years, but he thought it would be worse if he did nothing. He sat up on the bed and put on his shoes. He resisted being a part of his long-abandoned family again, not wanting to be snared by whatever afflicted his sister, but he overcame his reluctance. He walked warily into the hall and knocked lightly at Reggie's door. He didn't want to startle her. He turned the knob, but the door was locked, so he knocked a little harder.

"You okay in there?" he said. "Reggie, this is Ben. Are you all right?"

He heard sniffling and a groan, but no answer. He tapped harder on the door so there would be no mistaking his purpose. "Reggie, do you need help?" He decided she was probably all right, at least as all right as she was going to be. He would tell Watt about Reggie's sickness. Somebody should relieve her suffering.

He found Watt in the library, bent over, studying what looked to be architectural drawings unrolled on a long table. Watt straightened up and let the plans roll loosely back together.

"That was a quick rest," Watt said.

"I couldn't sleep," Ben said. "Too much puking next door. You said Reggie was sick, but she really sounds wretched. Maybe you should check on her."

As Ben talked, Watt inserted the rolled plans in a leather case, tightly buckled the end cap, and locked it in a cabinet. He leaned against the door and looked down at his feet.

"I'd hoped you wouldn't have to see her like this," he said. "She really was excited about seeing you again. She was nervous about how you'd react to her. She's not the little girl you once knew."

Watt pushed himself away from the cabinet and poured bourbon on the rocks. He sat in a low leather chair near the stone fireplace and gestured for Ben to have a seat in the sofa across the hearth from him.

"She wanted to play tennis more than anything. Be a pro. You know that? Course not. You were in the land of fish and cowboys." He took a deep sip. "She went to Vanderbilt on a tennis scholarship. After a while she got in a few pro matches but never made the top one hundred. Not even close. That's when the drinking started. I don't know if the drinking messed up her game or if she never had a good enough game and drank because of it. We'd dry her out, but after a while she'd be back in the booze. Most of our relationship is her getting into trouble and me getting her out. A lot of favors have been wasted cleaning up her shit."

Watt slunk down in the chair. His chin's folds of fat rested on his large chest and his damp lower lip extended out in a pout. He seemed far away in thought.

Ben remembered once watching Reggie play tennis at the country club. After she devastated her opponent, she celebrated with her friends by buying drinks on their parents' tab. Everyone wanted to bask in her radiance. That vision didn't fit the person Watt was describing.

"I remember her differently," Ben said. "She was so alive. The world was hers to conquer. I remember being envious of her — her ease in everything she did. I've thought all these years I wished I could have been like her."

Watt exhaled an exasperated laugh. "Hah! If you'd been like her your hands would tremble too much to type your name, much less a whole story. Be glad you didn't turn out like her." Watt drained his drink and set it on a side table. He folded his arms across his stomach, his hands gripping his elbows.

Ben had been like the person Watt was describing, at least on occasion, times when his thoughts could never find their way to paper. Trembling, fear and pain competed until another drink offered the only solution and salvation. One day he had headed for a bar after an editor in Bozeman, Montana, ridiculed a story he'd worked on for days. As he reached for the door, a cowboy stumbled out of the bar's darkness toward the street corner and vomited in the gutter. He turned and shrugged sheepishly at Ben, then lurched down the street into another bar. Ben's hand still gripped the half-opened door. Lonely country music floated outside along with the air-conditioned smoke. He let the door close. From that time on, the only thing he drank was an occasional glass of wine or beer.

"You don't know that I didn't," Ben said. He scanned a cluster of photographs, finally finding Reggie's young face. Wearing a bikini, she leaned back on her elbow on a rock in the middle of a river, her face scrunched up in an insolent pout. Sunglasses rested on her hair. He couldn't imagine what had crushed that spirit and left her wallowing in self-torture. Might her life have turned out differently if he had been around? Go ahead and torture yourself, he thought. Unleash your ego, you prick. Maybe you could just do a little laying on of hands.

"I don't know a lot of things about you, Ben," Watt said. "Wish I hadn't done some of the things I did. Maybe helped drive you away from the family. I can't undo it, but I'm sorry for the wasted years."

Watt's gaze turned from Ben to the ice melting in his glass. He swirled the cubes around several times and sipped the residue.

Ben wondered if the apology hinted at sincere reconciliation or just regret at a botched assignment that
should have resulted in a different outcome. He wondered if their parents blamed Watt for screwing up the
revelation about Ben's fiancée loving money more than
she loved Ben. The consequences for Watt couldn't have
been too bad because he seemed to end up with most of
their money. But what were their choices? Ben guessed
his parents really didn't have much leeway about who
got their estate. It cost Watt nothing to show some sympathy. Ben couldn't imagine Watt having real regrets.

"The years are what they are. We lived them," Ben
said as he stretched out on the leather sofa across from
Watt. He leaned his head back on a cushion and shut
his eyes.

"I didn't come here to bury the hatchet. Whatever
we had as a family is gone. All I'm interested in is the
money. You and Reggie have your own lives that aren't
part of mine and won't be." Ben peeked through the
slits of his eyelids to see Watt's reaction.

"Thanks for your candor," Watt said, looking up from
his almost empty glass. "I don't know what I expected
from you. Not thanks, but something close. Maybe I'd
feel the same way in your shoes. Anyway, what's the point
of trying to be a family now? Too many broken parts to
reassemble."

Ben smiled to himself. "We're too far apart to be a family," he said. "We might just settle for being civil for a little while. Sometimes that's an accomplishment in itself. Especially if we're going to be discussing money."

Watt raised his empty glass in the air. "Here's to civility. May it prevail when all other forms of behavior have failed."

CHAPTER 5

Ben walked quietly down the hall toward his room so Reggie wouldn't hear him. A board creaked beneath him as he passed Reggie's door, and he froze mid-step. He turned his ear to her door, heard no sounds of suffering and went to his room.

"Killer views," Watt had said. Windows on both sides of the corner walls framed the view beyond the front lawn to the valley below, where smoky blue mountain ridges bordered the wide valley. A tarnished brass bed butted against the wall next to one of the windows. In place of a closet was a black iron rack for hanging clothes, with a luggage shelf below it. Spartan, but I've had worse, he conceded.

He took a paperback copy of *A Sand County Almanac* from his bag and settled on the bed. The book was a gift from an editor who worried Ben didn't seem to get pleasure from the outdoors any more. He scanned the front and back covers and glanced at several blurbs, including one by Robert Redford.

"Your movie messed up fly fishing," Ben said.

He flipped through the pages until his eye caught a sentence that said all ethics are based on the premise that the individual and the community are essentially interdependent.

"And you're a lot happier the less interdependent you are," Ben said softly. "As for ethics . . .."

A sound came from across the room. He cocked his head and listened carefully to the soft and measured tapping. Watt wouldn't be that delicate, and Ben hadn't seen any ravens in the house. He closed the book and went to the door. The tapping started again with the same muted beat. Ben grasped the doorknob and pulled the door open quickly. Before him, with her knuckles poised to strike again was a haggard woman with tousled, graying hair. She wore a thin robe, open to reveal a protruding stomach straining against a long tee shirt. Half-closed eyes in her lined and pallid face suddenly popped open in surprise. They were rheumy with dilated pupils. She blinked harshly as she adjusted to the light, then returned to her sleepy gaze and opened her mouth. She exhaled vapors of booze, burned tobacco and vomit.

"Welcome back to our world, Bennie."

He hadn't heard that name in decades. When Reggie called him that a plea for a favor usually followed. He held his breath. Watt said their sister had a drinking problem, but he hadn't prepared Ben for this. She easily could have passed for a homeless woman pushing a shopping cart down back alleys in Atlanta. He couldn't get near enough to her to look into the hall. As she made a move in his direction, he stepped back into his room and put his hand on the door as he edged toward it for protection. He was embarrassed when he realized he was using the door as a shield.

"Reggie?" he asked with a puzzled frown.

She half-smiled through her sleepy gaze. "You expecting some other babe?" she laughed, but it quickly became a fit of deep, phlegmy coughing that turned her face crimson. Ben thought she might burst as the veins on her face bulged into an elaborate web. She finally caught her breath, took a long drag on the cigarette butt between her yellowed fingers and exhaled slowly. She dropped the butt on the runner carpet, looked at it smolder, and then crushed it with her slipper. "Don't want to burn it down yet."

"I thought maybe you were asleep. Watt said you weren't … you surprised me." The awkward reunion unsettled Ben. He didn't know what to say. She should be in serious rehab, not Mossback. He kept hoping she wouldn't throw up on him or hug him as her long lost brother. He wanted to close the door and make her go away.

"I have that effect on a lot of people. Even myself, sometimes. Come in? Sure. Nice of you to ask."

She pushed away from the doorjamb and shuffled into his room without touching him. She slumped on the bed and closed her eyes. Ben was afraid she was passing out.

"Watt told me you were coming. Didn't know it was today. What is today? Thursday? Friday? I remember Thursday. Yesterday, right?"

"Two days ago. It's Saturday. Afternoon. Late afternoon, almost dinner time," Ben said. He sat in a straight-backed wooden chair near the bed.

"The cocktail hour," she said, smiling with her eyes still closed. "Care for a libation? Why, I don't mind if I do. Please join me. I'm having whatever you're having. Make it a double."

"Sorry. Nothing here but water."

"After all those years away from home you can offer only plain water? Didn't you learn that woman cannot live by water alone? She must have something to kill the taste. You didn't bring any offering? What kind of prodigal son are you? How do you ever think you could get back in our good graces without special offerings? Why are you here?"

He had seen a few drunken women in the bars he had prowled during his heavy drinking days. He usually didn't think much of them, but the more he drank, the prettier they became, until late in the evening when he found them to be absolutely fascinating. His wife had been fascinating until he sobered up. Then they divorced.

Staring at Reggie spread over his bed, he figured this was part of the price for his sudden good fortune, or whatever it was.

"Watt found me," Ben finally said. "Something about money. That got my attention."

Waving her hand dismissively, she said, "He can get people's attention. Just flash cash and their tongues hang out."

Ben winced a little at her characterization.

She lay silent for a while. Ben watched her labored breathing and worried she had passed out. *Just what I need, a drunk tapped out in my bed.* He still had trouble believing this lost soul was the spirited teenager he remembered. He calculated that Reggie must now be over forty years old, although she could easily have passed for well beyond fifty with her pasty, slack skin. Her red nose flared out as she exhaled. A few bubbles swelled and popped at the corner of her down-turned mouth. He noticed an artery slowly pulsating beneath the thin skin on the side of her neck.

"He has a way with everything," she said suddenly, opening her left eye and staring at Ben. "His way. No use fighting it. Much easier to just float along. Less chance of injury." She closed her eye and sighed.

"Or you can walk away from it," Ben said.

The eye opened for a moment to scrutinize Ben, then closed again.

"Course *you* can. Free, white and twenty-one. That's the key. Add male to the list. That makes it easier to just walk away. The world opens its arms to you."

Ben realized she was right. The only skill he remembered she had was a scorching serve and volley. That might get her a gin and tonic in the clubhouse. He wondered what their parents said or did to squash her dream. Did they use Watt to deliver the message, or did they do it themselves? He decided they somehow shattered her belief she could be a star player. What a terrible clash that must have been, the anesthetized wreckage now sprawled over his bed. Instinct warned him to remain distant from her suffering, which he couldn't change.

Reggie snorted, then opened her eyes with rapid blinks. "Must have dozed off," she said with a slight smile. "Was I gone long?"

"Just a few minutes."

"Sorry to be a burden," she said as she tried to sit up on the bed. "Thanks for waiting."

Ben studied the tiny red capillaries spread across Reggie's nose, like little dead ends.

"For the longest time I thought I'd be reading about you in the sports pages. The queen of the tennis court vanquishing all challengers," he said.

She laughed her phlegmy laugh. "Everyone had hopes for me," she said. "The weight was crushing."

Reggie looked away from Ben toward the bed table. She reached for the table lamp and pulled the chain repeatedly as the bulb brightened and darkened.

"I started losing more than winning and just couldn't turn it around. Then nobody had any expectations, including me. About anything. I got really good at losing." Her rheumy eyes fixed on him. "After a while, I just didn't care anymore about anything. You sure you don't have anything to drink in here? Some things need drowning, you know?"

"Tried it, but it didn't help. The morning pain got worse than the memories," he said.

"Hair of the dog," she said.

"The dog always kept biting."

"You just didn't get to know it well enough," Reggie said, ignoring a tear flowing down her cheek.

A heavy knock at the door startled them. Another louder knock was followed by a deep bellow.

"Time to fuel up little brother," Watt said from the hallway. "You ready?"

Ben saw the disappointment on Reggie's face that their reunion moment was interrupted.

"On my way," Ben said. "Let me wash up. Didn't realize it was so late."

"Ten minutes," Watt said as he walked back down the hall.

They heard him stop at Reggie's room, pound on the door and command loudly, "Make yourself presentable, Reggie. Dinner's ready and we have a special guest. Get it in gear and behave." He didn't wait for a response, but went on downstairs.

"Maybe he hopes I'm still asleep," Reggie said as she swung her feet to the floor. "It didn't sound like a warm invitation, did it? I think I'll surprise him by making a grand entrance." She walked very deliberately to the door, turned and blew Ben a kiss and went to her room.

Ben thought he knew the way to the dining room as he walked downstairs. He sniffed the air in hopes of heading in the right direction. A single weak bulb cast a ghostly light in the hallway. Through a door on the right he saw Watt setting plates on a solid oak trestle table that stretched across the room. On a sideboard sat a large blue platter crowded with steaming baked potatoes and charred steaks, with a large wooden bowl of salad next to it. Nearby was a fireplace chiseled from large rectangular granite blocks darkened by years of smoldering fires. Freshly split burning logs hissed while damp smoke slowly drifted up the chimney. An iron chandelier entwined with spider webs cast uneven light from its few working bulbs dangling above the dining table. Watt turned when he heard Ben.

"Hope you have an appetite. Steaks seemed in order. You probably get all the fish you can stomach. Just sit anywhere. We're not formal like the old days with the parents."

Three places were set at one end of the table, one on each side and one at the end. Ben sat to one side of the table.

"I don't know if Reggie's up to having dinner with us," Watt said. "She's probably under the weather."

He served their plates and placed one in front of Ben. He put his own at the head of the table where Ben remembered their father presiding at dinner. Watt wore a brown herringbone tweed jacket with suede shooting patches on the shoulders. Underneath the jacket was a tattersall shirt tucked into jodhpurs. Highly polished riding boots completed the outfit. Ben remembered from years ago that Watt enjoyed playing the English country squire.

"We're not waiting for Reggie?"

Watt looked toward the hallway and listened for a moment.

"We might as well eat. I can warm it up if she gets here later," Watt said.

They began eating in silence, except for the sound of the knives and forks scraping the fine china plates. He preferred idle conversation to the silence but he resisted giving Watt a chance to be charming or a bully. Watt finally broke the silence.

"So, what's it like going around the country fishing and telling everybody about it? Sounds like every fisherman's dream," he said. He crammed a large piece of meat and fat into his mouth and chewed vigorously, his lips glistening with juices.

"It's okay, I guess," Ben said, mounding butter and sour cream on his potato. "Gets a little routine after a while. Places start to look alike. But it keeps me out of an office."

Watt had the look of a contemplative cow chewing its cud as he gazed across the room. Finally he said, "Sounds like you've lost your enthusiasm for the job. There's nothing worse than routine. You know every day what you'll be doing for the rest of your life. Where's the thrill in that?"

Ben stabbed a piece of meat and held it in front of him. *At least my life is far away from you.* "It might not be exciting to you, but I made my own way. Nobody greased the skids," he said, sitting up a little straighter in his chair.

"Hot damn!" Watt said. "There's nothing more satisfying than making your own way in the world, doing something no one's done before." He chewed meditatively for a moment, then added, "Unless you take what somebody started and become Midas."

Ben saw a smile on Watt's face. "Not everything's measured in money," Ben said.

Watt laughed. "Spoken like a man who's never had any," Watt said. His thick hand slapped the table and made the wine splash from his glass. "You've got to have money to appreciate what it really means. Not just the material aspect. That gets old faster than white bread. I'm talking about the power money brings. Real money. Enough to make people do things they normally wouldn't do. It's a real kick to watch people get all weak-kneed and salivating." Watt jabbed his steak and began slicing vigorously.

Being an outdoor writer didn't necessarily make Ben swell up with pride, but his profession didn't embarrass him either. He seldom reflected on his life's worth in the greater scheme of things. *I go to a river, try to catch fish and write about it. My writing's taken a lot of desk-bound slobs to Alaska, the Amazon, New Zealand and everywhere in the USA just for the price of a magazine.*

Ben noticed he had been slumping in his chair and straightened himself. "I give my readers a good time while they're slaving away for people like you."

Watt dropped his fork and clapped his thick hands. "How noble!" he shouted. "You and Mother Theresa.

Giving hope where there's only despair. You sound absolutely saintly."

Watt breathed deeply, leaned back in his chair and took a long swallow of wine. He smiled and tilted his head slightly. Ben noticed a small dribble of wine seep down a creased fold of skin by Watt's mouth.

"I really don't mean to dismiss what you do for a living. You went off on your own and survived. That's admirable. I know a lot of folks back in Memphis who couldn't have survived without family help. You did it all by yourself. Good for you," Watt said, extending his arms toward Ben.

He resumed slicing his steak.

"But didn't you ever want to do anything extraordinary, like write a novel? The great American novel," Watt said. "I thought every hack writer had the secret hope of becoming a famous novelist. Don't tell me you never had that dream. And then selling the movie rights for big bucks."

Ben played with his food as he remembered a time when outdoor writing started becoming routine, and he thought a plunge into fiction would rescue him. He'd have a couple of beers at night and sit at his desk and try to write a book. After a hundred pages he still didn't know his characters very well, much less have any idea where they were headed. There were so many choices to make. What if he made the wrong one and nothing worked out? He'd have to start over. Or maybe the book would be awful. He had slid the pages in a drawer.

"Fiction never really interested me," Ben said.

"Too bad. That's where the real money is, especially in movies. But money doesn't really get your juices flowing, right?"

Ben pushed a piece of meat through its juices toward some sour cream. Without looking up he said, "How did you go so far, Watt? I mean you went a lot further in real estate than Dad. Why did you follow in his tracks?"

Watt paused from his eating and gazed past Ben, then looked directly into Ben's eyes.

"It was the easiest path, really. I couldn't play football forever. The old pros were cripples or bums or announcers. All I had to do was what the old man said and I'd have plenty of money. It worked. But his vision really was small. For him, it was all about making enough to live well. That was easy. I wanted more. I love the game, but the score matters. The profit's the score, and I like to run it up as high as I can. It's not about having enough. It's about having more than anyone else."

Watt was wide-eyed when his finger jabbed the table. "Poor people call it greed. That's easy for people who never accomplished anything. They don't know what it takes to make things happen. Great projects don't get done by magic. There're a thousand things that can go wrong and dump you on your ass. It's a rare gift to juggle all those things and walk away at the end with all that money."

He shrugged and sat back with a look of enormous satisfaction.

Ben listened until he noticed how his brother parted his hair. How had he missed it before? Just above his left ear, Watt combed his hair up and over what obviously was a mostly bald dome. The hair on that side of the part must have been very long to travel from one side of Watt's head to the other, he thought, wondering what it looked like when he went swimming, if he ever did. Would Watt risk his vanity for such pleasure? Probably not, Ben decided.

"True genius," Ben said, as he studied Watt's combover.

"Nothing to do with genius," Watt said. "Everything to do with determination and hard work. And the utmost confidence that I can charm, buy or scare anyone."

"When you're awake in the middle of the night, what do you think about? Does anything scare or haunt you? Make you want to stay under the covers when morning comes?" Ben asked.

Watt gave a puzzled look and then snorted dismissively.

"Every day we have a choice of pulling up the covers or throwing them back and saying 'piss on it.' I like throwing back the covers. Makes me feel alive."

Watt's words depressed Ben, who struggled to face many days and survive till darkness. Ben tried to imagine the exhilaration Watt felt, and thought it's easier for a rich person to feel that way.

"What makes you feel alive?" Watt asked as he popped the last morsel of steak into his mouth. "A new river to explore? Catch a bigger fish? Write something really good?"

Ben shifted uneasily. His work excited him at first, but now it felt more like cheating to be paid for "fish and tell," the stories no more than fill-in-the-blanks exercises. But what was the alternative? Sell real estate? Easier to go with what you know.

"Oh, I think . . ."

As Ben started to speak, a gravely voice inquired, "Did somebody say dinner's served?"

Reggie stood in the doorway with one hand propped against the frame. Heavy makeup covered her face, accented by darkly lined eyes that reminded Ben of a raccoon caught in a hunter's spotlight. She wore a bright red knit dress that might have fit properly a few years ago.

"Thanks for waiting," she said. She walked to the sideboard and poured bourbon into a large water goblet. Sitting across from Ben, she lifted her glass. "Here's to the return of the prodigal son. Raise your glass, Watt. Aren't you glad to have Ben back? Maybe there's a glimmer of hope for this family after all."

"I don't mind drinking to that," Watt said. He lifted his glass to Ben, who was drinking only water. "This might be a special beginning for all of us." He raised his eyebrows in a question as he looked at Ben.

Reggie put out her cigarette in the butter dish and said: "What does a lady have to do to get a meal around here?"

Ben looked at Watt. They stared at each other for a moment before Ben said, "What can I get you Reggie?"

"Such a little gentleman. Pay attention, Watt." Reggie looked at the platters on the sideboard. "A real guy kind of meal, huh? Just a potato, Ben. I don't want anything too heavy on my stomach."

"Might interfere with the booze, huh Reggie," Watt said. He tightly gripped his knife and fork.

"Do you know how bad red meat is for you? All sorts of chemicals and drugs are fed to those critters before they march off to the supermarket. Bad for you. Causes cancer." She took a gulp of her drink and lit another cigarette.

"Our resident health guru," Watt said. "We thought you were too ill to join us. Thought it was something you drank cause you haven't eaten anything lately."

Ben put a plate in front of Reggie and sat down. No, you can't go home again, and who in his right mind would want to? Just take the money and split, he thought.

Reggie blew a stream of smoke toward Watt. An ash dropped on top of her potato.

"The first time Ben's home in a zillion years and you have to act like an ass. Can't you pretend to be human for Ben's sake?" she said. "He might even stay a while if you don't scare him off."

"Sure, Reggie. Ben's eager to get reacquainted with us. Right, Ben?" Watt put down his knife and fork and pushed himself back from the table. "Wouldn't you like to enjoy this family bliss every evening at dinner? Reminds you of Norman Rockwell . . . on acid."

"I'm just here briefly for some family business, according to Watt. I'm not going to stay," Ben said

Reggie frowned at Watt, then turned to Ben and smiled sweetly. "What kind of family business, Ben? I'm still in this family despite efforts to shut me away. Family business includes me too. Tough shit, Watt. Doesn't have something to do with this place, does it? The Wilderness, right, Watt? Isn't that what you call your big deal? It's a wilderness all right."

She drank, then inhaled deeply. Her focus on Ben and Watt seemed to become more tentative. Her head swayed back and forth to a sound only she heard.

"The ramblings of a lush," Watt said, glaring at his sister.

"What's she mean about wilderness and your big deal?" Ben said.

For the first time since he'd arrived, and for the first time in his memory, Ben saw an emotion close to rage ablaze in Watt, whose jaw muscles rippled over his grinding teeth. Blood rushed to his head. His eyes locked on Reggie, who returned his glare for a moment, then turned away and slumped in her chair. As Reggie seemed to withdraw into herself, Watt became more relaxed and the redness drained from his face.

"Reggie thinks she knows things, but she just imagines stuff from catching a word from eavesdropping," Watt said, still fixated on Reggie. "Just ignore her. She imagines a lot of things. Don't go chasing her phantoms."

Reggie's chin rested on her chest. A little string of drool dropped from her open mouth and stained her red dress. A gurgling snoring followed the drool.

"She'll be out for a while," Watt said. "This is her life. Has been for a long time. When things get really bad, I put her in a hospital to dry out. The cure never takes, though. It always comes back to this." He pushed away from the table and walked next to her.

"Aren't you afraid she'll hurt herself?" Ben asked.

"Not as long as we keep her away from sharp objects and cars," he said. "I'll take her on up and put her to bed. Finish your dinner."

Watt swept up Reggie in a quick motion Ben assumed had been performed many times. She appeared childlike in his massive arms, like a little girl being carried up to bed for the night, no longer able to keep pace with the grownups. Ben could hear her snoring in the hallway as Watt lugged her upstairs.

Listening to the groaning stair treads, he thought of Reggie's descent into her private hell and Watt's expression when she mentioned something about wilderness. "The Wilderness" she had said, as if it were a proper name. She called it his big deal. Ben wondered if she was merely delusional, as Watt implied, or did some revealed secret trigger Watt's reaction? Whatever the answer, Ben decided he didn't want to make it his business. Judging from tonight's farce, he made the right decision a long time ago. His life sure trumped this.

Ben looked at the half-eaten meals around the table. Reggie's glass of bourbon was drained. Cigarette residue littered her plate. He walked to the hallway and listened for voices, but there was only silence. He didn't want to talk to Watt again. The future might be a little different if Watt was truthful about the money. Some lawyer talk, some signed papers, and get a big check. It should be pretty routine and impersonal. Go to bed, wake up, and be richer than he had ever imagined. Keep it simple. No detours or distractions. It's a good plan, Ben decided.

He walked up the dark stairs. As he was about to enter his room, Watt came out of Reggie's. They looked at each other. Ben nodded goodnight and went into his room, to sleep and to wait.

CHAPTER 6

Ben jolted awake from his dreamless sleep and listened for some clue to what awakened him, but heard only the old log walls creaking as they shrank in the increasingly dry fall air. From deep within the walls, a mouse gnawed a passageway. The unanswered hooting of a barred owl drifted through the half-open window.

He pulled the down comforter over his head, nestling in the bed, hoping for more sleep, but his mind couldn't relax as he thought of Reggie and his brother. The possibility that last night's drama might resume dismayed him. Watt said the lawyer would arrive this morning. A check in the mail would've been simpler, he thought.

Ben was curious about what he was being asked to sell. He knew so little about this family retreat that strangers in Kelsey mentioned with awe and envy. Driving in, he saw a forest unlike anything he'd ever seen in the East.

He needed a closer look at what Watt so eagerly wanted to buy.

Outside, a faint pink glow dissolved the black night. He knew Reggie would sleep well past morning after her dinner performance, but he had no idea about Watt's habits. If he wanted to delay the reckoning of Mossback, Ben had to leave the house soon. He pushed back the covers and dressed quickly.

Placing his ear against Reggie's door, he heard sporadic snoring. At least she's alive, he thought. He felt sorry for her, and wondered if there was anything he could have done to help her, to ease the years of self-loathing she heaped upon herself. Probably not, because he knew that a drunk wasn't looking for salvation, just another drink. And he didn't expect to be around if Reggie ever decided to put the bottle aside.

He grabbed an apple from the kitchen and walked outside. A few birds were calling from the bushes bordering the woods. Ben zipped his jacket against the cool, damp air and walked into the front yard where he startled a rabbit nibbling the overgrown grass. He thought about the exquisite solitude of other early mornings beside rivers, the smell of coffee brewing over a campfire and the day born full of possibilities.

The edge of the lawn ended at a cliff that plunged to a valley a few hundred feet below. The crowns of the trees in their golden autumn foliage rustled above a thin fog rising up from the forest floor. As he stood at the edge of the fence, he recalled stern warnings he'd gotten as a child to never climb on the fence, much less go on the other side of it. You'll fall and we'll never find you, his mother had warned.

The house's gray chestnut logs reflected a rosy glow in the pink light, and he saw, in a small nook where chinking had fallen out, a flycatcher nest woven from twigs and moss. Staring at the house, he wondered who in his family had ever found happiness inside. He didn't know about his parents, but he was confident Reggie and Watt hadn't.

He watched the sun beginning to highlight the tips of the white pines and hemlocks behind the house. The green needles glistened in the first rays shining over the mountains. A pale mist rose from the damp limbs as sunlight warmed the bark. Ben leaned against the fence and listened to a Carolina wren's exuberant trills.

The notion of a permanent home was alien to Ben, a working drifter all his adult life, but he realized life could be a lot worse than living here. He laughed at his sudden sentimentality. If I keep this up, I'll be married with kids before I know what hit me, he thought.

When light came on in the upstairs window of Watt's room, Ben shoved away from the fence and walked toward the woods on the side of the house away from the parking area. A stone path led to a gap in the mountain laurel edging the forest. By the time he passed through the opening, the long wet grass had soaked his boots. He saw lights come on in the kitchen, and he ducked into the woods.

The path was thick with leaves and pine needles covering the spongy earth that yielded to his weight on soil soft from centuries of forest litter. Narrow light shafts radiated through the vapor slowly rising from the fern-covered forest floor. The mist grew thicker and obscured the shape of things, leaving only a suggestion of what they might be. Tree trunks were only darker shades of fog, barely distinguishable. Ben followed the remnant of a trail for a few feet until it also dissolved in the dense mist. He stood still, waiting for the air to clear, and listened.

A few birds in the high branches sang to others that they survived the night. Far away, from a direction he couldn't discern, came the faint sound of metal clanking and grinding. It puzzled him that any activity would occur so early on a weekend morning in a place that he believed was all uninhabited forest. Of course, he really had no idea what might have happened since he last wandered in these woods. Watt said Ben owned part of this land, but he still felt like an intruder.

The atmosphere grew brighter as he stood listening until he saw the trail meandering several yards ahead through waist-high ferns. The mist moved slowly in one direction, and then reversed itself. The breeze swirled and pushed and lifted until Ben could see farther into the forest.

From off to the left came the sound of an old engine chugging along. Far through the trees he caught glimpses of a pickup truck traveling then disappearing into the distance.

Obviously some kind of road existed where the truck had traveled, and Ben left the trail and walked in that direction. He felt the weight of his drenched pants and boots. He reached the road and saw tire tracks pressed into the sandy gravel. The truck was a few dozen yards ahead pulled to the side, its red taillights still shining.

The first thing he noticed about the old man was his silky white hair escaping from underneath a battered straw hat. The man unloaded gear from the truck and stuffed it in a large blue backpack. Even though the man noticed Ben, he continued working as if Ben were no less expected than a shrub beside the road. Ben stopped ten feet from the man and wondered if he would ask Ben who he was, or, at least, explain his purpose in Ben's forest. Even though he appeared to be over seventy years old, his short body moved with a young man's easy grace and balance. He finished loading the pack, pulled tight a drawstring at the top, and secured the top flap. Lifting it with one hand, he swung it up on the truck's tailgate. The man finally looked directly at Ben with a perfunctory smile.

Ben nodded back as the old man sat on the tailgate and slid his arms through his backpack's shoulder straps.

"What're you doing here?" Ben said at last, fearful the man would dash into the forest without any explanation at all.

"Just a little inventory work," he said. He stood up and let the pack settle on his back. Fastening the pack's belt around his waist, he tightened the straps.

"What kind of inventory?" Ben said, moving a little closer.

"Flora and fauna." Patting his pockets and glancing around, the man showed no interest in Ben or his questions.

"You got permission?" Ben said, and immediately regretted the question. In just a few moments, he had become territorial and possessive of land that only yesterday he was eager to sell for whatever Watt was offering. He still felt that way. He just disliked being ignored by a stranger who seemed very comfortable on Ben's land.

The man leaned against the tailgate and put his hands in his pockets.

"I work for the owner," he said, as he took off his glasses to clean them with his shirttail. "That's all the permission I need. Anything else?" He looked at Ben with exasperated impatience.

Ben felt stupid as he stood twisting one foot in the gravel like a kid who has just learned he is not as clever as he thought.

"Didn't mean to keep you," Ben said. "Just curious. I live here, too. Not really live here, but I have, I mean . . . Well, I'm sort of an owner, too." He was embarrassed when he announced his tentative claim, as if he had no right to assert it.

The old man examined Ben a little closer, taking more care to observe this new claimant. "You related to Mr. Phelps?" he said.

"His brother."

"Any problems?"

Ben wasn't sure what he meant. "Not that I know of," he said. He realized the man was standing again and adjusting his pack in preparation to depart. "I just got here yesterday," Ben said. "Haven't been here in a long time. Decades."

"Hasn't changed much," the man said with a quick smile. "Been pretty much like this for centuries. Except for the chestnuts, of course. Just big snags to remind us."

"What kind of inventory you doing?" Ben said. "Plants and animals, I know. But why does Watt want to know what's on this place? He hates the outdoors."

"He hired me to look around and see if there's anything rare or endangered. It's an unusual forest. Never been cut, so it's all old growth and a lot of it. There might be something here that doesn't exist anywhere else."

Ben had ignored Mossback for so long, he was only partly aware of its nature. Driving in, he knew there was something unusual about the place, but his mind had been distracted.

"Found anything yet?" Ben said. "I mean, anything unexpected?"

The old man stopped fiddling with his gear long enough to regard Ben more closely. He tilted his head slightly. "If I do, your brother will be the first to know. He gave me clear instructions that I report to him alone. It's a written contract. Nothing personal, just business."

He smiled again, shrugged his shoulders and disappeared through a break in the wall of rhododendron like an apparition. Ben again felt like an intruder.

He decided to return to the house. Might as well get this over with, he concluded. Lingering around here would only bring problems. This place wasn't his, never was and never would be. The best thing to do would be to sign whatever papers Watt shoved in front of him and enjoy a check with lots of zeros.

As he started walking up the road, Ben realized he didn't know the way back. He had a general sense of where the house should be, but he had gone off the trail and through unmarked woods. Look for trampled ferns, he thought. The sun was burning off the morning mist, intensifying the light. Like an Indian tracker, he walked slowly along the road looking for signs that would reveal where he had emerged. Finally, he saw some broken ferns. He peered into the woods and noticed more bent ferns. But they were so thick and tall he couldn't be certain they showed his route. He watched a breeze sweep low over the forest floor making the ferns sway rhythmically back and forth in an emerald ballet until he decided his return began where he stood, and he stepped from the road into the deep forest.

The mid-September air had become crystalline and the sunshine brightly backlit the forest's high canopy of, red, orange and scarlet leaves. A quick breeze ruffled the canopy, dislodging leaves that clattered down though twigs and branches to the ground. Fat moss and shaggy lichen crept into the trees' deeply grooved bark. If elves exist, this is where they would be prancing in the woods, he thought.

The rhododendron thickets with their hard, twisted branches thinned out, letting Ben see clearly into the forest for more than a hundred yards. A soft carpet of myriad ferns and buckberry bushes turning purple covered the ground and swayed from the same breeze rustling the leaves a hundred feet above him. Dense colonies of dew-coated galax and shortia glittered in the leaf mold.

He touched immense poplar trees he knew were saplings when the first European explorers set foot on the Atlantic's sandy dunes, at a time when many people still believed in a flat Earth and only a fool would sail the oceans much beyond the sight of land. Saplings now rose hopefully above the ferns and waited patiently in the certainty nature eventually would provide an opening to reach toward the sun.

Ben rested on an old fallen tree rotting very slowly back into the spongy soil, blanketed by thick moss, ferns and foamflowers. In a hundred years, only a long mound would mark this leviathan whose canopy once brushed against the sky. He loved that everything in the forest nurtured something else, including him. Speculating what his brother intended for Mossback saddened him as he contemplated this forest's fate.

The centuries-old trunks rose imperially, their surface deeply grooved as if a mammoth tiger regularly honed its claws down their solid bulk. Their branches were the size of most tree trunks. He saw enormous beech trees with bark like the skin of a prehistoric beast, polished smooth by centuries of wind and water. Unseen birds chirruped, twittered, peeped and cawed. Hearing a soft swoosh, he turned to see a horned owl glide lazily by him to perch on a low branch snag, then swivel its head to observe wide-eyed the interloper below.

Suddenly a deep drumming erupted, as if some mad percussionist were beating a hollow log. The thumping stopped, followed by shrill, rapid laughing. Ben was glad to hear the pileated woodpecker greet him on his visit.

In the distance, where ferns grew especially thick and tall, he saw what looked like a tawny rope rising up. It was curved and twitched occasionally as it moved in a wide arc around Ben. When it came to an area where the ferns were slightly lower and less dense, Ben saw the unmistakable silhouette of a panther and was fascinated by the possibility that it could be living free at Mossback. He knew black bears flourished along the edges of vacation-home developments where they could raid garbage cans and bird feeders. That a creature thought hunted to extinction in the East actually existed in his forest pleased Ben. The panther vanished into the forest. His nerves tingled because the panther could make a drawn-out meal of him.

He scanned the area where the cat's path might have taken it and hoped it kept walking a steady course, but only ferns and buckberries were visible. When he fished out west, where grizzly bears or mountain lions might threaten him, he usually carried a .45 automatic. He never had to use it but he appreciated the comfort it provided. Here, a sudden attack might never be discovered in this vast forest. His flesh would become panther shit, and his bones would sink into the earth, and who would know, or care? He felt very small and insignificant. He also felt scared. His life hadn't been of much importance, but he wasn't ready for it to end. Sweat dripped from his armpits down the sides of his chest. He wondered if the panther could smell his fear and be emboldened.

Slowly, Ben backed toward the direction where he thought the house was. He knew better than to run and encourage the panther to attack. Without breaking into a sprint, Ben quickened his pace until he finally found the trail. He could see more light ahead where the forest thinned.

He needed only a few more minutes to get to the clearing where civilization might discourage the predator. As he came through the opening in the wall of rhododendron and mountain laurel leading to the lawn, Ben sprinted to the closest door and dashed through.

He sat on the floor and sucked air. His breathing a little under control, he peered through the door to the break in the rhododendron wall he had just come from. He wondered if the panther waited in the shadows, twitching its tail and purring, and remembering.

CHAPTER 7

"You look like you saw something evil." Watt stood in the doorway of the library holding a mug of coffee, its steam swirling in the cool air of the unheated house. "Saw you tearing across the yard. Something after you?"

Ben didn't say a panther was stalking him, because Watt would want it killed.

"Stirred up some yellow jackets," Ben said. "Didn't see them till I was on top of their nest. I outran them"

Watt sipped his coffee and studied Ben over the rim of the mug.

"You'll have to show me the nest so I can have the caretaker spray it," he said.

"Yeh, after they've calmed a little." Ben said, remembering he had heard about the caretaker yesterday.

"Let's get some breakfast," Watt said, heading for the kitchen. "There's some cereal and milk, a few bananas."

Ben surveyed the wide kitchen. The wood-burning cook stove stood out from the log wall. The other appliances had a 1950s look. Ben wondered if the refrigerator worked, then heard its loud, labored vibrations. Opening the door, he found a carton of milk along with a lot of imported beer, Chardonnay, Gilbey's gin, mixers, lemons and limes. Watt pointed to several boxes of cereal across the kitchen on an old linoleum-covered table.

"No one goes thirsty around here," Ben said, sitting at the table. He ate his breakfast slowly, gazing out a window toward the parking area. Watt poured another cup of coffee and sat at the other end of the table. Ben watched him put three teaspoons of sugar in his coffee and stir methodically.

"How was your walk?" Watt said, tapping the spoon on the side of the cup. "Hope you didn't get lost. Kinda easy with all the trails overgrown."

Ben chewed thoroughly before answering. He almost asked about the man he had met who worked for Watt. What possible reason would Watt have for a detailed inventory of plants and animals at Mossback? He doubted Watt was a nature lover who enjoyed the outdoors or cared about the creatures calling Mossback home.

"It was okay," Ben said.

"See anything interesting?"

Ben didn't want to show any interest in Watt's business. The more detached he appeared, the less chance for conflict. "Any panthers been seen around here?"

"Not that I've seen. There's always rumors, but I haven't been here much," Watt said. "See any signs out there?"

"Just wondering. There're some out West so I have to be careful on wilderness trips. Grizzlies too. Pack a pistol sometimes, but never used it yet."

"Bring it with you?" Watt said.

"Don't worry, I didn't pack heat," Ben said. "You're safe."

Watt laughed loudly and slapped the table. "That's good to know. Can't be too careful in my business," he said, rocking back in his chair.

Ben wondered if Watt ever faced life-threatening dangers in real estate development. He guessed it was cut-throat, with a lot of money at stake. But the risks were economic, not deadly. And Watt certainly couldn't regard Ben as a threat. Even though he'd hated his brother for years, Ben never considered bloodying his own hands.

Watt wiped up the coffee he spilled and tossed the damp towel toward an open trashcan. It hit the side and fell to the floor. They were silent for several minutes. Finally, after Ben finished his breakfast, Watt stood up. He carelessly rinsed his cup in the sink and put it in the dish drainer.

"My lawyer will be here about ten o'clock with the papers for you to sign. He'll have a certified check for you. Your life's gonna get real good." Watt had his hand on the doorframe as he spoke. "You've got the run of the place. I've got some calls to make. Try not to wake Reggie. Things get squirrelly when she's awake. I'll let you know when you're needed."

He slapped the doorframe and disappeared down a hallway. Watt's shift in demeanor surprised Ben. It was as if Watt had made some kind of assessment of Ben and drawn conclusions, and further social pleasantries were unnecessary. While Ben still had a lot of unanswered questions, Watt obviously didn't. Ben tried to understand what their brief conversation contained that prompted Watt's changed attitude.

He decided Watt had little curiosity about Ben's life, or maybe he knew all he wanted to know. With Watt's resources, he could learn anything he was willing to pay for. Ben regretted there were no dark or thrilling aspects to his life that expensive detectives might ferret out and report to Watt, who would be surprised, shocked or, maybe envious. By now, the old county jail sentence seemed just a youthful indiscretion compared to the drug dealers, pedophiles and politicians parading through the current news cycles.

It was only two hours until Watt and his lawyer would summon Ben. He didn't feel like waiting around the house with only the prospect of talking to Reggie, poor company after last night. He went quietly to his room to put on dry shoes and socks. As he walked out of his room into the hall, he saw Reggie's door was open. As he looked in, her bleary eyes locked on his. There was no escape. She was sitting on the end of her bed, arms on her knees, a cigarette smoldering from her lips.

"Hope you don't feel like me," she said, frowning through red-tinged eyelids. "You'd kill yourself so you'd feel better." She tried to laugh but it came out as a hacking cough.

"Sort of like little people roller skating in your head?" Ben said.

She took the cigarette from her mouth. "More like big people, and they've got spikes on their wheels."

"Anything I can do?" Ben entered her room. It smelled like a cheap bar the morning after a mean night.

"Just stay a bit till I come to the surface." She faced the open door even though Ben sat in a chair beside the bed. They sat silently for a few minutes. Reggie kept smoking unfiltered cigarettes. Ben looked at the window, wondering if it opened. A spider web covered the inside.

"What was it like?" Reggie finally said through a cloud of smoke. "Being away from all this."

Ben glanced at her, slumped on the end of the bed.

"Okay I guess," he said, looking at his fingers locked together. "Necessary. Lonely at times. A little scary. But I survived."

"We settle for survival. I survive. Too bad we don't reach a little higher."

Ben wondered how Reggie might have turned out if he had not gone west. "Sorry I wasn't around. Maybe I could have helped."

"Unlikely."

He noticed her hand reaching behind her for his, but he pretended not to notice and studied his hands, wondering if she was right. She let her hand drop to her side.

"You headed west and I headed into the bottle," she said. "There's more room out west, isn't there?"

Ben looked at her sagging body. "I just ran. Don't make it more than it was."

"You missed all the fun of family life. Could have enjoyed home and hearth. The warm bosom of . . . "

Reggie's voice faded. Ben felt the bed shake a little. He saw Reggie quivering as she tried not to cry. He touched her shoulder, but she jerked away.

"You could have taken me with you, or at least written. We coulda been there for each other," she said through sobs. "God, Ben, I needed you so much and you didn't even know I was alive. I hated you for it. I just died when you left. Very slowly. One day at a time. This is all that's left." She shrugged and placed her limp hands in her lap.

Ben wanted to say something that would explain why he had not contacted her. Tell her about all the letters he wrote her, but threw away rather than mail. How could he tell her he was afraid that if he got in touch with anyone he knew, his parents would have eventually discovered that, and then discovered him? He had refused to leave any trace.

"A lot died when I left. I couldn't have saved you, Reggie. I could barely save myself. Not that much was saved."

She turned to him. "At least you had some choices. You did something. You decided."

She surprised him. He didn't regard his life as resulting from the best decisions. He simply did what he could do and kept doing it for a long time without much introspection. If safety was a choice, then that was it.

"Don't make more of my life than it is," he said. "Writing about fishing trips doesn't demand much talent. I did what was easy. How hard is it to go fishing at somebody else's expense?"

Reggie flopped back on the bed with her arms outstretched. "That sounds so pleasant. You just went fishing for years and wrote about it. What I Did on My

Perpetual Vacation, by Ben Phelps. You don't know how good you had it."

Ben wanted to leave the room's stale air and Reggie's irritating whining. He couldn't make her life different. He could think of nothing to compensate for his absence.

"This land thing with Mossback – you involved? I mean, are you getting any money from Watt like he wants to give me?" Ben said.

She laughed a gravely laugh, which became a deep cough.

"I'm not trusted with any real money," she said when she could breathe again. "Watt got control over my money a long time ago. For my own good, the court said. They don't trust some of my acquaintances. Or me, either."

Ben imagined that controlling all of her wealth gave Watt a lot of leverage in whatever he wanted to do.

"Why does Watt want this place?" Ben said. "He told me he never really liked coming here."

Turning her head toward Ben, Reggie smiled at him as a parent smiles at a child's innocence, then turned her gaze toward the ceiling.

"Just take the money. You'll be happy with a lot of money. See what it's done for the rest of us." She raised her head and folded her hands behind it. "Let's just enjoy today, Bennie. No talk of money or the past or the future. Let's just have a good time, go to town for lunch. Buy something sinfully expensive. Be carefree and happy for a few hours. Can't we just do that, Bennie?" Her eyes implored Ben.

He could see her tears forming. "I'm supposed to meet with Watt and his lawyer at ten. After that, the day is yours. Do with me as you please."

Ben felt himself being drawn into Reggie's orbit. He wanted to resist, but what harm could come from a few hours spent together in self-indulgent idleness? He had been away for so many years, years when she could have used a friend, a real brother.

"Why, I won't even drink today, that's how much I want to savor this day, to remember when I got back my prodigal brother. And I intend to find out just how prodigal you've been. I want to learn all your dark secrets. You will tell all. I can be very persuasive."

Ben sat on the bed at her feet. He put his hand on her leg and squeezed and patted it. "There's not a lot to tell, but you're welcome to whatever there is. You'll be bored and very disappointed."

"Oh, Bennie, you won't disappoint me now. You're here, with me, right now. There are so many years to make up for."

Now he turned away, unable to face her with the feeling that whatever she had suffered when he ran away was partly his fault. He was irritated for letting that notion taunt him.

"We'll head up to town as soon as you finish your business. Surely you'll be done by lunch. I'll make reservations somewhere. You won't be sorry. It'll be great fun."

He kept silent about being at Mossback only for the weekend, calculating she remembered little of last night's dinner conversation. Ben dreaded her finding out he was leaving again, when she would be left to her meager resources and Watt.

"I'm glad I'm back too," he said, as he looked into her eyes without blinking. I'm just like Reggie, he thought. Today is now, and tomorrow's a long way off.

"Tell me something, Bennie," she said as she sat up in bed against the headboard. She fluffed the pillows behind her. "Did you think about me all those years? Did you miss me?"

Just a few hours and then I'll be gone, he thought. I can say anything today.

"A lot of years passed since I saw you. You were just a kid. We didn't have much to remember. I mean in the way of experiences. We were off at school or in camp. But I did think about you. What you'd become, how things turned out. Yeh, I thought about the tennis star."

She studied her hands folded across her belly. "Looking ahead's so easy when you're a kid. After a while you quit looking that far. I can't remember what we looked forward to then, do you?"

Ben laughed. "It's all sort of fuzzy. I don't remember happiness. Then, there's just anger after Watt showed up at college. I guess I just stayed that way."

She snorted and shook her head. "I remember days on the court. Serving an ace to win a match. It was a sweet time."

They were silent for several minutes. Her eyes seemed to see something very distant. Her face slowly lit up in a smile, and he thought she seemed absorbed in a reverie of a time where possibilities existed.

Ben wondered what would happen to her, how long her body could endure hopelessness and despair drenched in alcohol. The happiness she was feeling now would vanish when he left. It was not his fault he had to leave. He kept reminding himself that her life was in her hands, not his. He kept repeating it to the point it was almost credible. But one thing she had said confused him.

"You said you hated me for leaving," he said. "You should have been mad at our parents. They put Watt up to it."

Reggie frowned at Ben as if he'd said the dumbest thing she'd ever heard. She made a few false starts at speaking, then finally said, "They were crushed when you disappeared. For years they tried to find you. You were gone without a trace. Even Dad's money couldn't sniff you out of your hole."

At first, Ben didn't really absorb Reggie's words, much less their meaning, as a deadness spread through him.

"They were crushed when you disappeared" was what she just said, he was certain. This pathetic alcoholic couldn't possibly be right. She's been in a drunken stupor for years. She said as much and so did Watt. Why should she suddenly say something so preposterous and false?

"How could they be crushed?" he said, looking at her with disbelief. "They told Watt to do it. It was their idea!"

Ben stood at the edge of the bed. His fists were clenched as if he were about to beat the truth out of this drunken liar. Reggie cringed into the bed.

"Don't hit me," she cried, as she pulled the pillow over her head and turned away from him.

Seeing his sister trembling with the real fear of attack frightened Ben. He had never hit anyone, at least not in his sober adult life. He wouldn't strike a dog, much less a human.

"No one's going to beat you Reggie. Don't be afraid."

Her sobbing continued until it subsided in exhausted groaning. He was ashamed at his outburst, and pulled up a chair beside the bed and softly put his hand on her shoulder. She flinched but didn't pull away. He left his hand on her until she stopped crying. Reggie became still, but didn't face him. She was curled up around the tear-stained pillow.

"I'm sorry I frightened you. You just said something weird. I mean, I know the folks didn't want me to marry that woman. Watt was doing what they wanted, to prove it was all about money. It worked. I just couldn't live with that. I hated them."

Reggie turned her head slightly toward Ben, but she still avoided his eyes.

"I see a lot, Ben. People think I'm a stupid drunk, but I know things. I know our parents did some dumb things, but they didn't send Watt. You have to believe that. All they knew was that you disappeared. Watt never told them anything. They searched for years, but, poof, you were gone into some great void."

She finally turned to him.

"After the folks died, he told me about his visit to you. He even admitted it was his idea. Said he didn't want some gold digger after the family money. I didn't know if you were dead or alive, and figured I never would."

CHAPTER 8

Reggie's ragged fingernails dug into Ben's arms like talons. She said something, but he could only think of how his parents were dead to him long before their real deaths because of Watt's lie. The magnitude of his brother's betrayal stunned him.

Ben carefully removed her fingers from his arm. "Why?" Ben said. "Did he ever explain why he told this lie about our parents?"

"He explains nothing," she said, as she relaxed. "He just does stuff and watches what happens. He's not that way about business. But with people, he's like a cat with a mouse, only meaner."

That his life was the result of Watt's whimsy made Ben bristle. He despised his passivity in never challenging his brother or confronting his parents. *I let myself believe the worst about everyone, my brother, which was deserved, and my parents, which was not.*

"Does the mouse ever win?" Ben asked, as he gazed out the window.

Reggie draped her arm over his shoulder and hugged him. He smelled her sour breath as she kissed him on his cheek. He didn't withdraw.

"This little mouse never has," she said, leaning her head on his shoulder.

As Ben was thinking about revenge, he heard tires crunching the gravel in the driveway. Looking out the window, he saw a large Hummer pull into the parking area. A tall, gray-haired man wearing a dark suit climbed down. He gripped a thick leather briefcase. The lawyer had arrived.

"Looks like it's time for a wealth check," Ben said, stepping from the window and Reggie's embrace. "I don't know what's going to happen. It's like driving into fog."

Reggie frowned at Ben. "I wish I knew what's going on. He doesn't tell me anything. He controls my stuff 'cause of my problems."

Ben silently embraced her, walked down the hall to the stairs and wondered what level of Hell he was descending into. He heard voices as he approached the library and grew queasy as everything familiar in his life now juddered like sand in an earthquake. He couldn't stop thinking about his parents.

He could ease his cascading anxieties if he just walked out of the house, got in his van and drove away somewhere, anywhere. He'd always found that delaying unpleasant confrontations offered plenty of time to prepare for various threats. Half the battle was bracing for what happens, he knew, and that takes time. Some people called it procrastination, but that was too negative. He embraced the Boy Scout motto of being prepared, a noble sentiment, immune to criticism. He also knew avoiding Watt was the best way to keep from slugging him and getting worse in return.

He hesitated in the hallway as laughter glanced off the walls toward him. Feeling the keys in his pocket, he turned toward the door leading to the parking lot. In a moment he was driving up the twisting road toward town. A little time among strangers would provide a chance to sift through everything he had heard in the past several hours, he convinced himself as he waved at the gate guard and headed into Kelsey.

Ben parked in front of the fly-fishing shop. He walked in and saw the man he'd talked to yesterday at the cash register.

Across the room near the fly case, another man sat at a small table tying flies. Hunched over and seeming small, he had long gray hair pulled into a ponytail, and an indifferently trimmed beard with a pink scar emerging from it on his left cheek. A pipe jutted from his gray tangle, and smoke drifted lazily from the bowl as he wrapped a long black feather around a curved hook. He glanced up at Ben with pale blue eyes. He stared a moment, then resumed winding the feather and tied it off with fine black thread.

"Welcome back," the owner said, as he slammed the cash drawer closed. "Decide on a trip?" He smiled expectantly. "Got the best guide around," he said, nodding in the direction of the man tying flies. "Knows the best spots."

"We'll see," Ben said, as he wandered back toward the man tying trout flies.

"Zeke, see what you can do for the man," the owner yelled across the room.

A thick haze of smoke floated around Zeke's head. He didn't look up as he sorted through more feathers.

Ben poked through the assortment of flies in the open case with its small compartments for each size and variety.

"I'm just here to kill some time," Ben said.

"Lot'a that's been killed here," the guide said, smoke following his words.

"Good fishing here?" Ben asked indifferently.

"In the right places."

"Where's that?"

"That's what you'd pay me to show you."

Ben liked the man's directness. It was not rude, just businesslike. After all, guides made their living guiding, not talking about fishing. Ben knew that the guides who talked the most were doing what they did best, talking about fishing.

"I'm here for a couple of days," Ben said. "Family business."

"Maybe next time," the guide muttered past his pipe stem.

Ben didn't say there probably wouldn't be a next time if the family business got completed this weekend. He picked up a large fly he hadn't seen before. It was similar to western salmon fly patterns but different in the wings, which were white bucktail instead of tan, and the body had thick iridescent dubbing with a red quill feather tail. He noticed the box compartment label identified it as a "#10 Zeke's hopper."

"This your pattern?" Ben said.

The guide glanced up. "Yup."

Most fly names were just descriptions of the pattern. Sometimes a wildly effective fly honored the creator by being named after him.

"Works pretty good?" Ben said.

"Put it in the right spot it does."

Ben put several in a plastic cup.

"Where you fish?" Zeke said.

Ben hesitated to say he wrote about fly fishing, which would trigger an endless stream of chatter and questions about where he had been and what were his favorite places. Today, Ben wanted anonymity. "Go out west sometimes."

"Nice waters out west."

Ben was relieved the guide didn't seem curious about his fishing pedigree. But years of habit and journalistic training overcame him. Ben's curiosity took over. "Where do you like to fish . . . around here, I mean?" he asked.

Zeke put a drop of glue on the thread that completed the fly. He took the pipe from his mouth and scratched his beard, releasing a flurry of dandruff.

"Depends on who I'm with."

"Just by yourself. When you want the best time," Ben said.

"Place where I caretake, I suppose. Purest waters and big native brookies. Like nothing you've ever seen."

Ben had nudged Zeke this far, he decided to see how much he could extract from this reticent fisherman. A guide's marketable asset was his knowledge for sale to customers. Giving away that asset never brought in any beer money.

"The place where you caretake, can you bring other people?"

The guide kept staring at Ben, who picked at the flies in his cup. Ben wondered if the guide would rise to the bait.

"Maybe."

Ben knew he should be elsewhere rather than postponing the inevitable. He put a lid on the plastic cup and decided to return to Mossback. "Where is this place that has such great fishing?"

Zeke lit his pipe with a wooden match and sucked a few deep puffs to get the tobacco glowing. Ben heard the spittle gurgling in the pipe stem.

"I watch out for the Phelps place down in the valley. Nobody fishes it. Owner's never there. Kinda like having seven thousand acres to myself. Fish there rarely seen a human or felt a hook." Zeke took the pipe from his mouth and exhaled a stream of blue-gray smoke.

Ben saw a very contented look in the man's face. "So that's the special place that guy was talking about?" he said, nodding toward the counter. "He hinted you sometimes guide there. Can't blame you. I'd do the same if I could. Just take the right people who can keep their mouths shut and wallets open."

Ben noticed Zeke's pipe stopped smoking briefly. He wondered if his friendly collusion would disarm the man.

"I really wish I had time to see it," Ben said. "Be the trip of a lifetime, huh?"

Smoke resumed from the pipe as Zeke seemed to relax.

"Some folks think so," he said. "But just a few. Don't want to abuse it and get fired." He grinned a twisted smile and looked away.

"Too nice a set up," Ben said, thinking about how Zeke was taking advantage of his own property without permission. As soon as he considered the transgression, Ben realized whom he resembled. He was embarrassed to compare himself to Watt and he felt tainted. How easy it was to betray the most innocent confidence, he thought. The exhilaration of his brief god-like omniscience collapsed as Ben thought of his own life and how Watt's meddling changed everything. That judgment was unnerving.

Ben said good-bye to Zeke and walked to the counter to pay for the flies. He handed his business credit card to the owner, since the purchase could be regarded as a business expense. The owner processed the card, and then read the front before returning it.

"Benjamin Phelps," he said. "Same last name as the folks who own that big valley where Zeke works. Wouldn't happen to be related?"

Ben grimaced as he retrieved his card. He glanced back at Zeke who had overheard the exchange and waited for Ben's answer. He stood up and walked to the counter. Ben wished he'd paid cash. Zeke leaned an elbow on the counter and faced Ben.

"You one of those Phelps?" he said in a very quiet way with undertones that discomforted Ben. There was no room for evasion. He cursed his lack of control as his face reddened.

"Guess I'm guilty," he said. "Shouldn't have taken advantage of you. Hope you'll forgive me."

Ben learned long ago, in his brief stint in Alcoholics Anonymous, that immediately asking forgiveness caught people off guard enough to diffuse all but the worst offenses. The lesson stayed with him even though he had not been to a meeting in years. He held out his hand. "Ben Phelps," he said, with a submissive smile.

Zeke looked at his hand. He delayed his response for a moment before taking Ben's hand in a hard, calloused grip. Ben noticed Zeke's expression flicker just a second as if he just grasped some new awareness.

"Think you almost got us twice," he said.

Ben wrinkled his brow in puzzlement.

"You're the writer, huh? Fishing stories in magazines."

Ben felt a little puff of pride, never doubting the recognition carried a degree of respect. "Guilty again," he said.

Zeke turned to the owner who had been listening carefully.

"This guy's probably caught more fish in more places than you or me ever hoped to," Zeke said. "Right well known . . . in fishing circles anyway. Don't think we said anything too stupid. At least, not me." He raised his eyebrows at the owner.

The owner reached across the counter to shake the hand of fame. Ben cooperated.

"Want to do some fishing while you're here?" Zeke said. "I might still have a little leeway, maybe."

"Guess you still got enough," Ben said. "It's tempting, but I'm only here for a little bit. Probably be gone by Monday."

Zeke shrugged.

"Didn't know you existed. As an owner, I mean. I always dealt with Watt. He never mentioned you. No reason to, I suppose."

Ben felt the ready curiosity of both men. He was not sure how to explain his absence.

"I've been away fishing a long time."

The owner leaned over the counter with outstretched arms.

"You really ought to have Zeke show you the place. Nobody knows those creeks like him. You won't ever find better fishing. Hey, no charge since you live there."

"He's been away a long time, Hank. Maybe he just wants to get reacquainted at his own pace," Zeke said

Ben appreciated Zeke's intervention. It was time to get back to Mossback. The longer he stayed, the greater the likelihood of encounters like this one. The curious might be more insistent to know how could anyone be gone so long from such a magnificent place and be such a stranger to his home and family? How could he explain that he turned his back on his family because his brother bribed a girlfriend years ago? Trying to explain that to anyone might sound as peculiar as it was beginning to sound to him. His ability to deflect unpleasant intrusions into his life was getting more difficult.

"Maybe I'll see you later," Ben said, without conviction he would ever see this place again, much less the two men. Kelsey would be in his rearview mirror very soon.

Ben wondered what Zeke knew about Watt. Was Watt aware Zeke had a profitable sideline taking people fishing at Mossback? Ben concluded Zeke did his job and kept his little enterprise very private. Considering Mossback's size, Zeke had plenty of territory to fish, assuming there were a couple of good size streams. Exclusive fishing in very private waters could bring Zeke a fat premium. That might make a very good story for a magazine, he thought. As an owner, he had certain access to the subject matter. I can do whatever I want at Mossback, he realized.

CHAPTER 9

Hope that he could postpone the inevitable vanished when Ben noticed the lawyer's car still parked at the house. On the winding drive from town, Ben still waffled on how he would avenge Watt's lie. He really wanted to know how his interest in more than seven thousand acres of virgin forest had been overlooked. "Seven-fucking-thousand acres!" he shouted over his van's sputtering cylinders.

Ben heard muffled conversation as he walked to the library door. He took a deep breath, and walked in. Watt and the lawyer looked up from long, unrolled maps they were holding down on a table. They removed their hands and the maps snapped closed.

"We thought you were avoiding us for some reason," Watt said, as he looked at the lawyer. "Herb here thought you might be prejudiced against lawyers or something." Watt laughed and slapped the man on his shoulder. "Ben, want you to meet Herb Funk. Herb, this is my long lost brother Ben I told you about."

Nodding at the lawyer, Ben glanced at the table to see if there were any clues about what they had been discussing. The lawyer's briefcase was open on the table, but the top shielded its contents. He noticed Ben's glance, and closed the briefcase, clicking the latches.

"Ben, I understand you've been away fishing and writing," Funk said. "Must be fun to get paid for such a pleasant pastime. A lot of people I know would give anything to have your job."

Ben gave a small smile to acknowledge the remark and looked at Watt. "I guess this is when you tell me why you asked me here. The big payoff."

Watt grinned and turned to Funk. "This is my kind of guy. Likes to get right to the bone. No extraneous bullshit. Bottom line kind of guy. Gotta like his approach to money."

"It's not every day a brother you haven't seen in forty years calls and says you're rich," Ben said. "So, tell me all about it."

Watt and Funk looked at each other, and Watt cleared his throat. Funk shifted to the side a little to give Watt center stage.

"That's a fair request after so many years," Watt said. "Let's all have a seat while I explain." Watt gestured to the chairs placed around the table. Watt and Funk sat on one side, and Ben sat directly across from them. The rolled up maps were between them on the wide, oak plank table.

"Basically, Ben, the situation is this," Watt said. "Our parents put Mossback into a private, closely-held corporation."

Watt went on to explain that the stock had been evenly divided among the five family members: the parents and three children. When the parents died, their shares went to Watt and Reggie. In time, Watt bought enough of Reggie's stock to gain voting control of the corporation. Any sale of stock had to be made to another shareholder at a pre-determined price based on an established formula. Ben could sell his twenty-percent share only to another shareholder. The value had been kept low through the years because the land was placed in a twenty-year conservation easement to reduce the property taxes.

"So, you see, you can only sell to me," and, he added with a laugh, "or Reggie."

"I'm wondering if I shouldn't check with a lawyer first," Ben said. "I'm sure you have my best interests at heart, but . . .."

"We assumed you would," Herb Funk said. "You'd be foolish not to."

Watt glanced at his lawyer with a disgusted look. "Sure, check things out," he said. "But lawyers are pricey. I should know. They always want their money, so you better have a lot of it before you have one open his trap. They charge by the word sometimes."

Watt grinned at Funk as if daring a reaction. Funk quietly looked at some papers in his hands. Ben sensed Watt knew that a couple of months rent money comprised Ben's available funds.

"Please be aware that just because you are an owner of shares, you don't have any proprietary rights over Mossback," Funk said, looking up from his clutch of papers to Watt. "This place is not a residence anymore, it's a corporate asset."

"That's a lawyer for you," Watt said. "Of course, you can stay here as long as the C.E.O. says so, and I say so. Want you to feel welcome."

Ben nodded despite all the questions churning in his mind, including how he could afford a lawyer.

"Anyway, Ben, an oversight was discovered and now needs to be corrected. I want to put Mossback in another corporation and need full control to do it. I'm willing to pay you a more than fair price for your share. Independent appraisal and all that. You can check around as much as you like. You'll see my offer is very fair under the circumstances."

Watt looked at Herb in expectation of something. Herb hesitated, and then pulled a folder from his briefcase. He opened the folder and extracted a bound document and a single sheet of paper. He pushed both of them across the table. Ben saw the appraisal and a certified check. He looked at the numbers and blinked in disbelief. He squinted at the numbers to be certain they were what he thought they were. No matter how hard he stared, the numbers kept saying five million dollars. The amount didn't really register at first. There must be some mistake. So many zeros. He picked up the appraisal and flipped through pages he did not understand. Near the beginning he caught a sentence that stood out in bold face type by itself:

"Based on all the calculations and comparable sales, it is my estimate that the twenty-percent share of the property known as Mossback, which is owned by the Phelps heirs, is worth four million dollars."

"Why's the check more than the appraisal?" Ben said.

Watt raised his eyebrows in Herb's direction.

"I told you this guy was smart," Watt said. "A good fisherman has to notice everything around him, get the lay of the land, or stream, I guess you should say." Watt leaned toward Ben with a sincere expression. "You've been without for a long time, little brother. I just thought it would be right to sweeten the pot 'cause of what you've been through, and what you got left out of by the folks.

I can't make up for everything you've been through, but an extra million might make up for something."

Ben resisted grabbing Watt by his throat and crushing it, steadily and very slowly. He wanted to burst into laughter at what he knew was a grotesque lie. But, he also remembered the numbers on the check. Ben leaned back to regard his brother from a distance that was safer for both of them.

"All you have to do now is sign the sales agreement, then the check and a new life are yours," Watt said with a big grin. "Isn't it great, Ben? One day you're just living your old life as always, then, boom! Out of nowhere comes money from the gods. Life can be so goddam funny at times, huh?"

Watt shook his head in amazement at the serendipitous nature of the whole series of events. He looked at Funk. "Have you ever seen anything like it, Herb? I mean, from nothing to everything in just a few hours. If we hadn't tracked him down, no telling where he'd end up in a few years. Not many retirement benefits in freelancing, huh?"

"You're right, Watt," Funk said. He straightened his shirt cuffs and smoothed his suit sleeves. "One of the most peculiar strokes of good luck I've ever seen. Ben, you're a fortunate man, thanks to your brother's refusal to give up looking for you. He had detectives searching everywhere. Not a penny was spared."

Ben wondered if they had ever heard of Google, but kept his mouth shut. As a writer of fish stories that often contained more fiction than he should have dared, Ben's bullshit detector was ready to blow. He was, however, too poor to be noble, arrogant or stupid. The money had a restraining influence on his felonious attitude toward his brother. Sometimes when you're playing a big fish in strong waters, you have to work downstream with it a ways until you see the best place to land it. Forcing the fish too early can cause it to break the line and make the fisherman lose everything.

They want my agreement very much, so the check won't evaporate any time soon, he decided. He was not going to refuse their offer, either. When the course isn't clear, he thought, the best thing to do is nothing, but in a way that makes nothing look like something.

"This is all a big shock to me as you can imagine," Ben said, looking more at Herb than Watt. "After so many years being reunited with what's left of my family. I never thought I'd see them again. And seeing poor Reggie this way." Ben looked at the floor and frowned. "And then there's the surprise of seeing our home again. Such happy childhood memories at Mossback. Then, I learn my brother wants to give me five millions dollars. That's a hell of a lot to swallow in just a few hours."

Ben looked at the two men across the table and sensed their discomfort. Herb adjusted the knot of his necktie. Watt's jaw muscles rippled quickly, then he wet his lips.

"You can certainly understand if I ask you to let me think about your offer," Ben said. "Just a little time. A few hours. Tomorrow I can give you an answer."

"I understand how you feel," Watt said, as he looked to Herb, then back at Ben. "You're right. We've heaped a lot on your plate. You have a lot to think about and we don't want to pressure you. But, if it's a matter of money, let me know. I thought the price was fair, but you might have other ideas. Nothing's in granite here."

Ben was glad to hear Watt was open to raising the price, not because he wanted more. He had no idea if he was getting a fair offer. Watt's openness indicated how badly he wanted control of Mossback, another bit of information that might be useful later. This was not a situation of Watt enticing some poor schmuck into selling a piece of land for some development deal. This was different, Ben knew, more personal, but he didn't know why.

"What do I know about money?" Ben said to Watt. "You're the expert here. Everybody knows you have the Midas touch. Our genes really separated there, huh? It's not the money, really. I just want a little time to think about everything. I'm not saying no. Just let me mull it over. I didn't think I had a home, and now I do. That's quite a jolt."

Watt just blinked a few times. Ben liked seeing his brother in a spot that made him squirm. Watt not getting his way pleased Ben, who grasped whatever advantage he could scrape together at this point. He clung to a slim branch when the powerful current wanted to pull him downstream, but he didn't know how long his grip would hold.

Suddenly Watt laughed and punched Herb in his shoulder. "How could we be so stupid," he bellowed. "Of course you can take some time to think about the offer. After what you've been through, who could expect you to do anything less? You're not stupid. Tomorrow's fine. I don't want to rush you into anything. I'm sure you want to get your bearings. Walk around a bit to clear your head, and you'll see this is a good deal for you."

Watt started clearing the table and with Herb's help, papers and maps were put into files, boxes and briefcases designed to hold expensive dreams and schemes.

"While you are doing your thinking, just keep this little bit of information in your formula," Watt said calmly, as he was snapping the lock on his brief case. "Each of us owns some of Mossback. I own controlling interest. Because of Reggie's condition, I have power of attorney over all her affairs. I can do whatever I want because I control the stock in our little corporation. Don't take that as a threat, just a valuable piece in your equation. So you can see my offer is really generous and heartfelt. You can guess I don't part with that kind of money every day just to be nice. You're special. I want to treat you that way."

Ben marveled at Watt's ability to disarm him and keep him a little off balance. Just for a moment he thought there might be a grain of truth in this brotherly sentiment. Ben looked out the window to keep from having to face Watt. The sky was clear except for a few fat, languidly drifting clouds.

"Just leave all the papers with me," Watt told the lawyer. "If Ben decides to accept, he can sign any time, take the check and be on his way to a rich life."

Funk frowned, then shrugged. "I guess someone can notarize the signature on your say so. Who could doubt you?" Funk said with a smirk only Ben could see.

Funk gathered his remaining papers and carefully placed them in various pockets in his briefcase, snapped it shut and looked around for any forgotten scraps.

"I'll be at the inn if you need me for anything," he said to Watt, who nodded as he guided him to the door. "Oh, Ben. Just to correct a misperception on your part, you don't suddenly have a home here. You only have some restricted stock that happens to have this house as part of its assets. It's an important distinction."

"You know your way out," Watt said, as Funk walked out of the room. "Cold-hearted bastard."

Silently they watched the lawyer leave, as the Hummer's tires crunched the gravel.

The mention of town reminded Ben of his encounter with Zeke that morning. He speculated how Watt's vague plan would affect his employment. Would he be kept on, or fired and lose his special fishing paradise? He knew almost nothing about this caretaker who doubled as a fishing guide.

"I met someone today who says he works here," Ben said. "Bearded guy named Zeke McCall who said he's Mossback's caretaker. Met him at that fly-fishing shop in town a few hours ago. Appears to be a popular fishing guide. He work here long?"

Watt looked at Ben inquisitively as he tilted his head slightly, apparently caught off guard by the mention of Zeke. How would Watt react when confronted with Reggie's revelation, Ben wondered smugly.

"Zeke McCall," Watt repeated the name. "Yeh, he's the caretaker. Done the job for as long as I can remember. Dad hired him long ago. He probably knows this place like you know your dick." Watt chuckled at his analogy. "So he works out of that fly shop? Didn't know he moonlights. Judging from his appearance, he sure looks the part. But that's half the game, right?"

"What do you know about him?" Ben said.

"Not much. We used to hang out when we were teens. Drank some beer, chased local pussy." Watt gazed at the ceiling. "There was this place across the state line called Mal's that was the only place to get beer. This state was dry then. Zeke drove us down some god-awful dirt road you wouldn't want to get lost on. Suddenly there was this tiny cinderblock building with a door and a drive-up window. Zeke'd pull up and say 'PBR' and a brown paper bag would be shoved through the window. We made a lot of trips down that road."

Watt's eyes narrowed, and Ben wondered if his brother was in pain. Then, just as quickly, Watt shook his head as if to shed an unwanted thought.

"When did he start working here?" Ben said.

"Seems like he's always been here. Can't remember when he wasn't. Just always been part of the place, like the trees, rocks and critters. Another critter, only on the payroll a long time."

"There must be some good-size streams here with nice wild trout," Ben said. "A fisherman like Zeke must be in heaven. Be a big temptation to bring some client here."

Watt's expression went blank. "Be the last thing he ever did here."

"You've told him, of course." Ben suddenly felt small and duplicitous.

"We've not talked much. He knows what to do. Place looks pretty good for nobody using it. He's got a little house near here at no charge. Overall, a pretty cushy job for hanging out in the woods. He's smart enough not to screw up."

Ben had no doubt Watt would destroy someone who crossed him. If Reggie's story was true, Watt was capable of anything.

"I guess you could ruin a person's life if it suits your needs," Ben said.

Watt glared at Ben, who tensed as he paused for an explosive outburst. An overwhelming anger boiled up in his throat as he remembered Reggie's words about Watt's solo trip to Ben's dorm room years ago.

"I understand you're even capable of destroying someone related to you, like a brother. Reggie told me that our parents didn't even know about your visit to me at the university. You told me they sent you. Is there any lie you won't tell?"

"Oh, shit Ben," Watt said. "Don't tell me you're going to believe a story told by a lush. Reggie hasn't had a sober week outside of detox that I know of. She's so miserable about her life she wants everyone to share. Misery loves company, you know, and will say anything to get it.

"What you know about your life is the truth. It all happened the way you remember it. You chose to run away. Nobody encouraged you or forced you. No one rejected you. What you did was what you thought necessary, but don't blame anyone else for your decision. Be man enough to accept what you did. The dead can't defend themselves, but I can. What we did was for your own good, and the fact the tramp took the money should be proof enough. Grow up, Ben. Get on with your life. Quit being a victim. Fuck somebody instead of letting them always fuck you."

Watt finished putting away papers, folders and bound reports in the desk, locked the drawer and put the key in his pocket. Sitting in a large leather chair next to the desk, he took a cigar from a mahogany case. As he rolled the dark cylinder of tobacco, he inhaled its dry aroma. A satisfied, dreamy smile spread across his face. He lit the end with a gold lighter, took a few puffs and watched the smoke drift slowly across the room in Ben's direction.

"Ben, no one can make up for what you've experienced but you," he said. "I'm giving you a chance to have a comfortable life. It's your right because of the nature of things. That's the truth. Enjoy it."

Ben understood his present life, where the only truth was that trout were hungry and easily fooled by skilled fishermen, and a lot of office-weary people were eager to know how it was done. That simple truth had sustained him for years. He had become so comfortable with the familiar, why change?

"Maybe you're right," Ben said finally. "Reggie's not the most credible witness, I guess."

CHAPTER 10

The sound of old slippers flapping on the wooden hallway floor signaled Reggie's approach. Her stained pale-blue robe barely covered the ruffled bottom of her flannel nightgown. She took a deep drag on her cigarette and blew the smoke into the room.

"What scheme's ya'll hatching?" she said, leaning her shoulder against the doorframe. "Up to no good, aren't you?"

"Just settling some old business," Watt said. "It's got nothing to do with you."

"That right, Bennie? Nothing to do with me? Bet it's got plenty to do with this place. You gonna sell out your birthright for a pot of . . . What was it a pot of? Money, if Watt's got anything to do with it. But a smaller pot than you deserve. Big brother never gives fair value, just what he can get away with. And count your fingers after shaking his hand."

"He's offered a lot of money for my share of Mossback," Ben said. "More than the appraised price."

"And who paid the appraiser?" Reggie flicked a long ash on the floor and scattered it with her slipper. She grinned at Watt.

Watt rose from his chair and walked toward Reggie. She dashed to Ben's side and threw her arms around him and buried her head in his chest.

"Don't let him hurt me," she said. "You don't know what he can do. If you did, you'd never sign anything. Tell him to go to hell."

Watt leaned against the oak table and folded his arms across his chest. He glared at Reggie clinging to Ben like a terrified monkey.

"See why I have her power of attorney?" Watt said. "She lives in a world of alcoholic delusion, off the deep end."

Reggie looked up at Ben as tears smeared across her puffy red face. "Ask him why he wants Mossback so bad. He won't tell you 'cause he doesn't want anyone to know. Top secret stuff, huh, Mr. Big Developer? Well, I know what he's doing. Big deal golf course, where the richest men can whack their balls in a virgin forest. Only one of its kind. No way in or out 'cept for that one road. Unless you're a billy goat. The Wilderness Club, he calls it. Bought off a lot of politicians. Thought of everything."

Ben looked at Watt as Reggie began coughing. The spasm made her release Ben. She kneeled on the floor and hugged her gut, then slumped back on her heels as the coughing subsided.

"Just sell out now and make it happen. You can be just like big brother," she mumbled from the floor.

"Her brain's soaked in bourbon," Watt said. "I'm really sorry you have to see this. Commitment in some asylum seems like the only way to help her."

"Like hell," she shot back. "A baby couldn't have an easier time getting booze in this house. Only time he cuts me off is when he throws me in detox. Rest of the time, the bar's always open."

Reggie was slumped on the floor, leaning against Ben's legs. He glanced at her hair, which looked like tangled snakes.

"Why do you want the place so badly?" he said, while he studied Reggie's hair.

"Reasonable question," Watt said. "I've got several concepts, but nothing has jelled yet. Of course, whatever happens will respect the place. But I like to act quickly when I do make up my mind, so having complete control is important."

Five million worth of importance, Ben thought, as he felt a tugging on his pant leg. He noticed Reggie thrusting an envelope toward him. "Here," she said.

Ben took the unsealed envelope which had his name scrawled across the front. He removed the contents, two hand-written pages of lined paper. At the top of the page, in capital block letters were the words "LAST WILL AND TESTAMENT OF REGINA ELIZABETH PHELPS." Ben could barely read the shaky script, but he deciphered the essence of the page: Reggie left anything she owned to Ben. He glanced at the short note acknowledging that she didn't have much control over her personal affairs because Tennessee courts had granted Watt power of attorney over her money. But she wanted Ben to have anything she had because he had suffered too much, and this might make his life a little better.

He held the pages down by his side as he stared at her dumbstruck. Watt finally asked what was going on.

"Seems she's making plans for the future," Ben said. "Reggie, this isn't necessary. You can be around a long time. Just take care of yourself."

"What plans?" Watt said, as he started walking toward Ben. "What's she done?"

"I'm leaving everything to Ben!" Reggie screamed from the floor. She turned to Watt. "Everything I own goes to him. Your lies ruined his life. He deserves better."

He wanted to run away but couldn't move with Reggie wrapped around his legs. He speculated what past holiday gatherings must have been like. It's too much like a bad movie, he thought. My brother wants to control everything and Reggie just wants to be out of control. One drunk on power and the other just drunk.

Watt moved slowly toward his entangled brother and sister. He held out his hand for Ben to show him the two pages.

"Don't let him touch them," Reggie said.

Ben handed them to Watt, who glanced at them and handed them back to Ben.

"They're worthless, at least the will is," Watt said.

"I can make a hand-written will," Reggie growled from the floor. "I saw it on TV. It's legal."

"A holographic will is legal if you're in your right mind," Watt said. "The key words being 'right mind.' A lot of legal and medical talent says that just ain't the case, honey."

"I was when I wrote it. That's all that counts."

Watt looked questioningly at Ben.

"Your call, little brother."

Ben resolved to stick with his original instinct to postpone any decision until the next day. He pulled away from Reggie's grasp and she slumped prostrate on the floor as she looked up at her brothers.

"Like I said, I'm going to sleep on it. The money sounds great, but I hate to rush into anything. I did that once, long ago."

Ben was pleased with his comparison. The only intelligent thing I've said all day, he thought.

"That's fine," Watt said, as he squatted down to look at Reggie. "Just remember, anything she says is completely without effect. That's not my opinion, it's the court's. That piece of paper is worthless."

Watt hesitated a minute as he regarded his sister. He turned his face toward Ben.

"Be careful nothing happens to her," Watt said. "You're the only one to gain by her death now if you believe her scribbling is worth anything. If she died under questionable circumstances that might look suspicious. Gives you a motive. You would never consider such a thing, but you can't tell what other people might think. She really hasn't done you a favor. Of course, that's what happens to her good intentions."

Watt sat back and laughed heartily at the picture he painted. As he tried to catch his breath, he didn't notice Reggie get to her knees and pull herself up by the sofa. She grabbed an ashtray from a side table and hurled it at Watt, hitting his foot.

"You goddamn arrogant bastard," she yelled. "Think you know every fucking thing about everything. You and your asshole lawyers and judges don't know me. They just bend over for you and do whatever the fuck you tell them. You got the best dickheads money can buy."

Reggie was sputtering, drool running down her chin. Her face reddened with veins bulging in her neck and temple. Her fingers grasped imaginary objects as they tightened and relaxed and tightened.

"You can't ruin our lives forever. Your shit-ass ways are gonna end 'cause I'm gonna end 'em. I know every fucking thing about you. You think I'm just pissing drunk all the time, but I hear things, and see things. I know what a pile of dog shit you are, and I'm gonna tell every goddamn thing I know."

Reggie screamed so hard she didn't notice Watt rise up and lean forward. She didn't see his thick hand swing around and catch her on the side of her face. After she bounced off the sofa onto the floor she shut her eyes tightly, rigidly tucked her arms by her side and growled like a trapped panther. Finally she yelled, "You gonna kill me like you did that girl? Tell Ben about that, you girl killer, fuck head."

She kicked her feet on the floor and twisted back and forth. Ben froze. At first he wanted to defend Reggie by smashing his fist into Watt's face. But Reggie was acting crazy, making accusations of murder. His siblings' lurid histories were best left undiscovered. He only needed to remember why he came to Mossback.

"Maybe it's time for Bolivar again, for a very long stretch," Watt said, as he looked down on Reggie.

Reggie stopped her twisting and clutched a pillow next to her and put it over her head. "No electricity, please. No more. They'll kill me next time. You fucker, please, no," she groaned into the pillow.

It took a minute for Ben to recall when he was a child his parents jokingly threatened that the boys would be put into the Bolivar Institute for the Insane in West Tennessee if they didn't behave and quit acting like wild animals. Maybe Watt had made good on the threat, for vastly different reasons.

Watt looked at Ben with a relaxed expression. "I think things will calm down a little now," Watt said. "She'll probably sleep a long time. I'll get her up to her room. We don't want anything to happen to her, especially now that you're her heir."

Watt grunted as he lifted Reggie's limp body. Ben heard Watt's heavy footsteps on the stairs and the hallway floor as he headed for Reggie's room.

Ben stood in the middle of the room feeling light-headed and realized he still held the papers Reggie gave him. She bequeathed him everything she thought she possessed, in return for what?

If only it had been nothing more than a simple real estate deal, Ben sighed. Too bad all this couldn't have been done through the mail without the drama. He wondered what would happen if history repeated itself.

Running away had led to many peaceful years. Peaceful, he scoffed. More like dead. Sometimes the loneliness nibbled at him, but usually it didn't last too long.

Ben shook his head to clear the vapors and headed out the door, hoping a long walk would focus his thinking. Where the drive connected to the road he could head left where it led back to town or take the way to the right, which stretched a ways until it disappeared into the woods. Ben turned right.

CHAPTER 11

Fragments of light filtering through the leaves glittered on the gravel as Ben wandered away from the house. The elation of a five million dollar windfall couldn't dislodge Reggie's wild accusations of Watt's lying and his somehow being involved in a girl's death. Her claims seemed no less bizarre than Watt's explanation that the ownership of seven thousand acres of virgin forest had been an innocent oversight for years. Thoughts of money, lies and death collided in his mind. What had his family become?

Despite the time of day, Ben thought some strong whisky would be a calming tonic, or, at worst, a lovely escape.

"Welcome home," he yelled down the road. He kicked at stones in the road and almost lost his balance.

He missed his days as a young reporter in West Yellowstone. Whenever life confused, angered or saddened him, some camaraderie and a tapped beer keg always smoothed the jagged edges. From the jukebox, Willie Nelson, Merle Haggard and Waylon Jennings

invited Ben into their worlds of lost love, broken promises and wasted lives. Soon he would be floating in a
bourbon and beer fog, eager for warm comforting arms,
all of which would be a painfully blurred memory come
morning.

Mulling over his predicament, Ben didn't hear the approaching vehicle behind him. A sharp blast from a horn
made Ben lurch to the side and stumble into a clump
of galax. Looking up, Ben saw a battered, sky-blue Ford
truck pull up beside him. Zeke leaned out the window, a
tobacco-stained grin spreading through his beard.

"Didn't mean to make you dirty your drawers," he
said. "You sorta had a monopoly on the road. Course, I
guess it is your road, but lunch is waiting and my empty
gut's got no manners."

Ben sat up and brushed his arms and legs, adrenalin
still racing through his veins. "No worry. You're not on
my payroll," he muttered loudly enough to be heard.
"Watt wouldn't be so understanding."

Zeke regarded Ben's position a little longer while
his grin receded. "Let me make up by offering lunch.
Nothing fancy. Soup and fresh bread. Homemade by a
great cook, and I don't mean me."

Ben welcomed the diversion and wondered who was
doing the home cooking, because Zeke hadn't mentioned any family.

"If you're not too picky about your guests," Ben said, climbing aboard. Zeke was silent as the truck rattled along the gravel road deeper into the woods. Ben contentedly listened to the truck creak and clatter as it bounced along the rutted surface. When the truck struck a deep pothole, Ben's door popped open. He grabbed the handle, which came off in his hand after the door slammed shut.

"Sorry about the handle," he said. "Didn't mean to break your truck."

Zeke laughed. "Not my truck," he said. "It's sorta yours, such as it is. Piece of shit, really."

My truck? Then he understood the statement was directed at him as an owner of Mossback, a title Ben wore uneasily.

As the truck picked up speed, Ben saw another truck coming toward them. It was the small Japanese model he had seen recently. Zeke slowed down and pulled off to the right as the truck approached. Both trucks stopped alongside each other, and Ben recognized the old man he saw at dawn in the woods.

"Find anything worth selling, Bob?" Zeke asked the old man.

"Nothing you don't already know about," the man said in a high pitched, quavering voice. "Who's the passenger?"

Zeke looked back at Ben as he considered the question.

"One of the owners, guess you could say. Ben, meet Bob Parker, our notorious naturalist. Bob, Ben's one of the owners of Mossback. Watt's little brother."

Parker looked a little sheepish as he acknowledged the introduction. "Sort of met this morning," he said. "You my boss too, now?"

"That's Watt's privilege," Ben said. "He signs your check."

"Anything new?" Zeke asked.

"Like he said, Watt signs the check, so Watt gets the report," Parker said. "Anyway, you've seen everything I've seen."

"I know what's here but it don't seem special 'cause I've seen it all my life," Zeke said.

"You and I might be the only ones to have seen it then," Parker said.

"Can't you make him talk straight?" Zeke said, as he half-turned to Ben.

"I'm just an innocent bystander," Ben said, raising his hands in helplessness.

"Just tell you this, Zeke, there are a lot more than fish on this place that are worth notice. A lot more." Parker waived as he put his truck in gear and slowly drove away.

"I hate people who talk in circles instead of straight lines," Zeke said, mashing the accelerator, making the truck spew gravel and fishtail down the road. "Academics! They specialize in torturing the English language."

"That old guy someone special?" Ben said. "Ran into him this morning on the road. Just about as informative."

Zeke thought a moment, smiled, and then told Ben that Parker was the most respected naturalist in the South. Parker was the head of environmental studies at Duke University when he retired to the lucrative life of a private consultant in conservation biology. Any time a large developer started planning the latest golf course, they hired Parker to discover any problem areas, like rare plants or animals living in potential fairways or building lots.

"But, you know," Zeke said, "the old fart never fudges a report. His word is solid, and he's well paid. Plans might have to change because of what he finds, but it saves the big boys a lot of bucks to have him on their side. With his connections, he can bring down protest hell on a project. He even got the U.S. Forest Service to change the way it logged forests around here. There haven't been big clearcuts for years. All kinds of people listen to him. Wonder why Watt's got Parker sniffing around Mossback?"

Ben also wondered why Watt hired the kind of person Zeke described. If he could believe a drunk, he might already know the answer.

Zeke turned onto a dirt track road that ended at a cabin with a rusty metal roof and chestnut-bark shingle siding. Thin smoke drifted lazily from a stovepipe chimney. Zeke led the way into the cabin.

The cabin's cleanliness surprised Ben because he assumed Zeke lived alone. Ben expected bachelor carelessness and indifference, perhaps reflecting his own domestic habits. An overstuffed sofa and chair and a bare rocking chair were set in front of a granite fireplace filled with cold ashes. Beyond that area, toward the back, Ben saw an open kitchen with exposed shelves, on old porcelain sink beneath a window, and an ancient wood-burning cook-stove with a kettle on top. The smell of simmering meat and vegetables filled the room. On the other side of the cabin were two closed doors Ben assumed led to bedrooms. On a wall by the fireplace was a bookshelf filled with fading books that had lost their dust covers. The floors were worn, wide-plank pine that had been painted a long time ago. The deep woods and small windows made the cabin seem dim and isolated in the world.

"Smells good," Ben said as he stood in the middle of the room, inhaling the aroma of herbs and garlic. "Your wife must be a good cook."

Zeke laughed. "She was, but she died years ago. Mama handles the domestics."

Ben wondered how old Zeke's mother must be because Zeke seemed at least as old as Watt, maybe a few years older, even though he was lean and apparently in good condition.

"Sorry about your wife," Ben said.

"Mama takes pretty good care of things," Zeke said. He walked to one of the bedroom doors and listened. He quietly opened the door to peek inside, and then closed it. "She's asleep. Don't worry about waking her. She's pretty deaf."

Zeke went to the stove and spooned soup into bowls and set them on the kitchen table covered in blue and white vinyl cloth. Zeke put a round loaf of dark bread and a bowl of soft butter on the table.

"Simple, but filling," he said as he sat down.

They ate in silence. Ben had eaten in a lot of places out in the country and in cities, but he had never tasted anything like the thick soup he consumed with growing pleasure.

"This is incredible," Ben said when he stopped eating long enough to take a deep breath. "What's in it?"

"All grown outside or killed on the place. Deer meat, some squirrel or rabbit. Turnips, carrots, onions and garden herbs. Whatever mama decides is right. Nothing from a store, 'cept salt and pepper, I guess."

They both swiped chunks of the crusty bread around their bowls until they shined. Zeke belched loudly as he patted his flat stomach.

"Not bad for a deaf old woman way in her eighties," Zeke said as he pushed away from the table. He put the bowls and utensils in the sink.

On the cabin walls a few photographs captured special moments in their lives. A bamboo fly rod and double-barrel shotgun hung over the fireplace. Clumps of dried herbs and flowers dangled from a beam in the kitchen ceiling.

"How long have you been here?" Ben said.

"All my life."

"I'm sorry, I guess I should have known," he said. "I've been away a long time. I was only a kid when I was here before. I don't remember seeing you."

Zeke stuffed his pipe with fresh tobacco. He lit it and took several long puffs. "I wasn't supposed to be seen," he said through a cloud of fragrant smoke. "Mom worked up at the house. I was told to keep away and not bother anyone. Didn't for the most part. Fished a lot. That's why you didn't see me. I saw you sometimes, but you were little."

Zeke talked fondly about growing up at Mossback and running wild in the woods, a magic place most boys never imagined. Sometimes he was called to the big house to play with Watt when he didn't have friends staying with him. Zeke tried to get him interested in fishing, but Watt was indifferent, said he liked team sports. "He didn't take much to nature."

Zeke said that when he was old enough, Ben's father offered him the care-taking job. That was after two years in the army. "Didn't see you around then," he said.

"What did your dad do?" Ben said.

"Never knew him," Zeke said, gazing into the cold fireplace. "Mom never talks about him."

Ben thought he had imposed enough. He felt a twitch of jealousy for Zeke's unpretentious life.

"Have you noticed anything unusual going on around Mossback?" Ben said. "I mean, strangers poking around . . . other than that old guy Parker?"

Zeke knocked the pipe's ashes into the fireplace and pulled out the tobacco pouch. He looked at it, decided against another smoke and put the pipe and pouch on the table beside his chair. He coughed up a large wad of phlegm and spit it into the fireplace.

"Seen some things, like planes flying over a lot, real low. Engineers and surveyors snooping around, drilling, digging and marking things. Said Watt hired them. Showed me a paper. Watt sent me a letter telling me they were doing research for him and don't get in their way. No explanation, nothing. I know this place better than anybody. Stay out of their way, he says."

Zeke spit into the fireplace again and wiped his mouth with his sleeve.

"Any guesses about the purpose?" Ben said.

Zeke shook his head.

"My sister thinks Watt wants to put in a golf course here. Some really expensive development."

Ben watched Zeke for some kind of reaction. The only change he saw was Zeke squinting as if trying to see something far in the distance.

"Be a travesty, a god-awful travesty," Zeke finally said. "Could be done. Land lies well in this broad valley."

Zeke grabbed his pipe, filled it to the brim, lit it and puffed furiously.

"Lot of golf courses around here," Zeke said. "Each one claiming to be more luxurious than anything before. Bulldozers come in and scrape every wild thing, then they replant with scrawny little plants. Smothers a stream, kills it dead with silt. Just so a bunch of pampered city folks can ride around chasing balls and telling lies, and think they're in nature. Wouldn't know nature if it bit 'em in the ass. They'd be terrified."

Zeke blew out a deep cloud of smoke. He seemed to sink into his chair in resignation. His head leaned back as he stared at the ceiling. "He could probably get big bucks for lots around here. Guess he really needs the money," Zeke said.

"The money just keeps score," Ben said. "Maybe Reggie's wrong. Could be something else. She's not the most sober witness."

Zeke turned to Ben and raised an eyebrow. "Glad I'm not the only one to notice," he said. "That girl's gonna get hurt real bad, she keeps up her consumption. Found her wandering in the woods day before you got here. She was stumbling and babbling. Something about a prodigal son. She have any children?"

Ben doubted it, but anything was possible. He had a notion what prodigal son she was thinking about.

"Reggie's heard something," Ben said. "You got any sources."

"I got a friend at the county courthouse with a nose like a Walker Hound," Zeke said.

Ben was about to stand up to leave, then hesitated. Despite knowing Zeke only for a few hours, he felt comfortable with him, a kinship that he welcomed.

"You ought to know something," he said, unsure if he should confess what Watt had offered that morning. Ben felt he could trust Zeke; he needed to trust someone. He told him about Watt wanting to buy Ben's share of Mossback and expecting an answer in the morning. He told Zeke about the threat that Ben's refusal wouldn't stop Watt's plans. Ben said he left Watt with the impression the offer would be accepted, but that he wanted to think about it overnight. He couldn't tell Zeke what his answer would be because he didn't know. Zeke didn't ask, either.

"Get out of the house before anyone wakes up and stay away till at least noon," Zeke said. "I might learn something by then."

Zeke offered to take Ben back to the house. As they were standing on the porch, Ben remembered the other accusation Reggie made. It was so vague, without any context, but he decided Zeke probably knew more about the Phelps family history than he did.

"Reggie said something else about Watt. Something about killing a girl. I don't know what she meant, but it got a violent reaction from Watt. He slapped her, hard."

Zeke was stepping down with his hand on the railing when Ben made his remark. Ben noticed Zeke stumble, then recover quickly. He stood on the step, tightly gripping the handrail. Ben saw Zeke's jaws clenching even through his thick beard. His lips squeezed together. After a few deep breaths, Zeke said, "Get in the truck. We need to revisit some ghosts."

CHAPTER 12

They traveled only as far as the end of the driveway when Zeke stopped the truck and stared absently out the windshield drumming his fingers on the steering wheel. After a few minutes, he turned to Ben. "How well you know your brother?" he asked.

"Not too well. We were never really close. The age difference. And I've been gone a long time."

"From what you remember, what do you think he's capable of?" Zeke persisted.

"You mean as a developer?" Ben said. "What he can accomplish?"

Zeke chuckled. "Not much mystery there. No, I mean his dark side. What would he do if somebody threatened him, or made him super pissed off?"

If Reggie's version of Watt's visit to the university years ago was right, he was capable of astonishing lies and manipulations. A flash of memory reminded Ben of how lethal Watt's rage could be.

"There was something," Ben said, "a long time ago. But it answers your question."

"Tell me," Zeke said.

"You have to be any place?"

Zeke turned off the motor, settled back in the seat and took out his pipe.

"Take as long as you need," he said, as he filled his pipe and lit it. He leaned his head back and listened.

I was almost eighteen. Watt had just leased a fish camp on a lake near West Memphis, a swampy place full of hungry mosquitoes. He was going to turn it into a duck-hunting club. It was in a good location along the Mississippi flyway, not too far from the river.

It was going to be a great way for him to entertain potential investors for his real estate developments. I remember telling him that we should just use it for our own fun, take friends and girls and party all weekend. He gave me a pitiful look. You can't hunt with the big dogs with that attitude, he told me. He and I were interested in hunting different things back then.

I'll never forget the day of the first hunt. It was important for me, because Watt was letting me into the world of deal making. He took the club's business potential seriously. We worked hard and he spent a lot of money to make sure everything was perfect and was going according to plan. He'd never asked for my help before, so I wanted us to succeed, because my big brother needed me to make his plan work.

We spent most weekends that summer scouting good sites for duck blinds, hacking out paths to them through the slough and fixing up the old fish shack for a clubhouse.

Making the place perfect wasn't enough for Watt. He had to get himself in prime condition for the first hunt. He went to England to refine his shooting skills at the Holland and Holland Shooting School and returned in two weeks with new shotguns, tweed hunting jackets, Barbour coats and some Wellies.

I might have laughed at his new hunting clothes, but the laughter stopped when Watt took me to the gun club. After a couple of hours of shooting, I was a believer. In four rounds of twenty-four clay pigeons a round, he turned each one to dust. A lot of money was lost that afternoon by those who bet against him.

He also wanted a good gun dog. I've been on hunts where you heard across the marsh and woods the most violent profanity from hunters whose dog forgot everything they ever learned about retrieving dead ducks from cold water once the shooting began.

At Ducks Unlimited dinners, when hunters bragged about great retrievers, Bart Cowan's name was often mentioned as the breeder or trainer. So we went to Cowan's farm in Grand Junction, Tennessee. By October, it was too late to buy a pup and have it trained. Watt would have to get a young dog already trained and learn to handle it himself. Cowan said he had the dog. Watt had read everything he could about training and handling retrievers, as well as stories about hunting dogs. He wanted his dog sense, his mastery of the nuances of hunting with a dog, and his command of his dog to appear as natural as scratching fleas.

Cowan got results from hardheaded labs without beating them into obedience. He said he had a gun-ready dog eager to hit the water and know what it was doing. It was a Labrador bitch with nothing wrong other than a little white patch on her chest. She was named Star and tagged along Cowan's side like they were from the same litter. Star immediately sniffed Watt's feet, then worked her way up his leg to his crotch. Watt twisted sideways to fend off the probing muzzle.

They went through basic obedience commands pretty quickly, and then headed to the lake for more complex commands and signals to show how Star could retrieve under actual conditions, short of real ducks falling out of the sky.

They spent the rest of the afternoon going over voice commands and hand signals. Cowan had Watt work with Star so they could get used to each other. Cowan thought they got along fine and should have a good season if Watt kept up the training. I could see Watt swell with pride when Star eagerly obeyed his commands. He scratched her on her white patch and she twitched reflexively, and then rolled over on her back.

Watt wrote a check for five thousand dollars. On the way home Watt boasted how everybody would talk about Watt Phelps, his famous dog, and the great duck hunting at his club.

Watt's first guests that December were perfect prospects for the duck club. Both men were rich and loved to hunt. We reached the camp well before sunrise. A cold front had pushed freezing air into the South and driven ducks and geese down from the Midwest.

I was bragging how Watt would shoot the most ducks because he was a natural shot and was refined by his schooling in England. One guy said he hoped Star would retrieve enough ducks to justify her cost. Watt told him that she'd retrieve anything he could shoot straight enough to kill. The duck club was open for business.

From a small channel upriver, we drifted down into the main current and hugged the bank till we reached the blinds. Sunrise was about fifteen minutes away as each boat slid quietly under its blind and was tied up. Watt set out the decoys and let them drift until their anchors found river bottom to grab to keep them bobbing in the small ripples.

We could see the black outline of the bare trees across the river as dawn came. It was time. With his duck call, one man began the shrill quacking, clucking and chucking to lure a flock within range of the guns. Star shifted nervously as the moments passed.

I heard from up river a few sporadic quacks beyond a grove of sweet gum trees. They were answered by more quacks, then a lot of quacks and chattering through the woods. The caller recited all the calls he knew in rapid succession. The flock came in cautiously over the treetops and inspected our decoys. There must have been more than a hundred ducks, one of the largest flocks of mallard I'd ever seen. They flew by without landing, but the lead ducks circled around over land across the river and made another pass. The flock followed and descended slowly.

By the time half the flock had landed, all of us were blasting away. The ducks were not more than ten to twenty yards from our blinds. The setup made for perfect passing shots. In the first round, we all got ducks.

Watt commanded Star to fetch and she hit the water. She swam keeping her head and shoulders high in the brown water so she could easily spot her targets. But, as she passed near a decoy, she turned toward it and her head lunged as she took it in her eager mouth. She then turned and headed toward the blind where she deposited it and returned to the open river and repeated the act.

By the time Star retrieved the second decoy, Watt's cursing could barely be heard above the hysterical laughter of our guests. I used all my self-control to keep my reaction to a few sputters. I didn't want to worsen Watt's humiliation. Star continued tirelessly retrieving decoys as the dead ducks slowly drifted down river.

Watt stopped screaming at Star. He sat in the blind and his shoulders sagged. Everything Watt hoped to accomplish had become the kind of event that would be retold at cocktail parties for years.

One of the men pushed our boat into the river and began picking up the dead ducks. We got most of them and pulled up to Watt's boat. Behind him, Star had managed to pile up ten decoys on the riverbank and was eagerly prancing back and forth, her tail wagging furiously, her red tongue hanging from the side of her mouth. She would occasionally stop and bow in Watt's direction. He didn't look at her. He was sitting slump-shouldered in the boat. The other man tossed some of the dead ducks in Watt's boat and said his retrieval efforts cost a lot less than what Watt had paid for his retriever. He said he couldn't wait to tell his partners about the best decoy retriever in the South.

Watt's shoulders stiffened imperceptibly. The skin around his eyes tightened. I noticed it because his eyes made me afraid to be near him. He took a deep breath, and then let out the stale air slowly through his flared nostrils. He seemed to relax a little and a faint smile crept across his lips. He told the men to keep the ducks and agreed the hunt was a bust.

They said maybe Cowan would refund the money for Star to save his reputation. The dog was certainly going back were she came from, Watt said.

After they left, Watt and I retrieved the decoys Star had overlooked. Despite her workout, Star was energetic and playful and eager to keep retrieving. She barked and trotted back and forth along the bank, urging us to keep up the game. I picked *up a stick and tossed it into the river, shouting for Star to fetch it. She crashed into the river, got the stick, dropped it at my feet and waited for me to throw it again. I thought Watt might have had enough retrieving for one day, but asked him if I could work Star some more. She can have a last swim, he said, as he stood on the riverbank with his gun cradled in his arms.*

I threw the stick far out into the river. Star dashed up the bank a few yards, and then cut toward the river from a spot where part of the bank had fallen and left a small drop off. From this spot, Star made her leap toward the river. At the same time I heard the explosion, I saw her twist in the air, then plunge into the muddy water. After the splash subsided, Star floated motionless just at the water's surface as she began drifting downstream. I looked over at Watt who was returning his shotgun to rest. A little wisp of smoke drifted from the barrel's end.

"Back where she came from," Watt said. I yelled at him, but he just looked at me, his eyes tightening as they dared me to challenge him. I turned and watched Star float out of sight around the river's bend.

"So you ask me what Watt's capable of," Ben said, facing Zeke. "That's one answer."

Zeke clenched the pipe in his teeth. "Son of a bitch."

Ben didn't argue. "What's that got to do with Mossback or us?"

"Some people regard a good dog as higher on the evolutionary scale than humans. I fall into that category after exposure to some people. Any man that'd do that to a dog, I'd hate to think what he'd do to people," Zeke said, scratching his beard. "Wonder what he'd do to someone who really threatened him in a serious way?"

CHAPTER 13

They didn't speak driving back to the big house. At the driveway entrance, Zeke said, "Get out of the house early. We need a few hours to check some things, then meet at the shop in town and see what we know."

As the sound of the truck faded, Ben heard a crow caw in alarm and fly deeper into the woods. Crickets and katydids chirped and buzzed while overhead the leaves continued their colorful transformation.

Ben looked around and didn't see anyone. Watt's Range Rover was gone. He wished Reggie were away, too, so he could explore the house alone for a few hours. If he were lucky, she would be asleep, resting for her next round of self-destruction.

He walked through the hallway to the library where a gauzy curtain lazily flapped from a breeze drifting through an open window. He sat in a dusty captain's chair by the door and scanned the room, trying to remember how his parents looked and sounded.

Pictures hung on the walls and unfamiliar objects resting on shelves caught his attention. What books did his mother and father read, what pictures did they enjoy, what artifacts did they cherish enough to collect on a shelf?

Ben got up to examine a letter in a black dusty frame. It was typed on a manual typewriter and had a few corrections written in blue pen. The writer, Peter Taylor, encouraged Ben's father to keep up his efforts at fiction, and expressed pleasure seeing someone writing about Memphis. At the University of Virginia, Ben remembered, there had been a big fuss about Taylor accepting a teaching position there, and his father urging him to take the man's class, but at the time, he preferred truths revealed from history, not fiction. What other secret aspirations and longings did his father have? Ben had known his father as only a businessman.

He replaced the framed letter on its nail and wiped the dust from his fingers. On the shelf behind the letter Ben scanned the rows of books in fading dust covers. Some were by Taylor, but most of the books were by novelists from the early and mid-twentieth century. Farther along were mildew-covered books in finely tooled leather whose bindings were cracking from decades of climate extremes inside the uninsulated log house. Ben pulled out a small volume of love poems.

His father had inscribed the front page to his mother: "Sarah, Thank you for coming away with me and being my love. Sidney."

A slip of paper marked a poem called "A Shephard to his Love" by Christopher Marlowe. A four-leaf clover was pressed into the seam. He envied the love expressed by his father.

Farther along the bookshelves he looked at a framed watercolor of a sailboat in azure waters with bending palm trees along the beach. A faint signature said, "Homer 1899." It must be a reproduction, he thought, until closer inspection made him reconsider. He replaced it carefully.

On another shelf was a series of black and white photographs in simple dark frames showing his young parents happy in each other's company, horseback riding, sailing, playing tennis, picnicking, golfing, or sitting on a bare mountaintop. In all the photos they seemed full of joy.

He looked at other photos on another shelf showing his parents with him, Watt and Reggie. One photo showed Watt in his Tennessee football uniform, stretching mightily to catch a pass. There were several of Reggie playing tennis or posing with trophies. Ben was disappointed there were so few of him, and no triumphal athletic moments captured. One photo showed

Ben scowling in his military-school uniform as he held a rifle. He noticed one of him painting, as his mother pointed to something on the canvas. Another picture showed Ben and his father building something that appeared to be a doghouse. He touched the photo of him and his father as if to retrieve the moment.

An assortment of broken or warped wooden tennis racquets hung in a column on one shelf divider. He guessed each one represented a story his parents told over drinks at dinner parties.

Ben studied an old framed map darkened with mold and nibbled by silverfish. It had the name of a surveyor and the date 1809. He studied the topography that depicted a broad valley surrounded on three sides by mountains. The forth side was a river valley that eventually expanded beyond more mountains. The map depicted no signs of human intrusion, with the exception of a trail that ended at a dashed line labeled "The Escarpment" and a skull and crossbones, much like a pirate's icon. Taped to the bottom frame was a typewritten label that said "Mossback."

Another framed document was a bill, dated Sept. 23, 1903, for materials and labor for a log house. The hewn chestnut logs, nails, windows, roofing tin, doors and sawn oak flooring amounted to twelve hundred dollars. The labor of four men and "eight coloreds" amounted to six hundred and fifty-four dollars. Ben didn't recognize the recipient of the bill, but a handwritten label taped to the frame said "Mossback." A photograph next to the bill showed a new log house with a gathering of people standing in front. One dark-suited man sat on a gray horse to one side of the gathering of men and two women, Mossback's first owners, Ben guessed.

Ben sat slowly in a straight-backed chair next to a wall. For forty years, he had carefully fashioned a version of his parents very unlike the two people revealed in this room. The man and woman who carefully collected the books, paintings, artifacts, photographs and mementoes seemed so unlike the parents he vaguely remembered. He had no memory of his mother guiding his paintbrush. He didn't recall building a doghouse with his father. The two people whose images adorned this room were romantic, tender, curious and nurturing. They beckoned to him, yet he couldn't even summon the sound of their voices.

A wooden screen door slammed twice and echoed through the hallway from the kitchen. He sat very still.

He heard the sound of glass shattering, followed by Reggie's voice, angry and growling in her smoker's rasp, "god damn, damn, damn. Fuck, fucking son of a bitch," followed by a brief silence. The cursing didn't indicate any pain, so Ben ruled out serious injury. He speculated that she dropped a precious stash of bourbon, secreted away for the inevitable moment when Watt denied her lifeblood.

Listening by the door, he heard soft crying. He walked down the hall toward the kitchen where he saw Reggie sitting on the floor picking up pieces of glass scattered in a puddle of liquid. She looked up at Ben and shook her head.

"It slipped," she said. "Crystal's so heavy and smooth. Just trying to brighten up the place."

On the sink, he saw a bucket of goldenrod, asters and ferns tumbling over the sides.

"Don't cut yourself," he said. He helped her pick up the shattered vase and scolded himself for assuming she had dropped a bottle of booze.

"Same to you," she said.

As they gingerly picked up the slivers, Reggie sighed.

"I can't ever remember putting flowers in a vase. Seems like a simple thing. I forgot how heavy crystal is. Doesn't look heavy," she said, surveying the damage. "Don't tell Watt, please. He'll just say, 'Can't hold her liquor or a vase.' " She laughed. "I swore I wasn't going to take a drink today . . . in your honor, you know. But that promise seems flat right now. Care for a drink?"

"I'll pass," he said, hoping she would follow his lead.

"More for me," she said. She got up on her hands and knees, then tried to stand.

"Hold it," Ben said, as she reached to pull herself up by the sink.

"Change your mind?" she said.

Ben saw blood seeping through Reggie's pants in little dark spots. "You're bleeding."

"Wrong time of the month," she said, pulling herself up.

"Glass," he said. "You sat in glass. Don't you feel it?"

Reggie twisted to see behind her but couldn't turn far enough.

"Don't feel a thing. Gives new meaning to dead end," she said.

Ben told her to go upstairs and take off her pants while he looked for some tweezers.

"Sounds kind of kinky," she said. She walked up the stairs leaning heavily on the banister.

When Ben walked into the room she was lying on her stomach. Her pants were on the floor and her stained underwear was loose around an ankle. Ben saw little rivulets of blood on her bottom and thighs. Purple veins crisscrossed the backs of her calves to her ankles. He remembered her honey-colored legs rippling with muscles from hours of fierce tennis on clay courts.

He sat down beside her, noticing her stained skin and hoping there was some strong disinfectant in the house.

"Start plucking," she said into the pillow.

He spent the next half hour probing and picking fine crystal slivers from her loose flesh. He couldn't imagine Watt with tweezers plucking at Reggie's bloody bottom. He might hire someone to do it, and then never let her forget it.

Ben left the bedside in search of something to cleanse the wounds. He returned with a bottle of iodine, and Reggie began to stir as he dabbed the liquid into the wounds. She smacked her lips and turned her head.

"Felt that all right. You dropping hot coals on my butt?"

"Just about through. You might want to take a good hot bath later," he said. There were no Hallmark cards made for what ails this family, he thought.

That evening as he was going down to dinner, Ben knocked on Reggie's door.

"You coming to dinner?" he said.

He was about to knock again when he heard the bedsprings squeak.

"Down in a minute," Reggie mumbled.

He couldn't tell if he had waked her or if she was slurring her words for another reason. He hoped they wouldn't repeat the scene from last night. How could he physically restrain his brother, who had plenty of muscular pounds on him, from hitting Reggie again? He found the suspense of his siblings' behavior intriguing, in a detached way.

Watt was mixing a drink as Ben walked into the kitchen.

"Care for a little libation?" Watt said without turning around to notice who was entering the room. Ben figured the offer was not intended for Reggie.

"Maybe a beer," he said.

Watt got a beer from the refrigerator and handed it to Ben without opening it. "Dinner's just some takeout I got in town," Watt said. "We can eat anytime. Let's take our drinks outside."

Settling into the rocking chairs on the wide covered porch, they looked out over the valley beyond the granite escarpment. They rocked without speaking for a few moments in the cool evening air. The chairs' woven backs and seats creaked rhythmically as they moved back and forth. Ben delighted in the fall colors over the landscape he partly owned and was amused at his proprietary attitude.

"Any thoughts about my offer?" Watt said. "I'm not pressing, you know. Just wondered if you had any questions."

Ben doubted he would get truthful answers, at least about Watt's plans for Mossback.

"I did have some questions," Ben said, before taking a long swallow of beer. He let the brew bubble in his stomach, and then belched softly. "What do you remember about being here as a child? I mean the kind of memories – good or bad – not anything specific. You know, do you remember feeling good about being here with our parents?"

Watt looked annoyed the questions were not about the subject he wanted to discuss. "They were okay, I guess, nothing special."

"What do you recall about being with our parents?" Ben persisted. "Did you do stuff with them?"

Watt hesitated, and then said, "I wasn't much into the stuff they liked. Sports I liked, but there wasn't much of that around here. Just tennis. They seemed to take you around a lot, showing you stuff. You seemed like a special project for them."

Ben closed his eyes. "It all seems never to have happened. I try to remember, but it's all so vague."

"They really loved doing things with you. Mom wanted you to learn to paint. I remember that. You broke their hearts when you went away." Watt drained his drink and chewed on a piece of ice.

Who made my life so terrible that I wanted to run away? Ben almost said, but resisted the urge.

"Did they love us?" Ben said, startled he asked the question.

"I guess," Watt said. "Especially you. Little Ben was their favorite. They had great plans for you. Mom thought you were very talented. Too lazy, maybe, but great potential."

Watt stared at the horizon as he spoke. Ben studied the label on his beer bottle. He wanted to believe what he had felt in the library that afternoon, that he might have been part of a happy family.

"Didn't they think you had great potential?" Ben said

"Potential for making money," Watt said. "Dad liked that, I suppose, or he wouldn't have turned everything over to me. But they didn't love that potential." The resentment in Watt's voice seemed genuine. This was the first time any utterance from Watt's mouth seemed to carry a semblance of truth.

Reggie calling them from the hallway stopped any more revelations. They left the porch to join her.

"You two scheming my commitment?" she said when she entered the kitchen. "Don't get too chummy on me. Might look too much like a family. People wouldn't recognize us."

Reggie poured a glass of water at the sink. Ben and Watt looked at each other in surprise.

"The elixir of life," Reggie said, as she smacked her lips. "Tastes a little lonely by itself, though."

She drained the glass and set it on the drain board. She faced her brothers as she leaned against the sink. Her clean, damp hair was carefully combed, and her makeup almost masked her years.

"You guys look like you've seen a spook. I thought I looked a little better than that. Or do I just have that effect on men when I clean up a little?" She fluttered her eyelashes.

"You look just fine," Ben said. "How're you feeling?"

Reggie twirled around in a clumsy pirouette and finished with a deep curtsy.

"Feeling great!" she said. "Haven't had a drink all day. Might not have one tomorrow, either. You're a good doctor, Ben."

With a puzzled frown, Watt looked at Ben, who just shrugged innocently. Why give Watt another reason to belittle Reggie? he thought.

At Reggie's insistence they filled their plates with a microwaved pasta concoction and ate on the porch as the night shadows climbed the mountains. Small bats fluttered jerkily above the lawn. Night insects chattered in the deep grasses. The occasional flash of a firefly caught their attention as they ate quietly. An owl's hooting resonated from the deep, surrounding forest.

After they put their empty plates on the wide railing, Reggie turned her rocking chair to face her brothers.

"There's something I need to tell you," she said solemnly.

Ben sensed Watt stiffen in his chair as if preparing for an earth tremor. He hoped Reggie was not going to have another announcement about her share of Mossback. Ben welcomed several hours without argument about the control of the family home.

"God, you two look like I just said I'm carrying your child!" she said. "Relax." She rose up and sat on the railing. "I've made a decision about my future. I'm going to resume my tennis career. Not at the level I once played, of course. At the senior level. It'll take a while to get back in shape. Have to get a trainer and work hard. I can do it. I know I can. What's to stop me?"

Even in the fading light they could see Reggie's expression indicated she thought she had just uttered of the most rational pronouncements of her life, and that it was beyond question. Ben heard Watt snort as he slowly shook his head. "Same old crap," he muttered.

"That's a great idea," Ben said. He wondered what she would think in the morning when she sobered up, then realized he had not seen her take a drink all day.

Could she really mean it, or did he merely fail to recognize some strange form of D.T.'s? No harm in cheering her on, he thought. "You had it once. It'll come back to you like riding a bike."

Watt took their plates to the kitchen as they followed. Reggie clung to Ben's arm as she explained the training regimen she believed she needed in order to play by next summer. Her enthusiasm peeled away years from her spotted face. She smoldered with excitement as she stood more erect.

Watt put the dishes in the sink, looked at Ben and Reggie with unconcealed scorn, and walked out of the room. They could hear him upstairs.

"Mister Charm seems unmoved," Reggie said with a giggle. "He'll see."

Ben again told Reggie he thought she could be a serious competitor if she trained hard. He hugged her, and then said he was going to bed. She kissed him and said, "Your return's gonna change my life."

As Ben was walking out of the kitchen, he stopped to tell Reggie he might not be in the house when she woke up in the morning. As he turned, he saw her pouring bourbon into an old jelly glass. She saw him and grinned.

"Just a night cap for the sandman," she said.

CHAPTER 14

Ben felt the soft, damp breeze seeping through the window screens as he squinted at the bedside clock that told him sunrise was at least an hour away. He tossed back the bed covers, dressed quickly, felt his way through the dark to his van and headed for town. He thought about the guard but no one was at the unlocked gate, so he pushed it open and drove through with a fugitive's relief. Kelsey still slept as the eastern sky crept into dawn.

Ben drove aimlessly around Kelsey's deserted streets. A few lighted store windows clamored for attention. The wide main street was empty of cars. An early morning jogger, highlighted in reflective tape, ran toward him. The jogger waved, and Ben waved back. He mildly regretted he lacked motivation for running, but then began to think he actually had been running for the last forty years, just in the wrong way.

An early morning delivery truck pulled into a convenience store. Ben's empty stomach rumbled as he imagined coffee and chocolate-covered donuts. Why not, he decided, and headed to the store.

"First customer of the day," a voice shouted. "Coffee's on us."

Ben looked around but didn't see anyone.

"Help yourself," came a voice from behind the checkout counter. Ben finally saw a gray-haired woman rise up and place a moneybag on the counter. She was thin with a gaunt face and pursed mouth.

"Thanks," he said, as he made his coffee. He paid for a couple of doughnuts.

"Out early," she said. "Couldn't sleep?"

"I like to see a town when it's just waking up," he said, and immediately thought he sounded pretentious.

"You're new to here," she said, as she finished putting money in the cash register. "City folk sometimes can't take the quiet. Worries 'em. Think something's wrong."

He noticed her smirk.

"I used to come here as a kid," he said. "Town's changed a lot."

"Developers!" she said, slamming the cash drawer shut with a ring. "They just want to pack in more people, sell 'em a slice of heaven, then bag their loot and do the same somewhere else. Good for business, though. How long you been gone?"

"Decades," he said, and bit into a doughnut.

She chuckled and looked out the large plate glass window toward the street. "Progress ain't sentimental, though. Town you knew's gone. Never coming back, no matter how hard folks want it."

"I don't remember much about it," Ben said. "I was little."

The old clerk turned her gaze from the street to Ben. She studied him for a moment, and then unleashed a long lecture in which she told Ben about how Kelsey had been a quiet mountain village for many decades. Wealthy families from across the South spent summer months escaping the stifling lowland heat. The pattern brought good times in the summers, usually enough to get local people through the lean off-season if they were frugal, industrious and didn't drink. And having a productive vegetable garden didn't hurt any.

"In the nineteen eighties," she said, "Florida developers bought some large estates, built condos and that was the end of quiet summers."

Hordes of people attracted big retailers and outlet stores on the north side of town that bankrupted the family businesses. "Most people work for low wages," she said. "Now every scrap of vacant land not big enough for a golf course is being chopped up into town houses and condos. Politicians love the growing tax base.

Anybody who speaks against the developers is shouted down, accused of being against jobs and working folks. Meanwhile, we've become just like where all the tourists came from." She paused to sip some coffee.

"Progress," she said, as if she tasted something sour. "You live around here?" she asked. "Who your people?"

Considering her version of Kelsey's recent history, Ben dodged the truth. He didn't want her to regret the free coffee.

"I'm just visiting, a tourist," he said.

"Who?" she said. "Visiting who?"

"Going fishing," he said, concocting a plausible story. "Zeke McCall is taking me."

The old woman let out a yelp that startled Ben.

"You got the best! That old boy can catch 'em in his sleep. Not good for much else, but what do you care?"

"That good, huh?" Ben said grinning.

"If he can't find fish, they ain't there," she said. "He taking you to his special spot?"

Ben pretended he didn't understand her question.

"That place he caretakes," she said. "Got the best fishing in these parts. Only he don't let nobody on it without him as guide, and then only if he likes you."

"I'm not sure where he's taking me," Ben said. "The place he works, what's it like?"

The old woman smiled.

"Just a bit of heaven, a damn big bit," she said. "Thousands of acres of land that's never felt an ax. Developers would kill their mamas and kids to get a holt of it. Some family owned it. Parents died some years back. Tied up with lawyers, I hear. Went on it once when I was little. Thought I'd see Adam and Eve any second. Never did."

She took another sip of coffee, curled her lip and poured the rest of the coffee into a trash can. "Tell him to take you there. See what God intended a place to be."

Ben said he'd take her advice and went back to his van. As he chewed his donuts he wondered how he would spend the rest of the morning. He thought about the woman's version of Mossback. He had spent enough time outdoors in a lot of wild places to appreciate her assessment. He wondered who else saw the place with the same reverence. Ben sipped the bitter coffee, then opened the van door and poured the remainder onto the greasy asphalt.

Main Street picked up as more cars arrived, a couple of restaurants opened, and a few people wandered in search of their morning newspaper fix.

Ben drove aimlessly through the sparse streets to the edge of town until he saw a sign for a nature center. *Zahner Nature Center* said the raised letters of a gray wooden sign. Ben pulled into a gravel parking lot in front of a low, expansive building made from large, hand-cut granite blocks. A long row of wide windows were about two-thirds the way up the wall. A green metal roof sloped toward the front. Long-dormant images, sounds and smells stirred Ben as he stared at the closed building. He knew this place. He shut his eyes and leaned his head back on the seat.

A vision emerged of stuffed creatures aligned in neat rows, their arms and legs stretched out and their eyes stuffed with white cotton. They were labeled and looked like war casualties awaiting the burial squad. In his reverie, he saw glass display cases containing live snakes, frogs, turtles and salamanders wandering about their small spaces filled with rocks, sticks, moss, wood chips and little dishes of water. In one cage a tiny mouse trembled in a corner as a black snake, flicking its tongue, moved slowly toward it. Elsewhere, a beehive was mounted on a window and had a glass side revealing the waxy combs. Honeybees danced around in deceptive frenzy through the cramped hive as they came and went, searching for pollen.

He saw a giant cross section of log big enough for him to stretch across. At certain points along the growth rings were pins with strings leading to typed labels. One label near the center rings mentioned Christopher Columbus's first voyage of discovery to the new world. Another had the date for the Declaration of Independence, while one noted the Civil War.

In the next room he saw glass cases filled with rows of arrowheads, spear points and ax blades. Other cases held Cherokee baskets woven from different colored split reeds and grasses. A few clay pots reconstructed from various fragments looked like round mosaics. Against another wall rocks glowed in splendid colors when a fluorescent light shined on them.

He remembered the rooms smelled damp and musty, and on rainy days made his nose tingle. He and other children sat restlessly in a darkened room in split-cane chairs and watched an old man talk about reptiles and let the children stick their fingers in the mouth of a large water snake, held tightly behind its head by an assistant.

He clearly remembered now his mother picking him up from the classes at the nature center. He babbled excitedly about what he had learned that day. She kissed him and smelled of Lifebuoy soap and cigarettes. Gold bracelets jangled on her wrists. She smiled as she watched the road, barely seeing over the Ford's large steering wheel. When they returned to Mossback he scouted the edge of the yard for rocks and logs that might conceal some of the snakes or salamanders he had learned about that day. He was careful only to look at the creatures he discovered, just as his teachers had stressed. Leave them as you find them or they might die, he was cautioned. He usually followed their warnings unless he found an unusual specimen he had never seen before. Sometimes his father joined him to help lift heavy rocks or logs. Dressed in old khaki pants and a Yale sweatshirt, his father would listen attentively to Ben's recitation about the creatures they discovered.

"You're going to grow up to become a zoologist," his father said, and for a while Ben thought he was going to work in a zoo.

The nature center was as familiar now as if he had just been there the day before, and as real as his time yesterday gazing around Mossback's library.

The underpinnings of the last few decades of Ben's life crumbled rapidly. The elation confused Ben, who was suspicious of unrestrained happiness.

Ben saw someone unlock the nature center's front door, and he remembered why he was waiting outside: to understand more about Mossback's value, not the commercial worth, but its natural qualities. Why was old man Parker so secretive about his investigation into Mossback's deep forest? Someone finally flipped an open sign in the window.

Ben gazed around the large main room through the eyes of the twelve-year-old boy he used to be. Gone were the stuffed animals splayed on slanting boards, their identities given in Latin and English. Contemporary displays explained the mountain ecosystem in photographs, text and digital maps. The room smelled of Lysol. On a far wall, however, he saw the beehive built into a large plate glass window. Nearby the huge hemlock log's timelines still recounted the nation's history through its rings.

"Are you here for the taxonomy class?" a soft, clear voice asked.

Ben turned to see a woman slightly shorter than he and, he guessed, a little younger. She was slender, and her snug clothes revealed a figure accustomed to regular exercise. Gray strands at her temples streaked her black hair, giving her an air of mature authority. Her deep green eyes enchanted him. Fine lines in her smooth skin radiated from her eyes as she smiled at him and waited for his answer. He was examining her face, the high cheekbones and square jaw, the pink lips curved slightly up, when he realized his mesmerized silence could be taken for rudeness, or dumbness.

"What?" he said. "The what class?"

"Taxonomy," she said. "It doesn't start till nine. You're a little early."

She smiled at him and fingered reading glasses that hung from a cord around her neck and rested across a deep cleavage he pretended not to notice. He forced his attention back to her face.

"I'm not here for a class," he said, fearful she would dismiss him as unimportant. "I used to come here as a kid, years ago. It's changed some. All those stuffed animals are gone," he said, looking back across the room.

She laughed and he noticed that behind her straight white teeth she had a small stud in her tongue.

"Yeh, we had to throw them away. At least what the moths and silverfish hadn't eaten. They were pretty pitiful." She tilted her head as if she were waiting for an explanation of Ben's presence.

Ben was relieved to know his memory was true.

"I did want to learn something," he said, hoping to keep her attention. "I'm a reporter, working on a story about old-growth forests. I heard about one near here, called Mossback?"

An old writer told him that if you say you're a journalist, people sometimes begin confessing whatever you want to know, as if you're the same status as a priest. "Just buy them a drink and nudge 'em in the direction they're already inclined," the friend said.

Her expression darkened a little when he mentioned Mossback, and she became tense. "Mossback," she said. "It's the most threatened land we have around here. I wish your writing about it could save it, but I doubt it."

She seemed to be waiting for a nudge, and he complied happily.

"How's it threatened?" he said.

She breathed deeply and said, "A few centuries ago, the forests were so vast a squirrel could travel from the Atlantic to the Mississippi without touching the ground."

She explained that Mossback's thousands of untouched and unspoiled acres in the valley were the last, large old-growth forest east of the Mississippi River.

"A forest like that might shelter plants and animals in unknown ways," she said. "Different creatures can thrive in different levels in that kind of forest. It's like fragile living strands all woven into a web of life that used to be immense, but now's mostly vanished. The web's unraveling."

She held out her open hands in a beseeching gesture. "Just take the cerulean warbler. A seventy-percent population decline since the nineteen sixties because of forest destruction. It thrives eating insects in high forest canopy. Mossback's a natural nirvana for that doomed little blue bird."

He couldn't recall a cerulean warbler, but her passion charmed him as he listened and watched her brow furrow with serious purpose. Her moral outrage bewitched him.

She said there were rumors that the family who had owned Mossback for decades was selling out, that

Mossback was going to become a theme park, a golf course, or both.

"That's the asphalt dwellers version of nature without regard for the natural world and all its messy beauty," she said.

Ben thought about clients he had taken fishing who suffered asphalt withdrawal. "Yeh, some people love the idea of nature but get mighty nervous in the middle of it."

Without seeming to have heard him, she explained that the White House put industry lobbyists in charge of writing the environmental laws and regulations, so the foxes were not only in the hen house, they were creating culinary chicken dishes for their friends and serving them up gratis.

"And our congressman – Buzzsaw Billy – is one of the worst foxes," she said.

Ben remembered a congressman leaving Mossback when he arrived a couple of days ago.

"He helped pull the teeth out of the Endangered Species Act," she said. "They brand good research as bad science whenever it threatens what they want to exploit. It's all about money."

As she spoke, Ben consumed her anger, passion and moral certitude like a very thirsty man in the desert, despite what the drink might cost him.

"God, will you listen to me?" she said. "I'm becoming too bitter for my own good. You really pushed the right button asking about Mossback."

She walked away into an office and Ben wondered why her impassioned monolog ended so suddenly. She returned and thrust a card at Ben.

"I've got a class in a few minutes," she said. "Here's my card. You can call me if you want to talk some more. I'll try to be a little more restrained. But no promises."

She smiled at Ben, and turned to greet some people entering the nature center.

Katherine Howell, Ph. D., Director, Zahner Nature Center, the card said. Did she go by Katherine or, maybe Kate or Katie? There was no doubt in his mind he would call her.

Ben watched her talking to people coming in for the class. She was relaxed and friendly as she put the students at ease. Her small hands gestured as she talked, and her single long braid swung like a pendulum across her back as it brushed her waist. He fingered the card in his hand and noticed the raised letters, his thumb feeling the impression of her name as he tried to discern the individual letters. The contours of her name on his fingertips pleased him.

In his meditation, Ben barely noticed her turn toward him. She smiled and nodded. In clumsy frustration, he grinned and waved her business card at her, to signify he knew how to contact her and would follow up. Her attention returned to more people entering for the class. Did she understand his gesture? She herded the students into a room at the far end of the building and was gone. Ben forgot the reason he had entered the nature center as he gazed at the doorway the green-eyed woman disappeared through. He would see her again, but he was anxious about explaining himself to her, especially after her tirade about the Mossback owners selling a national treasure.

Ben still had a few hours until he was supposed to meet Zeke. He had learned more than he expected in his visit to the nature center, but he didn't trust his impressions, especially when they came from a good-looking woman. He wanted another source.

Holt, the newspaper editor who had given Ben directions to Mossback, had said to call again if he needed any help or information, so he drove to *The Kelsey Gazette*. The large woman was talking to the editor at the far end of the open room, when the man looked Ben's way, smiled and finished his conversation. He walked up to the counter.

"You didn't tell me you were famous," Holt said, as he shook his finger at Ben. The friendly smile on his face showed no malice. "A writer no less, in national magazines. You were being too modest."

Only in bars late at night did Ben occasionally claim to be a serious writer and sometimes the woman on the next stool would be impressed. "You're partly a good reporter," Ben said. "I'm guilty of being a writer, not so great, much less famous. I just plug fishing stories and a few products. How'd you find out?"

Holt gleamed with smugness at his detective skills. "Not many secrets can be kept at a fly-fishing shop," he said. "Maybe Zeke can hold his tongue, but not Henry, the owner. He can't resist showing off what he knows. Fortunately for me, there's not much of a filter between his brain and his mouth. He didn't filter out you're one of Mossback's owners, either."

So much for being anonymous in a small town, Ben thought, and worried about how well-connected Katherine was to the town's gossip network.

Ben confirmed he was one of Mossback's owners, and explained the circumstances of his return after so many years. He extracted a promise from Holt to keep the information quiet in exchange for giving the newspaper an exclusive story on Mossback's fate.

"Maybe you can educate me about a few things," Ben said.

Holt invited Ben into an office overflowing with old newspapers and press releases, reports and letters. Several Rotary International plaques of praise and recognition hung on a wall above a glowing computer screen.

"Ask away," Holt said. "I'll tell you anything that's not slanderous. Maybe even some of that, too, if I think I can trust you."

"I'm sort of curious about my family place," Ben said. He asked why Mossback would be so attractive, beyond being a very large tract of forestland. "Wouldn't it be hard to develop, with environmental regulations, that kind of stuff?"

The editor settled back in his chair and gazed out his dirty window overlooking a parking lot. Tapping an unsharpened pencil against his lower lip, he spun the chair around and leaned forward on his desk.

"The little bit you've told me makes a lot of things understandable," he said slowly, as if sorting through those things in his mind as he spoke.

"First, you may not be aware that a legal notice was issued several months ago, maybe a year, asking for information on your whereabouts. Nobody gave it much thought. But it was a legal notice of a missing person, so its publication had some legal purpose," Holt said. "Nobody gave much thought to Benjamin Morgan

Phelps. Who was he? Your parents have been dead quite a while, so there was no real connection with land that's now in a corporate name."

Holt frowned as he looked at Ben and resumed tapping the pencil against his lip. "That's one part of the interesting puzzle," he continued. Other things had happened that now made sense because they had a real-life application. Holt explained that federal and state legislation had recently passed, or was about to pass, that most people had ignored except a few environmental groups who were being increasingly dismissed as extremists and job killers. He confirmed what the nature center director told him about environmental laws being weakened in favor of developers.

Holt explained that their local congressman was the largest private timberland owner in the state and hated the U.S. Forest Service or anyone who wanted to restrict timber cutting. He had started the Healthy Forest Council, a poorly concealed front for the timber, mineral and grazing interests. It drafted local people to oppose any environmental concerns for land-use issues on public or private land.

"With all the industry lobbyists now in charge of government agencies, they just did away with the rules they didn't like," Holt said. "After all their campaign donations through the years, now they have easy access to public lands, and private lands are off-limits to most regulations. All in the name of jobs and free markets."

Ben was chagrined listening to Holt's list of rollbacks of environmental protection. He realized that some of the points sounded familiar, like complaints from people concerned about water quality in various places he had fished that he largely ignored because their fears were local issues unrelated to him. Remembering the chummy meeting with the local congressman known as Buzzsaw Billy, he now understood the nickname.

"So, what does all this mean for you and Mossback?" Holt said, raising his eyebrows behind his half glasses. "Just that whatever the owner wants to do, he can do with impunity. Developers and loggers and miners have the most unregulated field since the robber baron era, and that includes your brother, I suppose."

Ben didn't know how to respond. As the day began, he'd thought of his brother as a greedy bully who wanted to exploit the old family place in the mountains, a threat to no one other than family members. Now he realized Watt probably was paying people to chisel away at the regulations interfering with his developments. Reggie's drunken accusations suddenly sounded credible. A long chat with his little sister was in order. And what would Watt's reaction be if Ben told him no sale at any price? He assumed Watt had worked too long and paid too high a price to accept a refusal from the prodigal brother who had been off fishing while Watt was buying politicians to smooth the way for his dream development.

"Are you all right?" Holt said, placing a hand on Ben's arm.

"Not really" Ben said. "You've given me a lot to digest. Seems like I've been on another planet while all this was going on. Kinda happy in my ignorance. Now what?"

Holt sat back in his chair and frowned as he considered Ben's comments.

"Advertisers are always clamoring for more growth, more customers," he said. "Business people welcome development, and the chamber of commerce has a lot of support. Even the people who want to limit development don't want that to happen till they get their piece of land to build on. And there are lots of people who still want their piece of paradise." He tapped the pencil harder as if trying to dislodge a solution.

"Developers are so immune to public criticism around here, it hardly registers. I don't see what I can do." Holt said. "You'll have to find a way to get your brother's attention. I don't know much about him, other than his public image. Anything private that might make him reconsider what he wants to do, whatever it is?"

Ben couldn't imagine Watt suddenly moved by moral persuasion or public scrutiny. He figured developers were hardened to both and Watt was no exception, probably more intransigent than most. Watt said the offer to purchase Ben's share was made almost out of charity, not because absolute ownership was necessary to his plan, just more convenient. If that were true, Ben could not fathom what influence he might have to stop his brother.

"Maybe we'll think of something," Ben said. He stood up to leave. "Thanks for the information. Quite an education you've given me. Might make a good story for your paper."

"Maybe you could write it," Holt said.

"A story without fish. That would be a change," Ben said, as he walked for the door.

CHAPTER 15

Through the shop window, Ben saw Zeke in the rear of the store helping a fisherman select trout flies from the display box. Zeke glanced at Ben and nodded. Henry, the storeowner, was absorbed in a magazine. Wanting to avoid Henry's adoration of fly-fishing celebrities, Ben sat down on a sidewalk bench and watched a few early shoppers peering through windows. After a few minutes, Zeke came outside and sat next to Ben.

"What'd you learn at the courthouse?" Ben said, staring out at the slowly moving traffic on Main Street.

"Couple things," Zeke said. "One, there's damn few permits required any more. Seems like people can do pretty much what they want outside the city limits. No zoning, just what the state allows, which is pretty much what your checkbook can buy. Only thing that's on everybody's radar is drinking water. Gotta get permits for public drinking water systems."

Zeke lit his pipe and puffed for a while as the smoke drifted into the traffic. He seemed in no hurry to elaborate. Ben glanced at Zeke, who was absently bobbing his head to a primitive drumbeat vibrating from a car with oversized speakers in the rear and darkened windows obscuring the passengers.

"Wonder what their hearing'll be like in a few years," Zeke said.

Ben watched the car move slowly down the street, its music not much diminished by distance.

"Probably won't exist," Ben said. "What about the water permits?"

Zeke removed his pipe and reamed out the bowl of tobacco ash with his pocketknife.

"Your brother applied for one," he said, as he examined his pipe, then shook loose spit from the stem. "A big one. A water system that will serve at least three hundred and fifty homes, a hotel and other stuff. Seems nobody in the health department gave it much thought. Just another country club, they figured. The permit was in a corporate name: The Wilderness Club." He frowned at Ben. "The maps showed it was Mossback.

"It's not just another country club, you know. I've walked over most of it. Fished just about all of it. Ben, it's different from anything. The place is special, very special."

"Looks like Watt wants to do something really big, blockbuster," Ben said. "A lot of laws have been changed to let it happen, and his fingerprints are everywhere. Saw your local congressman at the house when I arrived."

"What're you gonna do?" Zeke said.

"Going against Watt's a little against my self interest, you know," Ben said. "I'm not known for being noble. Closest thing to acting noble was walking out on my alcoholic wife before she killed me. Kept her from going to jail."

"You will stop it," Zeke said.

Ben wasn't sure if that was a question or a command. "I don't know what I can do," he said. "Watt said he could go ahead without my consent. He has his share and controls my sister's. Says his offer's just a courtesy."

"Just tell him you're not gonna let him do what he wants. See what happens. How he reacts."

"He's not the kind of person you can scare or bully," Ben said. "He's the bully."

"Just see what happens," Zeke said calmly. "Try the simple stuff first. See if you can get him to tell you what he plans to do. Flatter him. His sort likes flattery, for a while anyway. Then tell him no, and see where it leads."

"I know where it'll lead," Ben said, the image of Reggie's bruised face in his mind. "He's deep into this. You got a plan B?"

Ben glanced sideways at Zeke, who was tapping the pocketknife's blade point on his calloused palm.

"If you can't reason with him, there might be another way to bring him to Jesus. Hope we don't have to 'cause it would be ugly. You don't need to be involved."

"I'm kinda involved already," Ben said, "like it or not."

"You don't always know what's involved in something," Zeke said. "Things can be connected like roots underground. They can spread and cross in ways you'd never guess."

Zeke stood up and stretched. He glanced up and down the street as if planning an escape route. "Just try the simple way first," he said. "That don't work, I might be able to reason with him. As old Lyndon Johnson used to say, 'Let us reason together.' Yeh, I might have to do that. Hope not."

"You know, in the end, I might take the money." Ben said, looking up at Zeke. "I haven't really decided what I'm going to do."

Zeke grinned at Ben as if he were stupid. "Yeh, you have. You just don't realize it yet."

Ben tried to make sense of Zeke's comments as he turned and walked away through the growing crowd of shoppers. That stuff about things being mysteriously connected like underground roots sounded like some country mysticism, he thought. It was hard to believe Zeke knew anything that would seriously rile Watt.

It was after noon, time to return to Mossback and his meeting with Watt. "Dead man walking," Ben muttered, as he crossed the street.

The guard was at the gatehouse again and waved him through. Ben nodded back without any expression.

As he drove into the parking area, Ben saw Watt in the yard, splitting thick logs into firewood with a heavy steel maul. He had a half-cord stacked by the back door. His blue shirt and the waist of his old khaki pants were soaked with sweat and rivulets dripped from his glistening head onto his collar. Watt drove the maul into a fresh log about three feet in diameter. The heavy steel head plunged into the wood and disappeared as the log collapsed into two large halves. Ben had split plenty of firewood, and Watt's strength and aim impressed him.

Watt looked up at Ben as he rested the maul on his shoulder. "Warms you twice," he said, as he dropped the maul and walked toward Ben. He pulled a white handkerchief from his pocket and wiped his face, head and neck. "Too bad I won't get the second heating in the winter."

Watt stuffed the damp handkerchief into his pocket and leaned against the split rail fence separating the parking area from the lawn. The weathered locust rail bent slightly under his weight. He was breathing heavily, but didn't appear winded.

"Couldn't find you this morning," Watt said. "Thought for a minute you might have fled the scene." He leaned forward to stretch his back and Ben could see muscles ripple through the sweat-drenched shirt. Watt arched his back, then relaxed. "How was your morning?"

Full of discoveries that confirm everything I thought about you, you wormy bastard. Why couldn't he say those words out loud? He rarely regretted what he said, but too often he regretted what he didn't say. Ben remembered Zeke's admonition to flatter Watt and try to learn his plans for Mossback. No fights, he warned himself.

"Just wandered around town thinking about your offer," Ben said. "Five million's a lot of money. I don't understand why you're being so generous after all these years. As you said, you could do anything you want with the place without my cooperation."

"I told you," Watt said in a comforting tone, "I just want you to be compensated for what you've been through. You missed out on a lot. Had to really struggle, far as I can see. Besides, I'm not giving the money away. That would be out of character."

Watt laughed heartily at his self-deprecation.

"You really going to build a golf course like Reggie said?" Ben asked. "It'd be a mighty beautiful spot.

Nothing like it. Of course, I'm no golfer. Don't know anything about the business of it."

"It could have possibilities," Watt said. Ben detected quiet smugness in Watt's voice. "It's a complicated business."

"How would it work?" Ben said. "I mean, there's a lot of golf courses around. They're sprouting like mushrooms. I saw all those billboards when I drove up."

"Those jerks don't know what they're doing," Watt said. "A lot of stupid money following the pack until the pack is exhausted. No vision. Very low end."

Ben sensed an opening. "You see a development that's different?"

Watt looked at Ben, sizing him up. Ben tried to look as naive as he possibly could without making Watt suspicious.

"What's really distinctive is something only a handful of people can afford," Watt said. Ben relaxed and prepared to be educated. "I mean a handful of people in the whole world, maybe three hundred families. I see a couple of golf courses meandering through an ancient forest. A polo field or two between them. Stables for dozens of horses that cost more than a house. Miles of trails through the forest, along the courses. They can ride to a trophy trout stream and fish in the morning, then in the afternoon play golf on the best course in the world. The houses will be on lots big enough for total privacy. There'll be a guest lodge and spa with gourmet dining, and town homes for people who don't want to bother with a house. And a heliport so they can get to their jets fast."

Watt's enthusiasm impressed Ben until he remembered his brother's vision for the old Arkansas duck club.

"And tight security," Watt continued. "Only one way in and out, unless you're a mountain goat. The people I'll attract put a very high premium on security. They can come here with their families and not worry about threats of any kind. Great for private conferences, away from the press. It'll have everything they want right here. And they'll be happy to pay. It'll be magnificent."

His brother was enthralled from what he envisioned, the status it would bring, the fortune he might make. "I guess the prices will be like no other place, too," Ben said.

Watt smiled. "Records will be set."

Kelsey had a reputation as a high-end resort community, but Watt's scheme would make the entrenched country club folks feel like poor country cousins. Ben could not imagine what a lot or membership might cost.

"What kind of records?" Ben said. "How much to join?"

"Way beyond what you could afford after you get your money," Watt said. "I still have to crunch some numbers, but it easily could be twice what you'll get."

The notion of paying ten million dollars for a club membership stunned Ben. That much money just to play golf where no one sees you but others just as rich as you. What were the limits to status? He did a quick calculation in his head. On the far side of three billion dollars, he estimated. He was suddenly aware of the stakes Watt was playing for. God, I'm about to plunge into a nest of white-faced hornets, Ben thought.

"What do you think, little brother?"

Ben thought the moment was surreal, as if he had just walked in on somebody else's dream he'd never comprehend.

"This has been a day full of insights," Ben said, shaking his head.

"Insight can be very useful," Watt said. "Helps clarify our thoughts, make better decisions. I believe in insights. What are yours?"

Ben thought, what it would feel like to make a wave? He wondered where the ripples would break. What would it be like to take one righteous step into the unknown and be unafraid of the consequences?

"Insights? I'll give you some insight," Ben said. "I had half a life because I believed you a long time ago. That's my fault as much as yours. Now you say you want to make up for all that by paying me for something I should have gotten years ago. You want to ruin Mossback. Our parents loved this place and I did too. God knows who you paid off to get this far." A sharp pain burning in Ben's spine almost made him drop to his knees. "You want me to make it easy for you. I won't."

Ben was certain he had done the stupidest thing in his life. Pissed away a fortune, for what? He anticipated Watt grabbing the heavy maul and inflicting the same fate on him as the firewood. Ben kept a sharp eye on Watt for any sudden moves toward the maul on the grass. Ben couldn't look at Watt's eyes for fear of bolting like a deer. Instead, he watched Watt's hands form a fist. The tendons and muscles stretched tightly as Watt flexed his thick hands, and then relaxed.

"Quite an insight, Ben," said Watt evenly. "You really don't want the money? The offer is sincere. You've suffered enough and deserve some comfort."

Ben looked sideways at Watt and saw his face was unperturbed, with a disarming smile. Ben bared his soul, and, yet, he was still standing, the earth still rotated, a bird sang in a nearby tree. He forced his breathing to resume a normal pace, and his lower back pain subsided. Guess the terrible ripples are not so terrible after all, he thought.

Watt shook his head slowly, his eyes closed. He stood to his full height. "I'm going to give you the benefit of the doubt that you're not nuts like your sister, and you've got some idea what you're saying, that you're not entirely delusional. I'll give you that much."

Watt moved a little closer to Ben, who could smell the sweat from his brother's clothing.

"You've made the wrong choice again, little brother," Watt said, looking straight into Ben's eyes. "You ran away from something you didn't like a long time ago. Now you're running away from the best offer you'll ever see in your life. I don't know what makes you tick, and I honestly don't care. You don't want a fair offer, fine. Then you're out of here. Like I told you, I don't need your consent. I control the stock. I'll do what I want. But I won't close out your options just yet, in case you sober up and see what's good for you."

"I'll get Reggie to help me fight you," Ben said.

A smirk spread across Watt's lips. "I absolutely control her share. She fought it in court and I won. Been there, done it. Besides, you don't have enough money to fight me. You have as much chance stopping me as that colored man Obama getting elected president next month."

Watt laughed as he began walking back to the house. "Don't hang around too long 'cause we're about to start doing business, and you'll just be in the way." He waved his hand in the air in a departing gesture.

A breeze blowing across the lawn scattered brightly colored leaves over the grass. Some leaves swirled in an upward spiral and then fluttered down. Ben didn't want to go inside the house where he would have to face Watt. He had no good news for Reggie, whose hopes were raised just by his presence. He turned and walked toward the road. The prospect of resuming his old life depressed him.

As he walked down the road, his hands thrust deeply in his pockets, he heard tires crunching gravel and saw Zeke's truck coming toward him.

"From your face I'd say your meeting went south," Zeke said, as he came to a stop next to Ben. He opened his door and turned in his seat to face Ben. "So he didn't fall apart at your decision?"

Ben kicked at the gravel. Zeke had been right about Ben already having made a decision. "No, he didn't fall apart," he said. "Just said he'd go ahead anyway. Didn't really need my share. The offer was a courtesy, for old time's sake. Watt knows every twist and turn. We're just dumb suckers who don't know the rules, if there are any."

Zeke spat on the dry gravel. "He plays by his own rules," he said. "Knows 'em pretty good." He sighed heavily. "I might be able to change the rules a little bit. Throw him off kilter. Maybe help him see things differently."

"There must be something about this place that encourages delusions," Ben said. "So, dazzle me. You must have some powerful ability to persuade."

Zeke looked at Ben with a hard stare. "There's stuff you don't know that can turn things upside down," he said.

Ben gave Zeke points for drama, but he was still waiting for some display of Zeke's persuasive powers.

"Dark family secrets only the faithful family servant would know?" Ben said, and immediately regretted his sarcasm. "Sorry, but Watt doesn't spook easily."

"Never thought he would." Zeke said. "Tell me, how far are you willing to go to keep this place like it is?"

"I don't know what you mean by 'how far,' " Ben said. "I'm new to power-politics business. I just write fish stories."

Zeke looked Ben up and down like someone about to buy a horse.

"You ain't done much with your life. No disrespect meant," Zeke said. "Fishing stories are all pretty much the same. Not much pride of ownership there. What if you had the chance to do something you could be seriously proud of? What are you willing to commit?"

"I'll go along with you," Ben said. "I want to hear how you're going to do all this."

"You're not hearing me," Zeke said. "I want to know if you'll hang around if I stick my neck out to help you save this place. You gonna help me, or you gonna cut bait? I can't do what I gotta do if you run away. I need you to see it through. You capable?"

"I need to know exactly what you intend to do before I answer you," Ben said. "I don't want to be a criminal, even to stop Watt."

"That's definitely not your problem," Zeke said, laughing. "I can't tell you unless you're on board. Once I tell you, there's no turning back. People could get hurt. But Mossback might be saved. No guarantees, but we have a good idea what'll happen if we just sit on our asses."

Ben couldn't make sense of Zeke's vague suggestions, but he knew Zeke was right about what would happen if they did nothing.

"What's it like," Ben said, "stepping into the unknown?"

"What's it like not stepping?" Zeke said. "You can't save Mossback, yourself or anybody, if you're scared what might go wrong," he said. "I think I can help. But if you aren't going to stick around, well, I may just be pissing into the wind. I want the odds on my side."

Ben looked around at the woods. "Tell me what you're going to do," he said. "What *we're* going to do."

Zeke shook his head in amusement. "You had me worried," he said. "Wasn't sure how much you cared."

"I'm willing to find out. Maybe I just can't stand writing about the last fish I caught anymore." Ben stared into the forest. "I don't have much practice caring about things."

"Get in the truck," Zeke said. "Before I start, I want your promise you'll use what I tell you to stop your brother from trashing this place. I don't know how we'll work it, but, if I'm right, Watt will listen to reason if he doesn't want to land in jail."

The man sure knows how to bait a hook, Ben thought. Jail time for Watt had the irresistible appeal of Old Testament justice.

"I promise," Ben said.

Zeke leaned back in the truck and stretched his legs.

"This all started when you were a little boy," Zeke said. "It was summertime when all your people were at Mossback. It was the summer Watt was named high-school All-American tight end. The best football colleges in the country wanted him. He could have gone anywhere he wanted, but he chose Alabama. Watt's head was really in the clouds that summer.

"Mama was keeping house for your folks. Kept things tidy and clean. Opened and closed the house. We lived near town. Not like now, on the place. That came later.

"Anyway, one day I saw Watt in town and we started talking, football I guess. He was sort of a local celebrity even though he wasn't from around here. The talk got around to girls and he wanted me to get him a date, somebody local and not too particular about her virtue. We agreed to go to Maggie's Barn that night to the square dance. He'd meet me there early. Time came and there he was in a fancy Chevy Impala, big engine. He said it was a graduation present. It was a Friday night and things weren't going to pick up till later, so he asked where could we get some beer. Town was dry back then. A couple of friends with me said we could go to Mal's across the state line. It was a little cinderblock room. You drove up to a window, named your brew, held out your money and drove off back across the line with a bag of beer. Everyone got in Watt's car and made the run. We got six-packs except Watt. He got a case. Said it was going to be a special night.

"We drove around for a while drinking beer, talking football and girls. Watt did most of the talking about football. He quizzed us a lot about the local girls, who was easy, who was hot. Just young bucks getting pumped up for the night. The beer was flowing pretty easy.

"Anyway, we're driving down this dirt road in a new subdivision right up there on Flat Mountain, above Mossback. Got a few creeks that flow down into Mossback. It was getting toward dark, near eight-thirty, nine. Watt was swerving the car back and forth on the dirt road, making it fishtail and showing off. We were all laughing and telling him to spin it around in a three-sixty. We came around a curve pretty fast and got into a slide.

"We really didn't see the girl at first. Just felt a bump, then heard a clatter. Watt stopped the car and we looked back. We saw a little bike in the road but no rider. I thought some kid had left it in the road, but Watt had this look on his face. We all got out and looked around. Beside the road near the bike was a little girl about six or seven. She slumped against a tree, sitting in some ferns. She looked right at us, not saying anything. A little trickle of blood came out of her hair down her cheek, stopped before it got to her chin. I'll never forget the empty look on her face.

"She was silent. I knew she was dead. I think the car bumped her bike and threw her into the tree. There we were with a car full of beer, heads full of beer, and a dead little girl. We panicked. We put her in the trunk with the bike. Watt was crying about his football scholarship and begged us to keep it quiet. The other two guys were moaning about going to jail. I thought about my mama, how this would just kill her. Then I thought about going to jail.

"We knew the area pretty well. The only thing we could think of was to make it look like she fell over a waterfall. There was a good steep one at the end of the road. We had to walk in the woods a way. I carried the bike. Lenny and Oscar, the guys in the back, carried the little girl. Watt carried a flashlight. We got to the top of the falls and then threw her over, then her bike, and then we all walked away.

"We swore to each other we would never tell anyone what happened. Lenny, Oscar and me never told anyone. Can't speak for Watt. Your family left early that summer, about a week after the accident, real sudden like. Few weeks later I heard Watt was going to Tennessee instead of Alabama for football.

"For days afterward, talk was about the missing girl from Flat Mountain. Search parties combed the woods looking for her. They had dogs sniffing the ground everywhere. Of course, she hadn't left a trail for them to sniff out. Someone got the notion of looking down the falls around Mossback, and that's when they found her, not far from here. Days had passed and she was pretty decomposed and all. The conclusion was she had taken her bike to the top of the falls and somehow fallen over.

Some bought it, others didn't. But there wasn't anything to head the law in a different direction. The girl's parents went back to Atlanta, sold their place here.

"Me, Lenny and Oscar all joined the army. They went to 'Nam and I went to Germany. When they got back, they were pretty messed up from drugs and the war. Lenny hung himself. Oscar fell off a cliff, they claim.

"Watt must have told your folks the story. That would explain the fast departure that summer. Your papa eventually thanked me for keeping Watt away from the law. Said mamma and me could live here as long as we wanted.

"I never mentioned it to anyone. Watt and I never spoke about it. We can hardly look each other in the eye.

"You know, Lenny and Oscar told me they kept getting envelops with cash, hundred dollar bills. Came every month they were alive. I got this caretaker job about that time. Just look after the place. I always got paid on time with a nice check from a Memphis bank.

"I've had a pretty good life. Watt surely has by all accounts. But, I never stop thinking about that little yellow-haired girl and the ribbon of blood on her cheek. Maybe she can save Mossback. You think?"

CHAPTER 16

Ben walked away from the truck with the sweet smell of Zeke's pipe tobacco following him. He couldn't shake the image of the little girl, the red ribbon of blood, and her bent bicycle. From somewhere deep in the forest, he heard the sound of water splashing over rocks and wondered if it was the same stream where she had been found. He imagined the horror and grief her parents suffered when they saw the child's body.

His own parents must have endured their own version of hell. Their star athlete son killed a little girl, and they helped conceal it to avoid losing their own child. How did Watt recall that distant summer night when he no longer owned the world? Did he even think about it?

Zeke seemed ready to reveal his part in that dreadful night. The confession was made, with atonement to follow. Ben imagined Watt wriggling out of any legal predicament with the help of thousand-dollar-an-hour criminal defense lawyers, but poor Zeke's future could be a small concrete and steel room without a view of the sky. He assumed Zeke knew what he was risking, and was humbled. But he wasn't too clear about his own role in this new strategy.

Ben walked back to the truck and leaned against the open driver's door. "How far are you willing to go with that story?" he said. "I mean, Watt's got to believe you'll go all the way. You thought about that?"

"Haw!" Zeke said. "Thought about a lot of things, too many things."

"What was her name – the little girl?" Ben said.

Zeke looked surprised, and then his cheeks flashed red. "I didn't want to know," he said, shrugging. "She was always the little dead girl. It was better not knowing. What I knew was enough."

Zeke's gaze was fixed on something very far away. He turned and his blue eyes locked onto Ben. "She's haunted me for too long. I was always afraid, for myself and mama. But if I do nothing, my soul will be lost."

Ben looked at the ground where a wooly caterpillar was wriggling along from underneath the truck on its way to the roadside. It was furry black, with a narrow brown band around it's middle.

"Watt will deny everything," Ben said. "He'll say you're lying, trying to destroy him because he's going to develop Mossback."

"He'd be half right, anyway," Zeke said. "I would be out to ruin him if it went public." Zeke grinned. "You'll have to trust I can back up anything I say about Watt." Zeke tightly pressed his lips; he had said all he was going to say on the subject.

"How should I approach Watt?" Ben said. "You want me to say anything, or wait for you to do something?" Although Zeke had leverage to get Watt's attention, Ben couldn't see that alone saving Mossback. Watt quivering in fear of Zeke and skulking back to Memphis was unlikely. At the University of Tennessee he didn't earn the nickname "Bonecrusher" by following the rules. He would react calmly, detect a weakness, and then use all his resources to smash the threat.

"I guess your situation's a little tricky about now," Zeke said. "You've challenged Watt. Told him to fuck himself, but you're still in the house. He'd like to toss you out, but maybe you've got some right to be there. He might try to have the guard throw you out. How big are your balls?"

Ben hesitated. His inclination was to let Zeke confront Watt, then see how the winds blew and ride the breeze. "Guess I'll do what I have to," Ben said, seeking refuge in vagueness.

"I'll take you at your word," Zeke said. "You might try scattering a few hints. See how he reacts. Say something like: 'I heard in town a little girl died here years ago.' Ask him if he knows about it. Watch him. See if he twitches, gives away anything. Just get him thinking about that night. Get it in the front of his mind."

Ben liked the sideways approach, the image of a subtle remark casually uttered over drinks or dinner, like in a movie. He'd have to do it out of Reggie's presence because he didn't want her influencing Watt's reaction with drunken accusations, true or imagined. No, Ben wanted to watch his brother caught off-guard. He would shrug innocently if Watt pressed him for details or sources.

"What will you be doing?" Ben said. "I mean, while I'm watching Watt's reaction, looking for twitches?"

"I got an idea or two," Zeke said, the corners of his eyes wrinkled. "Something I hope will soften up your brother a tad. Get him in the right frame of mind to pay heed when the proper time comes."

Ben didn't underestimate the grizzly old man, even though he hadn't known him long. "Guess it's time to fish," Ben said.

"Time to cast a delicate dry fly," Zeke said, and left in the old truck rattling down the road.

Ben shrugged and walked back toward the house. He thought about how his petty crime years ago had landed him in jail and scarred his life. Watt, however, was guilty of something far worse and had prospered in life as if nothing had happened. At least I didn't kill anyone, he thought.

As he pulled the kitchen screen door, the rusty hinges squeaked in the empty room. Ben stood in the kitchen and listened for sounds of his brother and sister. Faint operatic music came from upstairs. Watt didn't strike him as an opera lover, but Reggie might like it. He could imagine her shrieking along with some busty soprano. Aural agony.

Ben guessed Watt would be in the library, on the phone to lawyers who would be summoned to action against the reluctant shareholder. Watt would be bellowing orders to take no prisoners, annihilate the enemy. Walking quietly down the hallway toward the library, he stopped just before the doorway and heard the sounds of pages turning. He peeked around the doorframe and saw Watt flipping through the pages of a magazine.

"Your stories all sound alike," Watt said, without looking up.

Ben didn't want to give Watt the satisfaction of humiliating him. "After a while they are," he said, walking into the room. "The trick is fresh verbs, adverbs and adjectives. We have a special thesaurus just for fly fishing."

Ben studied the books on the shelves. Pulling an old copy of Nash Buckingham stories from a shelf, he thumbed through the yellowed pages as he improvised his strategy.

"Do you remember hearing anything about some kid dying around here?" Ben said, skimming through the book. "Years ago, when we were kids?" He glanced sideways to watch Watt.

Watt kept flipping the magazine pages without skipping a beat. Ben saw no change.

"Doesn't ring a bell," Watt said. "Why?"

Ben closed the book. "Just something I heard this morning when I was getting coffee. I told some woman I was staying at Mossback, and she said the place had a sad history. The owners dying in an accident around here, and before that, a little girl falling down some waterfall. Said it was days before she was found all decomposed on our property. It was a strange case, maybe not an accident, but nothing ever came of it. She said the girl's parents were convinced it wasn't an accident, but couldn't prove otherwise. You never heard the folks mention it?"

Watt stopped flipping the pages but continued to look at the magazine. "Sounds vaguely familiar, but I was never too interested in this place. Football was everything back then."

Ben picked up another book, but was watching his brother, whose demeanor remained unchanged, except Watt had begun licking his lips, as if they were parched.

"Maybe you could switch from fishing to crime stories," Watt said, tossing the magazine into a trashcan.

"No one said anything about an actual crime," Ben said. "Anyway, fishing stories are a lot easier."

"Nothing like the easy way."

"You'd think so," Ben said, replacing the book on its shelf and walking to the door.

"You reconsider selling your share of Mossback?" Watt said. "Last chance."

"Reconsideration you can't imagine," Ben said from the doorway. "But the answer's still the same. I won't help you ruin this place."

Watt laughed. "You have pretty lofty principles for a poor man. Most people would at least give more serious thought to five million. You want to piss it away over what? Something you can't do anything about? Don't think my over-priced lawyers haven't scrutinized this deal through a high-powered lens. Reggie's drunken talk misleads a lot of folks, including her. She can't help you, and I know the courts won't. And you won't beat me. Better men than you have tried."

Ben slapped the doorframe and said, "Well, we'll see." He turned and walked away down the hall to the stairway as he heard a muffled chuckle from the library. Several tall glasses of neat bourbon would taste especially good right now, and he had a sudden empathy for Reggie's boozy existence within Watt's world.

He passed Reggie's closed door and heard soft music, classical Spanish guitar, the melody deeply lonely. There was no answer to his knock. Glancing toward the open bathroom down the hall, he saw it was empty. He knocked a little harder.

"Yes," a weary voice said.

He entered and saw Reggie stretched out on a large chaise longue by an open window. A book was propped on a pillow on her lap. Half-lens reading glasses clung to the tip of her nose. She looked over the glasses and smiled when she realized who was in the doorway. Without marking her place, she closed the book, a collection of Peter Taylor short stories.

"Have you come to check up on me or is this a social call?" she said, wiggling into a more upright position.

"Just seeing how you are," he said. "A friendly check-up."

She patted the chaise. "Come sit down and check away." Reggie seemed a little more alert this afternoon, her eyes not so red and watery. He smelled faint perfume competing with her musty tobacco overtones. He sat where she indicated.

"You feeling okay?" he said.

"You mean am I hung over, or maybe drunk?" She looked at him without a hint of playfulness. Ben looked away from what he took as her rebuke. She nudged him with her foot. " I'm fine, really. Mostly red blood flowing in the veins and brain, for all the good it does."

She took a cigarette from a pack in her lap, lit it and inhaled with deep pleasure. She exhaled to her side, toward the open window. "My only sin of the day," she said, displaying the unfiltered Camel. "If you don't count thoughts."

"What sinful thoughts have you been enjoying?"

"About Watt, of course," she said, picking a shred of tobacco from her tongue. "And they weren't enjoyable for him." She flicked the shred away.

"Involved violence, I hope."

"A shit load," she said and laughed.

"He brings that out in people. At least in me. Just had a little talk with him, and I kept wanting to hit him with something lethal," he said. "Repeatedly."

"I'll keep quiet. Say the butler did it," she said. "We need a butler, quick!"

They both laughed. Ben patted her foot.

"I'm sorry I was gone so long," he said. "I thought about you a lot. Imagined you as some tennis star. That's how I remembered you. I wish things had worked out better."

"Please, no pity," she said. "We all end up where we put ourselves. I could have left like you did. I stayed. Tennis was one thing. A big thing, but not everything. I did other things. Junior League stuff. Even had a book-store for a while till family subsidies dried up. I never had any fire inside. Did you?"

Her question unnerved Ben. "Fire? You mean a passion to do something?"

"Yeh, that. You ever have a passion that couldn't be ignored? Is fishing a passion?"

Is hatred, he wondered? All these years, he hated Watt with a passion, but that was hardly a vocation.

"No real passions," he said. "Fishing's easy. Writing about it's easy. Well, making each story sound interesting is a challenge, hard work sometimes, but nothing involving passion."

Reggie gazed out the window toward the retreating layers of pale blue mountains. "Poor us. Such promising ingredients and the dough never even rose."

"I was at the nature center this morning," he said. "A lot of memories came back. They were actually kind of happy, of Mother picking me up after nature class-es, teaching me to paint. I remember Dad helping me build a doghouse, but I barely remember a dog. Do you know its name? Maybe you were around six years old?"

"Sounds like you're having a Norman Rockwell moment," Reggie said. "You're getting all gushy on me. Next you'll be having loving thoughts about Watt."

Ben felt his face getting warm and wondered if she knew he was blushing. He wished he hadn't told her.

"Memory's a tricky thing," he said, wondering whether or not he should mention what Zeke told him about the girl's death on Flat Mountain Road. After all, Reggie had blurted it out the other night. "You claimed something a couple nights ago when you were yelling at Watt. About a little girl being killed, and Watt having something to do with it. Remember?"

He was touching her foot and he could feel the skin and muscle beneath it tighten. Reggie removed her glasses and lit another cigarette. He noticed her hand tremble as she lifted the cigarette to her cracked lips.

"I say a lot of things when I'm drinking. Most of them I regret if I remember them. When I don't remember, people – Watt – remind me. I get angry sometimes and say things to hurt people. I shouldn't." She hesitated and smoked for a few moments. Ben waited. "Did I say something to Watt about a girl's death? That he had something to do with it? He hasn't said anything to me about it."

Her contrition about the accusation surprised Ben. She had been so vehement when she attacked Watt, so absolute in her certainty.

"You seemed pretty sure the other night about Watt killing someone," he said. "You'd been drinking a lot and might have forgotten. No reason for Watt to say anything, I guess. Maybe he figured you were just too blotto."

They sat quietly for a while as Reggie smoked. Ben gazed idly around the room while he speculated what hell, besides rehab, Watt threatened her with.

"I heard someone this morning in town talking about a kid dying around here years ago. Fell from one of the ridges," he said. "Was that what you were talking about?"

Reggie smashed out her cigarette, leaned back and closed her eyes. Her forehead furrowed deeply as if she were in pain.

"There was talk Watt was involved in an accident years ago," she said, almost in a whisper. "I overheard broken comments from Mom and Dad. Nothing direct, only references. Sometimes when I've been drinking, I believe Watt killed someone, a little girl. It's something I believe he could have done. But I don't know he actually did it. I'd never accuse him sober."

She sat up and groaned. "You just don't realize what Watt can do to me. He controls my money, and he can put me away. I don't mean to be bad . . . but it gets so lonely sometimes. I just need to relax a little, be in a happy place. Watt says I get crazy, but I don't remember.

When he can't deal with it, into rehab I go. Twenty-eight days later, full of good intentions, I'm out." She looked at Ben with basset hound eyes, and then turned away toward the window. "The intervals have been getting shorter lately. I'm so afraid some day I won't come out at all. Watt can do that."

Ben wanted to hug his sister and tell her she never had to be afraid of Watt again, that no one would put her away forever in a hospital. He wanted to tell her that she could live her life without fear. He knew better.

"Has it really been that bad for you?" he said.

"You can't imagine what looking for love will make you do," she said, her eyes filling with tears. "There have been times when I wanted Watt to love me, but he barely tolerates me."

Ben was afraid ask her what she meant by love. He didn't want to know the nature of her despair.

"What are you willing to do for yourself?" he said. "I mean to get better, happier?"

Reggie looked puzzled.

"You mean to improve my life?" she said. "Make something of myself? Be somebody?"

"Maybe just have a reason to go to bed sober," he said.

"Too many demons," she said. "Sometimes I have to drown the bastards."

"They tend to resist drowning," he said.

She stared at Ben, as if trying to decide whether his form had substance, whether or not he was real, or just an apparition feeding their mutual delusion.

"Who will kill the demons?" she said.

"You can," he said. "Maybe just ignore them."

"Alone?" she said.

Ben was quiet for a moment.

"With help," he said.

"Your help?"

"Well, we'll see," he said, remembering they were the same words he had just said to Watt.

"Are you listening to yourself?" she said.

He hesitated, and then said, "Yes."

"And you're not afraid?"

"Terrified," he admitted for the first time in many years.

CHAPTER 17

Ben slept fitfully that night as drowsy thoughts of Katherine from the nature center teased him. She wasn't like women he'd met who flattered easily while the drinks flowed. Katherine's serious purpose intrigued Ben, as well as intimidated him. She was serious about things he'd paid scant attention to until this weekend.

Maybe she would enjoy touring Mossback. She might even like to learn how to fly fish. He knew a lot of nature-girls didn't like killing things, so the fishing would be strictly catch and release, let the trout live to be caught again another day. He could prove his devotion for Mossback equaled hers, and the wilderness experience would appeal to her love of nature. These moments, of course, would come after he had somehow stopped his brother from destroying the treasure Katherine wanted preserved. As with so many nocturnal fantasies, he easily overlooked the details.

Ben dressed in the dark and headed through the unguarded gate to the nature center as pink morning light crept into town. Soon he was parked in the nature center lot among a few small vehicles plastered with bumper stickers touting Obama and scorning polluters and their enabling politicians. He wondered which one, and which message, belonged to Katherine. He almost missed her riding quietly up to the front door on a bicycle. Slinging a courier bag over her shoulder, she entered the building without noticing Ben.

She wore a loose blouse under a vest and cargo pants. He waited in his car for a few moments, and then followed.

Voices and laughter came from an open doorway near the back. Although he was bewitched by their encounter yesterday, he hadn't thought through just what he would say to her now. What is the purpose of your visit, sir? "To ogle your body," would be a pitiful approach. Still, desperate need bolstered him. Maybe he would tell her that although he was one of the owners of Mossback, he wasn't at all like his plundering brother, but merely a simple fisherman and a catch-and-release one at that. Promising that he shared her passion for the old growth forest and could help save it would surely hook her attention. How he was going to deliver on promises he could save Mossback from the evil developer was being devised as he walked. Saying he was going to expose his brother as a child killer might be too dramatic. For now, genuine concern, liberally laced with an invitation for her guidance, would have to be the seedbed for their relationship

He heard her talking and laughing with co-workers. He caught her eye briefly, but she looked away as if she didn't recognize him. She looked his way again with a puzzled expression, then smiled and gave a small wave while she finished her conversation. Ben's face flushed as she walked toward him in the middle of the lobby.

"You were here yesterday . . . just about this time," she said. "You must be an early riser. How's the story going?"

He had forgotten his ruse about being a writer working on a story investigating old forests. His lie left his tongue paralyzed. All he could manage was a smile and a nod of his head.

"Yes, quite an early bird," she said, as she held her smile and nodded. Ben returned her nod. A couple of bobble heads, he thought with exasperation.

"Gets the worm, though," he finally said, and his smile turned to a grimace as he realized how lame he sounded. He drew a deep breath and could smell the fragrance of peppermint soap coming from her skin.

"Actually, you said something yesterday, about Mossback," he said. "How it was threatened. Maybe I can help. I don't know. But there might be something."

She stopped smiling and squinted at Ben as if trying to assess his credibility.

"You must be a pretty influential writer," she said. "Its fate seems pretty well sealed, unless you've got some hidden powers."

Ben shifted uneasily from foot to foot. What he needed to say embarrassed him; he didn't want to appear to be bragging.

"There's something you don't know about me," he started.

"There's a lot I don't know about you," she said, tilting her head. "Other than you claim to be a writer."

"Well, yes," Ben said. "I mean something important. About Mossback."

Katherine watched him cautiously as she took a half step back.

"You see, I'm not really a writer," he said, and realized he was sinking into a misleading quagmire. "I mean, I am a writer but I'm not writing about forests or Mossback. I write about fishing."

She continued watching Ben carefully.

"I'm one of the owners of Mossback," he said. "I don't want it developed. My brother does. He's the developer. It's his idea. I didn't know anything."

Ben realized he sounded like too many crooks and spies he had watched on late-night television.

"I didn't even know about Mossback till a few days ago. I mean, I knew about it, but didn't know I was part owner. I thought Watt owned it, my brother. I've been gone a long time. I was out of touch."

He heard himself becoming more obtuse as he spoke, but didn't know how to reverse himself and make sense of his situation.

"Well, you seem a little confused, but harmless," Katherine finally said.

At first he was relieved at her comment, but "harmless" was not the persona he had fabricated overnight to impress this woman. Irresistibly bold was more the image he had in mind.

"You seem kind of sincere. Maybe you write fiction?"

"Would you like to see the place?" Ben asked, reaching for the only way to prove his claim of ownership. "I can take you there now."

He wouldn't have believed himself if he were a stranger listening to his babbling. His only identification was his driver's license and a fishing license, both showing he lived in another state. An altered state, he thought.

"I wish you could save Mossback. But I believe in lawyers, not fairy tales, and the lawyers tell me it's hopeless," she said.

Watt's lawyer told Ben the same thing, he remembered. But lawyers' opinions were easily bought and sold.

"Maybe they don't know everything," he said. "In a trial, at least one lawyer always loses."

She looked back toward the office at her friends, and Ben knew she wanted to be somewhere else, away from a stranger's rant.

"I had forgotten about this place until yesterday," he said. "When I was a kid, people here at the nature center showed me snakes and salamanders and fish. It was the beginning of a very long love affair."

Ben told her about how he had first discovered the natural world's mysteries in this very building. How his mother encouraged his curiosity. He detected Katherine's impatience receding, certain that she was listening.

"I've really enjoyed talking with you," she said, as she extended her hand. "I hope you come back for some of our workshops or lectures. They're very interesting."

Ben felt the soft warmth of her hand and did not want to let go. He felt her hand's slight tug.

"What will convince you I'm telling the truth about Mossback?" he said. "I don't have a deed in my pocket. All I can do is take you there. I'll even introduce you to my brother. You won't like him. No one does."

She pulled her hand away and tucked it under her arm. "The gallant knight of Mossback. I want to believe you."

"I can take you there right now. You can follow me in your car. If we don't make it past the guardhouse, you'll know I'm a fraud. It's that simple." Remembering she'd ridden to work on a bicycle and would probably need to ride with him, the plan looked even better.

"Don't you want to help save Mossback?" he said.

Ben thought his challenge might be working because she was scrunching her lips, obviously perplexed. She fingered her beaded necklace as if praying over his offer.

"Take a chance," he said, feeling her waver. Fishing was much easier than luring people. "At least you can say you tried."

She walked away and spoke to someone as she gestured toward Ben. She returned and confronted him with her fists on her hips. "You will be banned from this place if you turn out to be full of bullshit," she said, as she walked toward to door. "I mean it."

Ben hurried behind her into the parking lot. He was dismayed when she got into one of the small cars near his van. At least she's coming, he thought.

"Just follow me," he yelled, as he got into his car and fumbled for the ignition key. His hand trembled as he tried to jam the key in.

The excitement Ben felt distracted him as he pulled out of the parking lot. He didn't notice the heavy dump truck filled with gravel thundering toward him. The loud blast from the truck as it swerved around Ben jolted him. As his heart resumed a normal beat, he cursed himself for such a humiliating start, and hoped a respectful greeting by the guard at Mossback would make her forget his nearly fatal flub.

As they approached Mossback's entrance, Ben saw the guard slouched in a chair, learning against the guardhouse. He quickly stood up when he saw the approaching cars, one hand rested casually on his pistol handle. Ben rolled down his window as he pulled even with the guardhouse. The guard stood smartly and waved him through.

"She's with me," Ben said, as he passed through and nodded his head toward the following car. The guard watched Katherine closely as she drove past the gate.

Ben was pleased by the way the guard waved him through, almost in a crisp military manner. That gesture surely proved the truth about his claim on Mossback. Keeping his car on the road was a challenge as he kept glancing into the rear view mirror, straining to see some indication in her face that she was awed or at least pleased at being here.

They pulled into the parking lot, and Ben hesitated for a moment so Katherine would have enough time to absorb the surroundings. When he decided she should be sufficiently dazzled, he went to her car and opened the door.

"Welcome to my home," he said, bowing slightly as he swept his arm. He immediately regretted his dramatic gesture. He straightened up and looked toward the house to see if anyone else witnessed his behavior, but saw no one.

"You weren't kidding me," Katherine said as she got out and looked around with her mouth agape. "Did you see those trees as we drove in? Ancient."

Ben felt a sense of pride as he watched her astonished expression. How easy it would be to place his arm around her waist and walk her about, pointing out Mossback's unique natural features.

"Some of those trees are older than our country," he said, walking toward her. "There might even be some hemlocks that were sprouts when the pilgrims landed."

He wasn't really certain of the ancestry, but he might be accurate. And he had learned as a fishing guide that if you sounded like you knew what you were talking about, others might easily assume you did. Of course, he had to be cautious around people like Katherine who actually did know about trees, so he had to be within spitting distance of the truth.

"You really can't be certain without taking a boring," he said. "But the trees have never been cut, so they're really old virgins."

"I'd love to take some core samples, just to confirm my estimates," Katherine said, as she walked to a nearby hemlock. Its bark was deeply ridged, with moss and lichen turning its dark brown trunk into a damp pastel green. She moved her fingertips across the bark, and then craned her neck to look up at the first branches, which were at least sixty feet above her head. He imagined his lips on the curve of her throat.

"I've seen a few trees like this, but never in a forest this full of them."

The hemlock trunk made her look like a tiny child. It would have taken several people holding outstretched hands to encircle the tree.

"Trees this large create their own ecosystem," she said, as she disappeared behind the trunk. " . . . can't live without them," she said, coming back around.

"What can't live without them?" Ben said.

"Some species of birds and insects can't live without these ancient trees," she said. "Take away these old trees and forests, and other things die, too."

Her enthusiasm infected him. "Let's save them, then," he said, grinning.

She arched an eyebrow at him.

"I mean it!" he said. "We might be able to stop my brother." He didn't care that he was wandering blindly.

"Who's 'we,' " she said. "How many people are working on this?"

Ben couldn't expose Zeke's role yet. He was too vulnerable. The less anyone knew about their plans, the better.

"Just some people checking out different ideas right now," he said. "Nothing's certain, but we have some angles. I can't tell you any more. Not yet." He hoped she would try to tempt him into revealing secrets, and wondered how long he could resist her.

"I understand," she said. "Developers have ears everywhere. Don't tell me anything that might hurt your plans."

"Thanks for not prying," he said. Without an interrogation to resist, he wondered what to do next.

Katherine turned around several times, examining the forest edge next to the house and lawn.

"Any son of a bitch who turns this into a fucking golf course ought to be castrated and hung up by what's left," she said.

He resisted an impulse to put his hands over his groin even though he was on the good-guy's side. "That's fun to think about," he said. "I guess there are a lot of folks who would gladly sharpen your knife."

He was quiet for a moment. "Taking this away from Watt would hurt him more than that," Ben said, sweeping his hand toward the forest, and glimpsing the perfect revenge. "This is supposed to be his ultimate glory. His balls are nothing compared to his ego."

A slamming screen door turned their attention toward the house. They saw Watt striding toward his Range Rover while he furiously squeezed the remote entry key and thrust it like a sword, making the lights flash and horn blare in response to its master's demands. He paused as his hand grasped the door handle and he looked back at the house. Then he turned and noticed Ben and Katherine staring at him from across the parking area. He started to say something, but stopped as the screen door slammed again.

They all turned to see Reggie stumble down the few stairs to the walkway where she sprawled face down on the mossy bricks. She was wearing a pale cotton nightgown and flannel robe, untied and tangled around her as she struggled to rise. Steadying herself on one knee, she screamed, "Come back here, you cocksucker. You can't slither away. I'm not through with you."

Watt shook his head in disgust and got into his car. The engine hummed to life and gravel spewed from beneath the tires as Watt accelerated toward the road to town.

"Family?" Katherine said.

"Very Southern," he said. "Bordering on Gothic, I'm afraid. I had hoped for a little better introduction if there had to be one."

"Well, I only came to see their habitat," she said.

Ben watched Reggie rise unsteadily on both feet, and then collapse on her rear end. Her eyes widened in amazement at her predicament, then closed as she seemed to mumble something.

"I'd better see if she's okay," he said. Ben heard soft chanting, something like a prayer, as he got closer to Reggie, who had not moved from her seated position. He heard a hissing sound and realized she was repeating "shit" in a southern, two-syllable mantra.

"Anything hurt beside your dignity?" Ben said, as he offered his hand.

Reggie opened one eye. "Dignity? You must have me mistaken for someone else."

She reached up to grasp his hand. Ben pulled her to her feet, and she fell against him. He noticed her hair glistened in the morning light and smelled of herbal shampoo.

"Who's the granola girl?" Reggie said, looking over his shoulder. "Have you found a little playmate?"

Ben pulled back and looked into Reggie's red-veined eyes trying to focus on him.

"She's not my playmate, Reggie. She's the director at the nature center," he said, as he released his sister. "She's never seen Mossback. I'm just trying to be helpful."

"How 'bout helping me back to the house. Invite your playmate in, too," Reggie said, patting his cheek.

Ben put his arm around Reggie. As he turned to tell Katherine to follow, he saw Zeke's truck leading a county sheriff's car past them without slowing down. No sirens wailed or blue lights flashed. Why Zeke was leading someone from the sheriff's office puzzled him, and he figured Watt must have been just as confused as he passed them on his way to town.

"You gonna invite her in or not?" Reggie said, tugging on Ben's shirt.

He returned his attention to Katherine, who also had been watching the two vehicles.

"Let's go inside for a minute, then we can look around the place," he said to Katherine. She shrugged and followed them into the kitchen.

"Are you all right?" Katherine said, as Reggie collapsed into a chair by the kitchen table. Blood stained the front of her nightgown where it touched her knees. "You're bleeding."

Reggie looked down and laughed as she raised her gown off her knees.

"Maybe I should treat it with alcohol," she said. "Somebody bring me a drink."

She rocked back, her laughter turning into a deep smoker's hack. When she regained her breath, she said, "Where's the drink?"

"You've still got plenty inside you," Ben said. "No germ stands a chance of hurting you. Instant death."

"Not lately," she said.

"Let me do this," Katherine said. She knelt beside Reggie and lifted the stained gown above her knees. "Bring me a wet towel and some hydrogen peroxide," she told Ben. "We'll have you cleaned up in no time."

Reggie looked up at Ben with a mugging grin. "At least someone knows how to take charge around here." She patted Katherine's head. "Take lessons from this woman, Ben. You could learn something."

Ben returned with the ordered supplies and watched Katherine skillfully treat Reggie's scraped knees. The skin was broken enough to bleed, but not enough to require anything more than dabs of antiseptic. Reggie didn't seem to notice the hydrogen peroxide bubbling in her raw skin.

"Try not to pick at the scabs when they form," Katherine said.

"Reggie, you've just been treated by the nature center director, Katherine . . ." Ben hesitated and was embarrassed he could not remember Katherine's last name, even as he strained to visualize the words on her business card.

"Katherine Howell," she said, extending her hand to Reggie.

A lot of points lost there, he thought. "This is my sister, Reggie," he said.

Reggie weakly shook Katherine's hand. "Ben was raving about the nature center yesterday," Reggie said. "Said it brought back all sorts of pleasant memories. He didn't mention you."

Reggie turned to Ben. "Why don't you offer the lady a drink? She must need one after such a great introduction to the household."

"It's a little early . . ." Ben began to say.

"Tea would be fine," Katherine said.

"I was thinking of something with a little more authority," Reggie said. "Can't hurt."

"Tea, really."

As they waited for the water to boil, he told Reggie about Katherine's description of Mossback as the largest old growth forest in the East, and why developing the pristine property would be a crime.

Reggie smiled as Ben served her and Katherine cups of tea.

"I thought you were here for Ben," Reggie said, as she absently stirred her tea. "I see you have higher aspirations."

Katherine glanced at Ben, and then smiled at Reggie. "Your brother seems nice, but I'm just here to see the place. I've never seen an old-growth forest this big. He said he'd show me around. He also said he might be able save it from development."

"There's nothing set in granite," Ben said. "We're going to do our best."

Katherine looked at him sharply. "You said you have a plan. I hope you weren't leading me on," she said.

"Absolutely, I meant what I said. But, Watt hasn't read the script," he said. It's in development, he thought.

"You need to cut Bennie some slack," Reggie said, as she lit a cigarette. Katherine turned her head to avoid the smoke drifting toward her. "He's been gone a long time. He got some bad news years ago and it soured him on family life. Running away didn't seem to help, though."

Ben saw Katherine's bewildered expression. He wanted to stub out Reggie's cigarette into her mouth. "I'm sure Katherine has to get back to work," Ben said. "She wants to explore the place and there's lots of territory to cover."

Katherine went ahead toward the parking area as Ben hesitated. He stood in the doorway and turned back to Reggie.

"I thought you were on my side," he said.

Reggie's face feigned surprise. "Regarding what?"

Ben glared at her. As he walked to the car, Ben knew that Reggie had done nothing to promote him in Katherine's eyes. How hard would it have been for her to find one redeeming quality to point out?

"Not a great start," he said as he approached Katherine. "My family seems to have a way of living below expectations."

Katherine was leaning against her car with her arms folded across her chest. Ben thought she looked cross, perhaps agreeing with his comment about expectations.

"Maybe we can salvage something, if you show me around," she said. "You did make some promises."

A few strands of hair had escaped from her braid and curled against her cheek. Ben wanted very much to lift them gently from her head and tuck them into place.

"I'm ready to go," he said.

Getting in his car, he realized he really didn't know his way around Mossback other than the road to Zeke's house.

"Let's just wander the roads, and we can stop when there's something you want to see closer."

They drove in silence for a while as Katherine twisted, turned and gaped at the landscape. An occasional expletive punctuated her observations.

Ben wished he knew more about the place so he could understand what impressed her. During his years fishing, he had learned how trout lived in streams and what bugs they ate and when, but he was far below her level of knowledge.

The sun had burned away the last traces of morning mist. Clear, bright fall light saturated the leaves, casting a golden glow through the deep forest. The rough two-track Ben turned onto from the gravel road faded into a clearing, cluttered with weathered gray trunks of large trees long dead.

"Beaver pond," Katherine said. "Must be at least twenty acres across."

High grass, shrubs and saplings obscured the water. All Ben could see were flocks of birds flitting across the forest opening. They left the van and bushwhacked through an alder thicket to the water's edge. Concentric circles dimpled the glassy surface.

"Brookies rising to caddis flies," Katherine said in a low voice.

Ben stood slightly behind and to her side so she couldn't see his astonished expression. Looking at her a little closer, he noticed her vest was a simple fishing vest. He hadn't recognized it before because he'd been looking elsewhere.

"You fish much?" he said.

Katherine kept her eyes on the rising trout. "Only to eat. Nothing tastes better than wild trout cooked on a wood fire just after you catch it."

"No catch and release, huh?"

"Trout's to be eaten, not tortured," she said. "I only catch what I can eat on the spot. Honors the prey and the hunter. Anything else is just ego stroking."

Ben had caught many trout with mouths scared by too many hooks. He felt a little ashamed that his pleasures had come at a cruel cost to the fish.

"What would catch one of these?" he said.

After a moment, she said, "A number twelve tan caddis on a very long leader should work."

Ben wanted more time with this woman. She might know more about catching a trout than he did, and she wanted to transform Watt into a eunuch.

Katherine stood and turned. "Let's go," she said, scowling.

As they walked back to the van, Ben said, "Maybe we could fish here sometime. I'll cook."

Katherine kept walking without answering and returned to the van. Shaking her head, Katherine leaned back in her seat. She looked out the windshield and said, "Do you have an inkling of what you have here?"

Ben glanced at her. He feared being tested and dreaded a wrong answer.

"My parents really loved it," he said. "I understand why."

"Over in Highlands there was a forest of more than a thousand acres, a primeval forest," she said. "All of it was cut after the Second World War. For pulpwood. Now golf courses and McMansions cover it. Hardly anyone cared about saving it. Jobs were more important. Topo maps show this is at least seven times larger. And it hasn't changed since the first explorers. It's untouched. No paved roads, tourists, hunters."

Ben decided to keep Zeke's name out of the conversation.

"This is probably the most unprotected primeval forest in the country," she said. "Four hundred years ago, everything looked like this."

Ben watched her pink lips protruding and pressing to form words explaining the natural history of Mossback, from magma flows, colliding tectonic plates, erosion and ice ages. He noticed the gentle curve of her long eyelashes. Her ears were small, their lobes decorated with tiny jade stone clasped in a gold post. Pale freckles spread across her cheeks.

She was reciting a list of large animals that once roamed freely before settlers hunted them to extinction, but he was lost in his fantasy of unbraiding her long hair and letting it cascade over her shoulders and his. He wanted to be bathed in her spirit as well as be lost in her body, and for the first time he could remember, he was indifferent to which came first. What would he not do for her?

"And now your brother wants to turn this last, vast ancient forest into a goddamn golf course." She turned toward him, with a pleading look. "Promise me you won't let that happen."

Ben wanted to put his arm around her and promise that, over his dead body would anything threaten Mossback.

"Watt's going to see how cold revenge can be," he said.

Katherine reached out and put her hand on Ben's leg. He felt feverish from her touch. "I hope you can deliver," she said, giving his leg a squeeze before withdrawing her hand.

"I can," he said, wishing she would replace her hand on his leg.

CHAPTER 18

Ben watched Katherine drive away as he lingered over the memory of her warm hand on his leg and imagined it touching him other places. But the promise he'd made to stop Watt's plan interrupted his fantasy with the very real possibility that he could be exposed as a fraud. Too easily he imagined failing Katherine and throwing away a fortune at the same time. The money would be missed, but salvaging what remained of his soul would be some satisfaction if he could fulfill his promise.

As he drove to Zeke's cabin, he recalled he hadn't seen Zeke or the sheriff since they drove by earlier. If the case was closed, the death ruled an accident and the sheriff uninterested, then challenging Watt would be impossible. Watt would not succumb to moral appeal.

Don't be a backsliding coward, Ben muttered as he approached Zeke's house. You deserve your life, and it will never change if you don't grow some balls. His self-flagellation was interrupted when he saw Zeke and the sheriff sitting on the cabin's front steps, inspecting something in a small box. As he got closer he could see they were examining trout flies.

"Now here's a real expert," Zeke said as Ben approached. "He's seen flies all over the world."

"Bugs are bugs," Ben said. "Fish are always hungry for them. Going fishing?"

"Just showing Jenkins what'll really catch something worth mounting on the wall," Zeke said, elbowing his uniformed guest.

"Thought maybe you were getting arrested for something," Ben said.

"Fish stories aren't a crime yet, but he'll do hard time if they ever are," the sheriff said. He grinned at Zeke, as if imagining the possibility. "He'd probably just talk his way out of it."

Zeke introduced the sheriff and explained that Ben was an owner of Mossback. He said the sheriff needed some serious flies.

"Of course, it'll still be the same ole fisherman," Zeke said.

"I think I'll go arrest somebody who's really dangerous," Sheriff Jenkins said. He stuffed the box of flies in his shirt pocket. "Thanks for the flies, overrated as they are. And I'll check on your question, but I think I'm right. Good to meet you Ben. Beautiful place you got despite the ugly caretaker."

The sheriff hiked up his shiny leather belt around his sagging belly and headed for his squad car. Ben waited until the car was out of sight, and then asked Zeke what he'd learned about the case.

"It's dusty, but still open," Zeke said. "The official version says she probably fell accidentally off the mountain. Her body was so decomposed they couldn't be sure. The file said a shard of glass in the girl's skull couldn't be explained. That was troubling, but no conclusions.

"Jenkins was curious why I brought it up. I told him you mentioned it and asked if I ever heard anything. He did say that if the cause of death was anything but accidental, the law was still very interested – his words, not mine. Jenkins was just starting in the department back then. Said he remembers the parents were kind of like zombies when they found out their only child was dead." Zeke struggled to speak the last words.

"You sure you want to go through with this?" Ben said.

Zeke huffed. "I can almost forget, sometimes. Not often enough. Only thing that keeps me going is remembering I wasn't driving that night. That's something."

"There's a chance it'll all blow up in ways we don't expect," Ben said. "You know, the unintended consequences thing."

"Think about the consequences of doing nothing," Zeke said. "Who can live with that? I can't. Not any more. But I need your help." Zeke turned away as he wiped his nose with his sleeve.

"Gotta check on momma," Zeke said as he climbed the steps and went into the cabin.

Ben decided that Watt needed prodding to see where there might be a sign of weakness in his blustery facade. Ben assumed he was the only one with legal standing to confront his brother. Watt could contemptuously dismiss Katherine's plea for environmental justice, could fire Zeke without a flicker of remorse, and would gladly throw Reggie into a mental hospital.

It didn't look like Zeke was coming back outside, so Ben returned to his van.

He drove aimlessly along the gravel roads that wandered through Mossback. Once he stopped, turned off the engine and listened. From somewhere deep in the forest, he heard the reverberating warble of a wood thrush, a sound so sweet and tender it seemed as if it were singing from a crystal goblet, the trilling notes rising and falling. He imagined the shy, brown-spotted bird hiding among the low shrubs, relying on Ben for survival.

He didn't know what he would say to Watt, but Ben allowed himself a glimmer of hope that Zeke's accusation might be sufficient to panic Watt into abandoning his development plan. Their scheme was based solely on Zeke's claim. He decided a lot of things are based on faith in something a lot less substantial than an eyewitness to a crime.

"I'll just have to believe in maybe."

As he approached the house, Ben saw Watt's Range Rover. A familiar old red truck with a camper top was parked next to it. Ben walked toward Watt's office in the library, increasingly irritated his brother had commandeered the room in which their father had given their mother a love poem. He heard conversation coming from the room.

"Anything else?" Watt said.

"That's the sum of it," said a voice he had heard recently. "What's next?"

There was a hesitation, then, "There is no next," Watt said. "These maps and GPS files are all the originals? No copies? Your complete notes are here? Nothing held back?"

"Yes. That was the agreement."

Ben heard a match being struck.

"You're absolutely positive these things you've found don't exist anywhere else? Nowhere?"

"I can't say absolutely nowhere," the voice said. "It's just that there's no record, no evidence of their existence elsewhere. As far as I can tell, they're exclusive to this place. It's really not a surprise, you know. Mossback is unique. *Not* finding something new would have been a surprise. You're sitting on some exciting discoveries. It'll put this place on the map."

Ben edged along the wall outside the library toward the door. Several feet from the doorway he stopped, fearing his breathing would be detected.

"You will recall the contract you signed for your services," Watt said. "You read it carefully. Then you signed it before witnesses. You were very well paid. The checks cleared."

"Well, yes, but . . .."

"There are no buts, Dr. Parker. Everything was very explicit. Your services were to me exclusively. Any findings by you on my land are the absolute property of me, no one else. Everything you used in making those discoveries belongs to me. Nothing is yours. The divulgence of anything, the appropriation of any discovery, will result in severe and drastic penalties, very expensive lawsuits. You freely agreed to those terms. Right?"

There were no sounds from the room. Ben wished he could see their faces. He felt sorry for the man, who he now remembered. It was the naturalist he met in the woods the first day he explored Mossback. The encounter seemed so long ago.

"Well, yes, I know what I agreed to," Parker said. "This knowledge is so important to our understanding, especially about old-growth forests. Don't you understand? You can't . . .."

A loud bang, like a book slamming a tabletop, made Ben jump away from the wall.

"Don't ever make the mistake of telling me what I can't do. You have no idea what I can or can't do. If you ever reveal this information, you will learn in a very painful way what I can do."

"You are . . ." Parker stammered for expression. "I . . . I . . . I. This is just grotesque, madness."

"You know your way out," Watt said. "Don't make the mistake of doubting me."

Ben had no doubts as he pressed himself against the logs and remembered a black Labrador retriever floating dead.

Parker walked into the hallway and saw Ben. "Madness," he yelled, as if including Ben in his accusation. "Madness," he cried, as he stormed down the hall and outside. Ben heard the truck start and drive away. He didn't doubt the encounter had sapped a few precious years from the old man's life.

Ben stepped away from the wall and turned toward the kitchen. As he pivoted, one of the old oak floorboards creaked loudly. Ben froze in mid-turn.

"That you, Ben?" a voice growled from the library.

"Yeah," Ben said, and waited for the next barked order.

"Come on in," Watt said. The invitation was cheerful and welcoming, as if he were truly pleased to see his brother and eager for his company. Ben was wary, like prey sensing a predator. He breathed deeply and half-appeared in the doorway.

"I didn't want to bother you," said Ben, hoping Watt might be too busy to deal with someone not helping him make money.

Watt laughed heartily as he leaned back in his chair behind the large library table stacked with rolled maps, charts and thick documents.

"Always got time for you," he said, waving Ben to come into the room. "I was hoping we could have a friendly chat. There's been too much stress for everyone. This can't be easy for you after all these years."

Watt was cleaning his fingernails with a letter opener. He was quiet for a moment, as if meditating on the blade's performance beneath his finely buffed nails. Abruptly, he tossed the letter opener on the desk.

"I haven't been very helpful. Calling you up here on short notice, out of the blue. Throwing this offer at you.

Then you having to see Reggie this way. That's a piss-poor way to have a reunion. I'm really sorry."

Watt had such a forlorn look that Ben almost forgot the browbeating he had just overheard. Maybe a seldom-seen, gentler side to his brother existed, saved only for his wife and children. They were smiling happily in a magazine article he once read. There was even a black Labrador retriever too, but probably not bought for hunting.

"Not a great start," Ben said.

"That's right," Watt said. He sat up and slapped the table. "We've lost too much of our past to let the future slip away. Family is all that counts, right? We're not getting any younger. Gotta look out for each other. That's right. Family."

Ben studied his brother and wondered what memory Watt had of that night years ago in a university dorm room.

"Family is very important," Ben said, hoping his voice held a tone of sincerity.

"I know you're not real keen on what I want to do with Mossback. I really understand. I might not be either, looking at it from your vantage point. But I hope you won't reach any final conclusions till you think about something." Watt sorted through the clutter of charts, impatiently knocking unwanted ones to the floor until he found the one he wanted. He spread it across the long table and smoothed the ends flat.

"There's an aspect of this that could use your expertise. You were born to do this. Everything you've done has prepared you to do this."

Leaning over the plan, Watt scrutinized it as if for the first time. Ben carefully watched his brother. Ben had not regarded himself as being born to do anything.

"Do you know what this is?" Watt said. He straightened up and swept his heavy hand across the colored drawings. "This is every fly fisherman's dream. And only a few in the entire world will ever experience it. And you could be the one person who will let the chosen few have that experience."

Ben listened to Watt explain his vision for Mossback's fly-fishing program, a part of his master plan. Fly fishing was the elite way to catch fish, he said, and the trout streams flowing through Mossback were unequalled in the world. Nowhere else could you find native brook trout the size of the ones swimming in here. They had never seen a fisherman, much less been caught. The streams were so unexplored, they weren't even named on maps. Ben thought about the conversation he had earlier in the fly-fishing shop about Zeke taking special clients fishing at Mossback. Watt's ignorance pleased Ben.

"You can structure and manage the entire operation," Watt said. He was beaming at Ben, as if to encourage enthusiasm for the plan, and then explained how rubbing elbows with some of the world's richest men could be exploited in many ways.

"Only your imagination would limit your opportunities," Watt said.

The flattery didn't seduce Ben any more than the apparent sincerity of his job offer, but Ben marveled at his brother's audacity. Watt was inviting some kind of response to the offer by a questioning expression.

"I've never fished the waters here," Ben said, as he devised his response.

"Zeke says they're unlike anything anywhere," Watt said. He held his hands apart at least three feet. "Fish this big."

Fish tales were notorious fictions, Ben knew, especially second or third-hand ones. "Do you know where they are?"

Puzzlement crept across Watt's face, and Ben suspected Watt was less familiar with Mossback's streams than he was. Where Ben could recognize promising trout waters, Watt would only see a development feature or obstacle.

"Why don't you show me the waters you want me to manage," Ben said. "I'm not saying I'll accept, but at least I'll take a look."

Watt hesitated. "Well, I'm not the best guide for that. Zeke can show you."

Ben savored Watt's discomfort, his nervousness revealed as his eyes blinked rapidly, and he licked his lips.

"Your offer's intriguing," Ben continued, hoping to draw Watt further into unknown territory. "I really want to give it a fair hearing. Like you said, it fits what I know. But, I need more details about your offer, and you're the only one who can explain it. You need to show me yourself."

Watt's brow furrowed in frustration as he weighed options and came up short. "Come on, Watt. It's your idea after all."

Watt shuffled some papers, and then looked at the unrolled maps. "I guess there's no harm in doing a little reconnaissance," he said. He patted his pockets as if searching for something.

They got into the Range Rover. Watt studied a topographic map of Mossback while Ben settled comfortably in the plush leather seat. Watt's thick finger followed the main road until it closely paralleled a stream.

"We'll go there," said Watt, tapping the near convergence of the road and stream on the map.

They rode in silence until Ben finally spoke.

"How much you planning to pay me for this guide thing? I've guided in a lot of places," Ben said.

Watt drove a little farther, then said, "The plan's not fully formed. Lot of details to work out and salary's one of them. But certainly equal to your value."

Ben glanced sideways and caught the faint smirk on Watt's face. They were going through a performance, he realized. As far as he could discern, Watt really wanted Ben to disappear as soon as possible. This must be a grand gesture by Watt to pretend some generous family reconciliation that would later sooth whatever conscience he has, Ben concluded.

A little farther on, Watt stopped the Range Rover. Through the lowered windows they could hear the nearby sound of a river crashing over rocks, and the air felt damp. A few hundred feet into the forest Ben could see mist floating through the trees as light refracted through it into rainbow shards.

"Over there," Watt said, nodding his head in the direction of the mist.

They walked through ferns along a trail marked by bright orange surveyor's flags.

"This will be one of the main entry points," Watt said. "It's called a beat."

Ben couldn't decide whether to be amused or offended by Watt's effort to educate him about what a section of fishable water was called. He doubted Watt had ever fished the highly compartmentalized rivers in England.

"It's got a good beat," Ben said, as he turned his face from Watt.

"Yes, it does," Watt said.

They could see a clearing in the forest canopy as they approached the river, where, through the ages, it had carved a deep groove for itself through the granite. Because the terrain was relatively flat where they were, the river flowed smoothly, without any waterfalls. Only boulders broke the water's flow. Ben stopped before he got to the clearing in the rhododendron and instinctively put out his hand to stop Watt's forward movement. Slowly, Ben stepped to the edge where he was still screened from the water by the brush. He peered upstream, and then downstream, scanning the river surface in an instinctual assessment of the most likely places a trout might be holding in the current.

For the first time that weekend, Ben felt comfortable. Years of fishing had honed his sense of where a trout might be suspended in a slow part of river current, waiting patiently for an insect or smaller fish to come floating within easy striking distance. In the crystal-clear water, Ben saw numerous brook trout behind rocks, beside cuts across the other shore and in depressions in the river's gravely bottom. They were large, muscular and bejeweled. He could easily spot the white leading edge of their pectoral fins and the worm-like etchings on their backs. They would hold their positions lazily until a doomed insect in or on top of the water came close enough for the trout to slide into the current, gulp an effortless meal, and then glide back to its previous spot in the slower current.

The size and quality of the trout were impressive. There must be an abundance of insects to feed this many fat trout, he thought. His fingers flexed, as if grasping a fly rod. He wouldn't have minded making a few casts, if only to impress his brother. As a cat instinctively stalks a bird, Ben scanned the river for the best place to make a first cast, one that would entice the largest trout.

"Well, what do you think?" Watt said, stepping into the opening. Dozens of trout dashed for deeper cover as Watt swept his arm across the view.

Ben watched the startled fish scatter in frenzied flashes.

"The richest men in the world will fish here. And you could be in charge of it." Watt stood with his hands on his hips surveying his domain.

Ben sensed a diminished enthusiasm in Watt's sales pitch, less eagerness for Ben to take the bait that was eagerly offered back at the house.

"This might be a good break from ungrateful editors," Ben said, as he looked past Watt to the waters upstream.

The opening where they stood was about forty feet above the stream. It was a granite outcrop that long ago had cast off part of itself into the river. Centuries of harsh weather and flooding had worn the dropped boulders smooth and round. Just to the side, on the rock beyond Watt, grew a thick green carpet of moss saturated by water seeping beneath it and dripping to the stream. Ben knew the danger such a benign setting hid. He had once slipped on just such a patch of leaf-littered moss and tumbled into a river. That fall had been just a few feet into a deep pool, and he hadn't been injured. But his Orvis bamboo rod had shattered as he tried to slow his fall. A slip here would be fatal against the granite rocks far below.

Ben looked down at Watt's smooth-soled, leather loafers. One step in the right direction and Watt would be a bad memory. Watt's accident would resolve several issues including revenge for the Great Lie.

"How far up would this beat go?" Ben said.

Watt turned upstream, toward the bed of moss just a few feet away.

"I guess we'd have to figure it out," Watt said. "Or, you'd have to, maybe."

"Should we check it out?" Ben said. "I mean, we're already here."

Ben looked over the rock edge.

Watt glanced around. Ben knew his brother had not given much thought to the details an underling should solve, but his brother didn't want to look stupid or uninformed. Watt took a couple of steps in one direction, and then turned toward the moss patch. He leaned out a little toward the water, as if to get a better view upstream.

Watt seemed awkward being out of his element, but Ben knew Watt had to pretend to show interest since he had brought up the subject in the first place.

"Maybe we can walk up there and get a better view," Watt said, as he gestured upstream.

Ben had only to be patient and say nothing, let his brother step into his own fate. He glanced at the saturated moss, then at the river slamming over the boulders, foaming spray drenching their surface.

"Wait," Ben said.

"What's the matter?" Watt said.

Ben watched a large trout glide slowly to the surface and sip a small caddis fly without disturbing the water. The trout casually returned to its previous location beside a sunken log and waited.

"We don't need to go over all these details now," Ben said. "There's plenty of time later. I mean, I haven't even said yes to your offer. I might say no."

Watt snorted in disgust as he began walking away from the stream.

"Wouldn't surprise me," he grumbled, as he walked past Ben. "I've never known you to make smart choices."

Ben followed Watt back to the Range Rover and was inclined to agree with his brother.

CHAPTER 19

Watt pulled up to the house, turned off the ignition and gazed ahead.

"Let's try to have some resolution by morning," he said. "You need to decide about your life. Maybe you'll be happier just taking the money. Anybody will tell you I'm not easy to work for."

Ben detected some pride in that assessment. He got out, leaned on the open window and said, "I guess we ought to be able to sort through things by tomorrow." He pushed away from the Range Rover and walked to the house. Watt was still at the wheel as Ben went inside. Standing inside, he thought he heard a strange sound, somewhat muted and a little distant. He cocked his head and listened carefully.

"Thwock . . . thunk."

He waited for the sound to be repeated, and when it was, "thwock . . . thunk," he suspected it was coming from outside the house, on the other side from the parking area, from the clay tennis court. He remembered one of his last times at Mossback, a warm summer day, and several families gathered by the court, laughing, cheering, jeering and applauding. The players wore traditional white tennis outfits. Reggie met all challengers in a friendly tournament. With infinite energy she darted around the court, returning almost every shot, and there were some respectable players as he recalled. She could make killer shots that opponents could either gawk at as the white ball whizzed by or stretch vainly to return, often sliding or skidding along the damp clay on their hands and knees in the process.

The "thwock . . . thunk" continued erratically. Ben walked outside to the tennis court screened from the house by an overgrown hemlock hedge. He stood at one end of the hedge and saw Reggie swinging a racket at a tennis ball against an old wooden backstop that had a few boards missing. She had pulled enough weeds to give her space to hit the ball, which slammed against the wooden barrier. The old paint on the boards had mostly curled and flaked away, leaving the unprotected wood weathered or rotted. Reggie struggled to keep up a volley that often ended with the ball plopping into nearby weeds or ricocheting wildly off a warped board. Her shapeless house robe billowed and collapsed as she rushed to swat the ball. Sweat matted her hair against her face and neck. Her movements barely suggested her once-formidable skill. He watched a while, remembering his little sister from long ago. She suddenly drove the ball against a loose board that made it rebound high in the air in Ben's direction. Reggie turned to watch.

"You aced it," Ben said, as he applauded.

Reggie breathed heavily, the racket at her side. As she caught her breath, she grinned at Ben and curtsied, holding one side of her robe out to the side. Her sweat-drenched shirt clung to her body.

"The comeback begins," she said, gasping.

She raised her racket and waved it triumphantly. They settled down on an oak bench facing the weedy court.

"Told you I'd change," Reggie said, resting her arms on her thighs.

Ben thought about how many times he had made that promise to himself after a lost weekend. He wouldn't hold Reggie to her promise, although he hoped she could stay close to sober a while longer. Who knows what we can do, he thought, bolstering his own hopes. He needed her help.

Reggie took a cigarette from her pocket, lit it, and after the coughing subsided, leaned against the bench back.

"I can't remember the last time I hit a ball," she said. "Do you think it's too late?"

Ben hesitated. From what he had observed, the woman sitting next to him had as much chance of becoming a serious tennis player as he had of flapping his arms and taking flight, although the dream visited him occasionally. She had been knocked down so often by others, he wasn't going to steal her hope.

"Give yourself a little time, no telling what you can do," he said. He didn't think Reggie was ready for a lecture about living one day at a time.

Reggie, still panting, took a drag on her cigarette. He didn't expect her to embrace what he said because he wasn't sure he did. He wanted to change the subject to something more immediate to his needs.

"Something you said the other night about Watt hurting a child," he said, staring at the blackberry briars and goldenrod trying to claim the tennis court. A few birds flitted through the stalks. He hated to rock Reggie's delicate balance, but he needed her complicity. "I know you're afraid of Watt. He kinda scares me too. But I need to know anything more you can remember about that time. Anything. Watt doesn't need to know."

Ben glanced sideways and squeezed her arm. He could feel Reggie tremble. He wasn't sure if it was caused by her recent exertion or by his question. It could have been D.T.'s. It could have been all three.

"I was just a little girl then," Reggie said, almost in a whisper. "I remember Mom and Dad being awfully upset. We left here in a hurry, back to Memphis. You were going to camp then. We didn't come back for a while, and the trips were short when we did. Not like all summer."

"Do you remember our parents talking about an accident?" Ben said, with his hand still on Reggie's arm. "Maybe on the way home?"

Reggie weighed his question, and then said, "That time is really vague. I'm sorry. I just don't remember any details. But we never seemed to be happy anymore, not like before."

She turned to look at Ben, who recognized the pleading in her eyes. "Please don't let Watt do anything to me. I'll die if he puts me away again. I will."

"He'll have to go through me to get to you," Ben said. It was all he could say, afraid to promise anything else. He put his arm around Reggie and squeezed her shoulder.

"I just remember one thing," Reggie said. "Sometimes I'm not sure if I dreamed it or heard it."

Ben still had his arm around Reggie and smelled her mixture of sweat and tobacco.

"Our parents were talking in whispers, and I was drifting in and out, like I was napping," she said. "Someone said 'the child's dead and another sacrifice won't make her less dead. We have to protect him and live with it.' I don't know who said it, only the words."

She watched Ben and then looked away.

"Another time, I overheard them talking about a little girl being found dead at Mossback. Just snatches of conversation, all very hushed and guarded. Maybe when I'm drinking, I think Watt killed someone. Maybe I want to believe he could do something like that. But I don't know, do I?"

Ben wasn't sure if she was saying she didn't know, or asking him whether or not she really did know. Pressing further would only confuse her more.

"I think our folks knew things they wished they didn't," Ben said. "I hate to think what they lived with. Or without."

Throughout the day Ben tried to imagine scenarios for the meeting in which he would cleverly interrogate Watt about his role in the little girl's death. Ben would enjoy leading Watt along a cunning line of questions, with responses that would lure Watt into confessions, followed by contrition leading to the abandonment of his development plans. But as delicious as these fantasies were, Ben unhappily acknowledged the pathetic absurdity of his daydreams. He wasn't really certain of his own standing to participate in a legal process. The whole thing seemed an improbable crapshoot.

Ben regretted that Katherine had no better angle for derailing the development scheme; she was relying on Ben's resourcefulness. Nevertheless, he needed to phone her and hear her encouraging words in his ear, words that would bolster his spirit, and convince him he could beat his brother. Afraid Watt might overhear, he decided to wait until he could be sure of a private conversation.

Dinner that evening consisted of solitary foraging. Ben went downstairs in the late afternoon to rummage through the kitchen for something to relieve the anxiety that had settled in his stomach. On his way, he searched for a phone other than the one in Watt's office. Ben walked down the stairs by the library, stopped at the door and heard nothing. He couldn't see the parking area to know if Watt's Range Rover was there.

Ben couldn't find a telephone and cursed the anti-quated communications in the old house until he saw a wall phone just inside the kitchen door, reached for it, and then glanced toward the table. Watt was reading a newspaper while eating a bowl of ice cream covered with a heavy layer of chocolate sauce. Watt saw him, waved the spoon in Ben's direction and smiled. "My favorite weakness," Watt said and resumed eating.

"Looking for a snack," Ben said, as he searched the kitchen. He watched Watt lift an overflowing spoonful of ice cream. A large drip from the spoon dribbled down his chin and spread on his shirt before he could catch it. He wiped the back of his hand across his chin, and then licked the smeared ice cream.

Ben grabbed a bag of potato chips and munched them as he studied his brother.

"Did you see the sheriff's car go by this morning?" Ben said.

Watt cocked his head but continued with his ice cream.

"I ran into the sheriff at Zeke's house. They were arguing about the perfect fly for catching brookies. Sheriff's not having much luck lately."

Ben looked in the refrigerator and pulled out a beer. He took a long swallow and belched. "He seemed like a nice guy," Ben said, as he read the fine print on the beer label. "Very conscientious about his job. The earnest type. Hates loose ends in a case."

Watt slowed eating his melting ice cream.

"I asked him if there were any loose ends in the case of a young girl dying around here years ago. He said as far as he knew, the death was accidental. But one thing bothered him," Ben said, as he studied Watt for a flicker of interest. Watt kept eating.

"Do you remember our parents talking about it?" Ben asked. "Must have been about the time you went off to Tennessee, by the sheriff's calculation."

Watt paused between bites. "I have some vague recollection about an accident. Didn't seem to be a big deal. Negligent parents, I guess. Should have kept their eyes on her." He jabbed at his ice cream.

"Yeh, real negligent," Ben said. He drained the rest of his beer. He held the bottle by its neck and slapped it in the palm of his hand, while he remembered their trip to the river that morning and wondered if he had been too cautious.

"The thing that bothered the sheriff was the glass in her head," Ben said. He saw Watt hesitate as he raised his spoon and turned his head slightly toward Ben.

"It was embedded in her skull, as if she struck some glass really hard. Or something glass struck her really hard. Sheriff said it didn't fit the nature of accidental death because there wasn't any sign of glass where they found her. Said it just didn't make any sense."

Ben kept tapping the bottle in his hand. How deeply would the glass from this bottle go into that head? Ben imagined the green shards piercing Watt's skull, and that was satisfying enough for now.

"He said if someone on the mountain hit her with a car, and then threw her off the mountain, that would explain the glass." Watt resumed eating, but with less enthusiasm. "But, they never found any evidence up on the mountain. The girl had been dead a while and evidence disappears. They found a few things that didn't make sense, but nothing led anywhere. A cold case, but not forgotten."

Ben tossed his empty bottle in the trashcan.

"And our parents didn't talk about it? Seems like it would merit some conversation. It happened right here on their land. At least she was found on our place, below Flat Mountain. Nothing you remember, huh?"

Watt acted as if Ben were talking about finding a dead frog as he scraped the spoon around the bottom of the bowl to get the last smears of chocolate and licked the spoon. He carried the bowl to the sink and washed it and the spoon and placed them in the drainer. He wiped his hands thoroughly, then neatly folded the towel and hung it carefully on the towel rack. Watt walked over to Ben who was leaning against the cold stove.

"You've been gone a very long time," Watt said. Ben smelled the chocolaty sweetness of Watt's breath. "You're a stranger here — to me, to Reggie, to this house, this property. Don't dare think you can just walk in my house and make up for the wasted years of your life by trying to get in my way. Don't expect to come here and change my life. Or Reggie's. Your expectations far exceed your capabilities."

Ben felt naked under Watt's withering glare and detested his brother for making him feel this way.

Watt walked out of the kitchen, and Ben listened to his footsteps through the front hall and up the stairs until a bedroom door slammed. Ben was alone. He looked at the wall phone and decided to make a couple of quick calls.

He dialed the number on Katherine's business card. An assistant said Katherine was gone for the rest of the day. Ben didn't leave a message.

The next call was to Zeke.

"I think it's time," Ben said.

"You tell him anything?"

"Not much he didn't already know. Except the part about the glass."

"How'd you put it to him?"

Ben detected concern in Zeke's voice. "Just said what the sheriff told us. You know, case cold but not entirely forgotten. Nothing to arouse undue suspicion. The glass in her head got his attention. That got a twitch."

Ben looked around the room. "I can't talk on this phone now," he said. "Watt's in the house. Can you come by first thing in the morning?"

"The moment of truth, huh?" Zeke said.

Ben suggested Zeke arrive around nine o'clock.

"Make sure Watt's around," Zeke said.

"I'll tell him I'm ready to settle Mossback. Nothing interests him more."

CHAPTER 20

It was a recurring dream in which he stood among strangers and began flapping his arms as if they were wings. Gradually Ben rose above the crowd, which ignored his ascent. With slight effort he rose higher until he attained an altitude where he fully extended his arms and soared like a hawk. He flew carefree above the people and landscape. But, just as he was fully savoring the flight's exhilaration, he began descending to earth. Furious flapping was useless as the ground got closer. At the edge of sleep, he wanted to plunge back into his dream for another ascent, but consciousness intruded.

Ben shaved quickly while he rehearsed the upcoming confrontation with Watt. But without a script for any actor other than himself, the plot was up for grabs. As he dressed, his fingers trembled as he tried to button his shirt. He closed his eyes and prayed to any available deity to calm him.

In the hallway, he heard nothing from Reggie's room. Maybe she was exhausted by yesterday's tennis practice.

She had left the impression the previous evening she wasn't going to drink that night. He wanted to believe her.

He went into the kitchen where the clock showed it was past eight. He rummaged through the refrigerator and settled on a slice of cold pizza. As he chewed, he looked out the window and saw the silver Mercedes belonging to Watt's business lawyer. Ben wondered how effective he might be rescuing his client from dusty criminal charges involving homicide. As he gazed out the window, Ben envisioned Watt pushed across the parking area, hands cuffed behind him, and being shoved into the back seat of the sheriff's squad car with the blue lights pulsating.

Zeke's truck pulled slowly into the parking area next to Watt's Range Rover, and he sat for a while, occasionally glancing at Watt's car. Finally Zeke walked to the house carrying a manila folder he slapped against his leg. Ben was surprised to see him wearing a dark grey suit coat paired with sharply creased blue jeans.

"You look somber as a preacher," Ben said.

"Might be going to jail today," Zeke said as he passed through the kitchen door. His hair was still damp from washing and was combed back. A faint smell of soap mingled with his pipe tobacco. "Want to look my best."

"Watt's lawyer's here," Ben said. "They're expecting me to sell my share of Mossback today. He doesn't know you're coming."

"I remember coming in here when I was a kid," Zeke said, looking around. "Your folks had a colored woman for a cook. She'd give me thick bacon and biscuits she'd made in that old wood cook stove. It was like putting a taste of heaven in your mouth."

"How do you think we should handle this?" Ben said.

Zeke hugged the folder to his chest.

"What's in there?" Ben said, nodding at the folder.

"Plan B," Zeke said. "I guess we both have notions how to play this. Let's just go in and ask real nice for Watt to change his mind. If he refuses, then we do what's necessary."

"You got a lot to lose if we bring up the little girl," Ben said. "You sure you want to do this?"

Zeke put his hand on Ben's shoulder. "I'm not the only one who stands to lose something in this." He let his hand slide off Ben's shoulder. "Silence could be really golden for you."

There was no arguing with that. Ben resigned himself to the depressing fact that his impending confrontation with Watt would cost him plenty.

"Let's see what's in Pandora's box," Ben said.

Ben knocked on the library door, and the voices hushed.

"Come in," Watt said.

The lawyer looked puzzled at the sight of Ben and Zeke together. Watt frowned.

"What's he doing here?" Watt said. "This is family business."

Zeke remained at the doorway, examining his polished boots. Ben noticed Zeke's hands left sweat stains on the tightly gripped folder.

"I asked him," Ben said, stepping into the room.

Watt cocked his head, examining his brother as if he were some rare insect.

"You can go, Zeke," Watt said, waving the back of his hand in dismissal.

"He stays," Ben said, feeling the muscles tighten around his spine. He tried to breathe deeply and slowly to relax. The pain didn't disappear, but he didn't collapse either.

"He stays. And this isn't all about family business. For starters, I'm not selling my shares to you, officially."

Ben watched the lawyer glance uneasily at Watt, as if his understanding of what was supposed to happen wasn't unfolding as planned.

"I'm not going to see this place destroyed. There's nothing like this forest anywhere. You can't trash it," Ben said.

Watt burst into loud laughter and beat his thigh with his fist. "Can you believe this, Herb? My brother's become some goddamn Earth Firster in Birkenstocks. Gonna save the critters from the mean old developer. We've never seen that before, have we?"

The lawyer smiled nervously and thumbed some papers he was holding.

"Boy, didn't I tell you a while back that I didn't need your permission? My offer's out of kindness, doing you a very big favor. I control the stock, so I can do what I want. I was trying to help you. You're too stupid to know what's good for you, and your education's gonna get damned expensive." Watt turned to Funk. "Tell this dumb tree hugger how much we don't need him. And how much he's losing."

Funk straightened up, cleared his throat and faced Ben with his most grave, lawyerly expression. "Well, Ben, you should know . . ."

Any previous thought of appealing to Watt's better side vanished. Ben leapt into the abyss.

"This is just a lot of bullshit," Ben said. "You need a different kind of lawyer, Watt. Herb doesn't look like he's been around too many criminals."

Funk looked puzzled as he glanced at Watt for direction.

"You need to answer for killing that child," Ben said. His palms were wet and he felt sweat trickling down his spine. "The sheriff – I told you about him yesterday – he said there's no statute of limitations on homicide. You need to worry about the sheriff. He thinks there's a killer due for some justice."

The crimson color flashing across Watt's face unsettled Ben. Watt was either going to have a stroke or he was going to jump across the desk and throttle Ben, who tried to remember the exact location of the doorway behind him.

"This is outrageous and slanderous," Funk said. "You're talking your way into serious damages, even if you are his brother."

"Isn't truth a defense against slander?" Ben said. He watched a network of veins bulging along Watt's forehead and temple. "You killed a little girl and thought there wouldn't be any reckoning. There were witnesses. One is here now who's not afraid to talk." Ben turned to Zeke and nodded for him to enter the room. "Zeke was with you. He's willing to tell everything to the sheriff."

Watt was hunched over the desk with his arms folded on top. "You're fired!" he said. "Get off this place today.

And take your mother. Today, or my guard will throw you off. Both of you."

"That would be a mistake, Watt," Ben said.

"Keeping him around was a mistake," Watt said. "He's lived here rent-free, like it's his place. Not much to show for it. Everything's all overgrown and wild. You think he's going to say anything? If what you're saying was true, he could go to jail, too. An accessory, or something. Right, Herb?"

The lawyer stammered, trying to grasp a statute to confirm Watt's claim. "Well, if he was a witness or participant in a crime, and he didn't report it to the authorities, he could be exposed to some legal liability, as an accessory, yes, perhaps." Funk's eyes shifted uncomfortably between the men who were threatening his client.

Watt stood suddenly and pushed his chair back so hard it toppled over. He pointed a thick, stabbing finger at Zeke.

"If you're saying I was involved in somebody's death and you were with me – and I'm not admitting anything – then you'll go to jail, too. You ready for that? Who's gonna take care of your momma? She sure won't be living around here!"

Funk cleared his throat and leaned closer to Watt.

"I don't like the nature of this conversation," he said, in a low voice that was easily heard. "Accusations are being made before witnesses that carry grave consequences. Don't say another word about these allegations."

Watt's eyes narrowed as he studied his lawyer. Ben watched Watt's fingers tighten into fists, then relax. "I pay you to make things happen my way," Watt said. "I don't need you to tell me to cringe in front of an employee or my suddenly brave brother."

Watt shoved Funk aside as he came around the desk. "Zeke, I said get out. You don't work here any more. And you, you're out five million. Go back to peddling your fish tales. I try to be decent to a hack, and I get crap in return."

Zeke appeared unmoved by Watt's advance around the desk, breathing slowly, impervious to Watt's threats. Ben inhaled deeply and stepped closer to Zeke.

"I told you you're not going to develop Mossback. If you agree to turn it over to a land conservancy, all of it, we'll forget the criminal stuff, the hit and run," Ben said, feeling light headed. His armpits were soaked. "That's our offer. Save Mossback and you stay out of jail."

"You know what I expect from this project," Watt said, glaring at Ben. "You think you and this ex-caretaker can scare me into quitting like some spooked rabbit? It'll take more than your fucking threat to stop me."

"Don't forget I own part of Mossback and I'll get Reggie to vote her shares with me. We'll tie you up in court for years," said Ben, who had never negotiated anything other than a few extra expenses on an assignment.

Watt turned to his lawyer. "This is too easy, Herb," he said. "I don't even need you for this." He turned back, smirking. "A little flaw in your plan. Reggie's shares in Mossback are under my control. Something about power of attorney, right Herb?"

Ben watched the lawyer's eyes brighten. "Yes, of course she can't help Ben because you control her stock in Mossback."

Watt folded his arms across his chest and sneered.

"Reggie said she's giving me her power of attorney and naming me beneficiary of her will," Ben said, clinging to the memory of Reggie's drunken outburst the other night. "She revoked Watt's power."

Funk and Watt looked at each other and shook their heads in amused pity.

"Sorry, Ben, but the court in Memphis granted Watt Reggie's power of attorney as well as being her guardian," Funk said. "She has no legal authority to revoke it. That's the court's prerogative."

Watt smirked and nodded in agreement.

"Then she'll go to a judge here," Ben said. He had no idea what he was talking about, but hoped if he kept jabbering, like the monkey at the typewriter, he might ultimately say something effective, or at least unexpected. "Yes, she'll be a North Carolina resident. She's in North Carolina now. A different state, a different jurisdiction. A judge here might not like what you're up to."

Ben watched the lawyer for any sign his argument was having the desired effect. Funk frowned, apparently weighing the legal implications of Ben's threat. The lawyer opened his mouth as if he were about to say something.

"You're full of shit," Watt said to Ben. "You get your law degree through the classified ads in the back of one of your fishing magazines? I'm calling the guard house."

As Watt reached for the phone, Funk softly put his hand on Watt's arm. He whispered something in Watt's ear. Watt glared at him and dropped the phone back in its cradle. Ben didn't know what was going on, but he sensed vulnerability, just a hint.

"Face it, Watt, you're staring at a homicide charge. Reggie stays here with me and we'll fight you in court. She'll refuse to let you control her or her money. Then it's lawyers, briefs, motions, hearings, trials, and appeals. How many years for the dust to settle?"

Funk patted Watt's shoulder as if calming an overly excited child.

"Lawsuits are terribly easy to threaten," Funk said. "Do you have any idea what one might cost? Do you have fifty thousand dollars to retain counsel? I think that would be a minimum figure to start, probably much higher. And it's not the kind of case that some lawyer would take on contingency, if that's what you're contemplating. No pot of gold at the end to get a percentage from."

"You're still here," Watt said to Zeke. "You deaf as well as dumb?"

Ben heard Zeke clear his throat.

"You got no call to treat me or mama that way," Zeke said. "She's always treated you right. I've done a good job, too. Everything I've ever been asked, and more. You got no cause to put me down."

Ben was surprised by Zeke's outburst and relieved to hear him finally speak up.

"Doing right by folks may seem quaint to you, but it's got some value around here," Zeke said. "Treat folks wrong, do something bad, there's always an accounting. Things gotta balance out. Your account's way past due."

Ben was struck by Zeke's menacing tone. He watched Watt's face become darker and his neck veins engorge and expand.

"I'm not going to let some hillbilly threaten me," Watt said. "I've ground up people tougher than you'll ever be. What I've got riding on this ain't gonna be derailed by some stupid, fucking redneck, or his sidekick."

The acrimony was leading away from where Ben wanted the discussion to focus – on Mossback and saving it. This pissing contest was not going to help.

"Watt, there's nothing personal here," Ben said, astonished at his outrageous lie. "Mossback's too important to turn into some golf course. You don't appreciate how special Mossback is, but Zeke and I do. And you want to ruin it. That just can't happen.

"There are huge tax breaks you can get by preserving Mossback, like from land donations," Ben said. He struggled to recall the details of land conservation and taxes Katherine had explained to him. "You won't have to pay taxes for years. People will think you're a hero."

Ben fretted at the feebleness of his plea, but he couldn't think of anything else to say. If Katherine were here, she could make a much more reasoned, scientific argument, and more passionate, too. Watt looked at Funk and raised his eyebrows.

"This project already sets new benchmarks for tax breaks," Watt said. "There will be so many damned conservation easements it'll make your head spin. Everything we can't make a fat profit on will be conserved big time.

See, we're really tree huggers at heart. This will be the greenest golf course ever."

Zeke stepped a little closer until he was next to Ben. His lanky frame had a military erectness as he studied Watt and his lawyer. Zeke softly tapped the folder against his thigh, and then took a very deep breath.

"You're right stubborn," Zeke said. "Sometimes that's good, sometimes not. Right now, it's real stupid."

Watt looked stunned, not fearful, but amazed. Someone on his payroll just insulted him. "You don't work here anymore. Pack up. Get out, now," he said. "Herb, get an eviction order from the sheriff."

Zeke held the folder against his chest with crossed arms, as if it were a shield.

"Like I said, you're real stupid. Your brother's given you some choices, things you can do. Laid it all out. He's got a good grasp of the situation. You don't seem to see things clearly, so let me help you."

Zeke shifted his weight and relaxed a little.

"You can give up developing this place, be a good guy, all on your own. Lots of folks will appreciate that. If you don't want to do that, I'll help put you in jail. You and I know what happened to that little girl. Lenny and Oscar can't speak against you 'cause they're dead. *I can.* You'll go down, and I'll go with you. But this place won't get developed. I'm ready to pay that price. Don't bet against me. That'd be real dumb."

Watt studied the two men threatening his crowning business development, and then whispered to Funk, who whispered back. Watt's heavy fist gripped Funk's coat sleeve.

"Herb here's no criminal lawyer, so he's reluctant to get all twisted up in this thing," Watt said, releasing the crumpled sleeve. He patted Funk's shoulder, smoothed the sleeve and pushed the lawyer away. "But I know it's just your word against mine. No other witnesses. My word weighs more. Go ahead and call the sheriff. Tell him your lies. I'll tell my side and we'll see who wins. I promise you one thing." Watt was shaking his finger at Zeke. Spittle sprayed as he growled his words. He wiped his mouth with the back of his hand. "I'll win, you'll lose and you will be very, very sorry. I am unmerciful. Ben knows."

"Before we go any further, take a look in the parking lot," Zeke said. "Just so you know I'm not shoveling a lot of bullshit"

Watt nodded his head for Funk to see what Zeke was talking about. When Funk returned, he was frowning and whispered something in Watt's ear that made him shove the lawyer away.

"You're getting a little ahead of yourself by having the sheriff outside," Watt said. "Like I said, you got nothing. You're gonna look pretty stupid explaining that to the sheriff."

"Sheriff Jenkins trusts my word. But, there will be the word of another," Zeke said as he opened his file and pulled out a single sheet of paper. "Your father will speak for me."

Zeke held out the paper, which the lawyer took. Funk glanced at it with a puzzled expression. As he read, his demeanor became somber. He handed the paper to Watt who snatched it. He held it at arm's length, cursed and reached for his reading glasses. As he read, Ben watched the broad shoulders begin to sag.

Zeke handed Ben another copy of the paper. It was a photocopy of a hand-written letter bearing the name of Sidney W. Phelps at his home address in Memphis. It was dated March 13, 1990, and read:

Dear Zeke,

Many years ago you did Mrs. Phelps and me an enormous favor by helping keep our son Watt out of harms way. That poor child's death would not have been made any less tragic by revealing Watt as the driver of the car that killed her. No one meant to do harm. You saved all of us that night. Watt has been able to have a good life because you kept our secret.

We have always appreciated your loyalty and will continue to do so. I want you to know that you and your mother will

*always be able to live at Mossback as long as you wish, and you
will draw a decent stipend for your service. I will be sending
you a document giving you and your mother a life estate in the
cabin and ten acres surrounding it. Watt will be certain it is
honored.*

*Again, thank you for your loyalty to our family. Please let
me know if there is anything we can ever do for you. This letter
is for your benefit.*

Sincerely yours,

Sidney Phelps

"Sheriff told me the little girl's name was Sarah
Cummings," Zeke said. "We should know her name."

Watt looked up from the page. "This is just some
copy of something. Anyone could fake this. It's nothing.
You're threatening me with a copy of nothing."

"The original and the postmarked envelope it came
in are in a safe place," Zeke said. "Safe till it's needed in
court."

Funk leaned toward Watt and murmured. Watt nodded and smiled.

"While this writing may appear valid to the untrained
eye, I don't think it could withstand the scrutiny of an
expert witness," Funk said, as he examined his sleeve
and picked at a loose thread. "Who is to refute an argument that this alleged writing is nothing but a forgery?

Do you have any credible writing samples of Mr. Phelps you could compare it with? He has been dead for many years, and I don't think any samples of his handwriting still exist in your possession. Watt believes that to be the case." He raised an eyebrow at Ben as if to ask if he had any samples of he father's handwriting.

The lawyer turned to Watt with a complacent grin. "Once again they propose legal battle with insufficient ammunition," Funk said.

Ben looked at Zeke for some signal that the writing could be supported, its authenticity documented. Zeke's expression remained unchanged, but Ben noticed Zeke's empty hand trembling slightly. He couldn't tell if it was from anger or fear. There must be other samples of his father's handwriting, but he didn't know where to begin searching. Ben glanced around the room as he heard Watt ripping apart the letter. A book caught Ben's attention. It was the small one he had noticed a couple of days before when he was browsing the library for signs of his parents' personal lives. Ben walked to the bookshelf and removed the small leather-bound volume as Watt tossed the torn fragments into a wastebasket. Ben opened the book of poems to the inscription on the front flyleaf, than closed it and held it to his side.

" I guess I'm kinda ignorant about what the law requires as evidence or proof," Ben said, looking up at Funk.

"You've made that pretty clear. So, Herb, what would be the minimum the law would require to, you know, say that letter of Zeke's was really written by my father? You said there aren't any writings left by him. Would that be something we'd need to prove the letter is genuine?"

"That would be a starting point. Something irrefutably written by your father in his hand," Funk said. "And it would have to be something that could withstand physical examination to prove it's real, you know, forensic examination for age, ink type, paper, that kind of thing."

Ben beckoned Funk to come to him. Funk looked to Watt for guidance, and Watt shrugged with exasperation, as if to grant a final indulgence. Funk walked to Ben, who showed him the inscription in the book, the one Ben's father had written to Ben's mother thanking her for coming away to be his love.

"It's very, very genuine," Ben said. "Irrefutably genuine."

Ben handed it to Zeke for him to read.

Funk stood in the middle of the room, his bravado gone. He walked back to Watt shaking his head.

"Nobody knows how a trial will turn out. A lot of accusations, witnesses and evidence," Ben said. "It's a big gamble for everyone. But a jury hates people who kill children. I covered a few trials when I was a reporter. They go hard on people like you. And you know how prisoners deal with child abusers? How big a gambler are you, Watt? You think rich folks are going to flock to you when you're accused of killing a child and running away from it? You might have a taint about you."

"Get out," Watt said, sounding tired. "You two go outside so I can see you through the window. Herb and I need to talk."

Ben and Zeke left Watt and Funk to plot their next maneuver. They didn't speak until they were on the overgrown lawn outside the library window.

"Why didn't you show them that document giving you a life estate?" Ben said.

"That letter was mailed just a few days before he and your mother died. Somehow those papers never got sent. Things just kept going the way they always had, so I kept my mouth shut. I got a letter from Watt a few months later saying I could stay on till further notice. Further notice never came, till now," Zeke said. "How did you come across that book? You a poetry lover?"

"Just dumb luck," Ben said, still tightly clutching the small leather book.

"There's not enough of it in this world," Zeke said.

Through the window they could see Watt and Funk pacing and gesturing, Watt seeming to do most of the talking. Then they stopped and looked at the telephone. Watt grabbed it, listened for a few moments, yelled at the receiver from arm's length and thrust it at Funk. The lawyer listened quietly, spoke briefly and handed the receiver back to Watt, who listened and then beat the receiver on the desk until the hard plastic shattered.

"I wish those walls weren't so thick," Ben said.

Watt began to yell and shake his fists. Funk stepped back. The outburst filtering through the old log walls was indistinct. They watched as Watt grabbed papers and maps from the desk and flung them across the room. Funk backed away farther to a window and glanced nervously outside as if seeking an escape route. After Watt threw everything off the desk, he lifted one end of it and pushed it over. He appeared exhausted from his outburst as he bent over and gasped for air. Finally, he sank to his knees, his shaking head drooped on his chest.

"Think they're through talking?" Zeke said.

"One of 'em," Ben said.

They watched as Funk moved a small chair next to Watt and leaned toward him. He talked without apparent emotion as Watt stayed kneeling on the floor. It reminded Ben of a supplicant at confession. When he finished speaking, Funk leaned back in the chair and folded his hands in his lap, apparently having nothing more to offer. Neither one moved for several minutes. Then Watt reached out to grasp one of the overturned table legs. Slowly he pushed himself up and looked out the window at Ben and Zeke.

"Some phone call," Zeke said.

At the window, Watt motioned for them to come inside. Ben and Zeke walked into the library, stepping on the papers strewn across the floor. Watt was perched on the edge of the overturned desk. He was hunched over with his arms folded across his chest. He stared down at the floor without speaking.

"Watt asked me to reply to your demands," Funk said in a very modulated tone. "As his attorney, I have advised him to say nothing about your allegations, and we won't respond any further. He has also instructed me to say that he will abandon his plans to develop Mossback. The Wilderness Club will not be pursued. He will donate his share of Mossback to The Nature Conservancy, as well as his sister's share. That, of course, is contingent on Ben doing likewise with his share. There will be a provision in the conveyance giving Zeke and his mother a lifetime tenancy in their present house on the property. Upon the conveyance, the original letter and envelope from Mr. Phelps will be turned over to Watt. I think that about covers it. Any questions?"

Zeke and Ben looked at each other, trying to suppress their astonishment. Zeke grinned with relief, but then turned serious.

"One more thing," Zeke said. "Just a little thing."

Watt glanced up for the first time since the two reentered the room. He glared at Zeke, ready to puff up to his full, threatening height.

"What *fucking* little thing?" he said.

"Let Ben live in the house, like you're letting me and mama live in ours. Won't cost you nothing."

Ben was shocked to hear Zeke's request. They had never discussed it, and Ben had never seriously considered spending more time at Mossback. He assumed the place would be part of his past, regardless of what happened. He wished Zeke hadn't sprung this on Watt without discussing it with him.

Ben saw Watt was actually considering Zeke's proposal. Watt looked at Funk who shrugged, as if to indicate the request was not a deal breaker. Watt examined the floor for what seemed like too long a time. Ben, Zeke and Funk looked at each other, not wanting to disturb Watt's meditation. Watt raised his head. He was smiling as if he had heard an amusing joke. He looked calm and relaxed.

"Just a minor adjustment to your little thing," Watt said. "If Ben agrees, then everything's settled, and I'm out of here forever."

"Shoot," Zeke said.

Ben resented Zeke's takeover of the negotiations.

"Ben's into saving things," Watt said. "He thinks he's saved this place from the nasty developer. Just one little item, and Ben can be the new darling of all the tree huggers."

Watt folded his hands together and rested his chin on his forefingers.

"I'm going to let you take care of your sister. It's time you experienced the joy. A bank can be trustee for her money. You're into saving things. How about it? How bad you want to save this pile of logs?"

Ben felt he was entering a dark tunnel. "Where will she live?"

"Up to her guardian, of course," Watt said. "Guardian Ben. Has a nice sound, huh? Cheer up. There's always detox if things get really ugly."

"All right," Ben said. "How bad could it be?"

Watt laughed loudly as he walked over and slapped Ben on the shoulder.

"You're gonna find out, little brother. Goddamn, you're gonna find out real good. Herb, draw up whatever papers will get the job done. I'm going back to Memphis. Eat some Rendezvous ribs and drink a lot of Black Jack."

Watt left the room, cackling all the way up the stairs until he slammed the door to his bedroom.

"I'll contact you once I have the documents prepared," Funk said, as he collected the scattered papers on the floor. "It might be a few weeks to get everything finished. I assume I can reach you here?"

The assumption surprised Ben, unaccustomed to thinking of Mossback as home. What was the address?

Funk finished gathering the papers, put them in his thick document case and snapped it shut. He looked up and thoroughly examined the two men before him. Ben resented the inspection. Funk tilted his head as if listening for some specific sound. He apparently heard what he wanted.

"Could I speak to Ben alone?" he said. The polite tone of voice caught them off guard.

Zeke looked at Ben, shrugged and left the room.

Funk closed the door and turned to Ben. "You think you won some noble victory today," he said. "You could enjoy the grand delusion, but I'm going to tell you the truth. From what your brother's told me, you have a shaky relationship with truth."

Ben disliked the lawyer's smug attitude and uninvited intimacy.

"Watt doesn't want to go to jail, and that's all the truth I need to know," Ben said.

Funk nodded in agreement. "The threat of jail's a big deterrent to a lot of things, if it's real. Your threat's untested by a sharp criminal lawyer, though. Who knows if it would hold up?"

"Watt seemed to think it could."

Funk snorted. "Something greater than your puny threat sidetracked Watt," he said. "You don't know much about the economy or finance, do you?"

"It's not something I've needed to know about," he said.

"Most people feel the same way," Funk said as he walked to the overturned desk and picked up the remains of the telephone receiver. "Over the next few months, people will be paying a lot more attention to the economy. Credit is evaporating, and banks are terrified they'll fail. Watt got a call while you were outside. The bankers pulled the plug on his project. No money, no deal, no nothing. And he has a good track record."

What the lawyer was saying baffled Ben. "You mean what we said, all of it, didn't matter?" Ben said.

"Oh, it mattered, a little," Funk said. "The bankers matter a lot more. We can't fight them. You, maybe we could fight. Not them."

"Why not sell out then? Watt controls the stock."

Funk had an amused look on his face as he answered. "And you and Reggie would stand by passively, without challenge or impediment? Not likely. A sale of this magnitude needs very clear title, which might be difficult with lawsuits and criminal challenges. We don't dismiss you entirely."

He held out his arms expansively.

"All is not lost. The tax deductions alone will be large enough to finance future projects," he said. "And the public relations value will be priceless. It will be national news when Watt announces the preservation of the last old-growth forest in America, thank you very much."

He dropped the remains of the telephone on the floor.

"So there's the truth. You were a ripple. The bankers were the tsunami. It's not what anyone planned so don't congratulate yourself too much."

Funk glanced around the room in one last inspection. Satisfied, he turned for the door.

"As I said before, I'll have all the papers for you to sign in a couple of weeks. By the way, we never had this talk," he said, walking through the doorway.

Funk left through kitchen, the screen door bouncing against its frame. The lawyer's explanation of events swirled in Ben's mind, souring his elation and sense of accomplishment.

Ben was drawn to the framed letter he had noticed earlier from Peter Taylor encouraging Ben's father to pursue his fiction writing. Ben had no idea if his father ever followed the advice. Sometimes telling a story, especially a family story, was only one person's version of the truth, and each observer had a slightly different or even wildly different version. When everyone who had been in the library this day went his separate way, each would carry his own story of what happened.

A knock was followed by Zeke poking his head around the door.

"Everything okay?" he said. "I get worried about lawyers behind closed doors. Bad things can happen."

Zeke's whiskered face cheered Ben, and he hoped that Zeke felt the burden of the little girl's death lifted a little. He remembered her name was Sarah. "Just talking details about Mossback," Ben said.

"We should name something for Sarah. Maybe a stream, something special."

"Yes," was all Zeke could say before it seemed his throat got too tight to speak.

Ben wondered what justice Sarah had received this day, if any. He hoped saving Mossback would suffice. It would have to.

"Maybe I should call Katherine," Ben said, to change the mood. "She'll appreciate the deal enough to pay me some serious attention."

Ben was a little unsettled by the look Zeke gave him, a puzzled expression followed by something resembling pity.

"What's with the look?" Ben said.

"You interested in her?" Zeke said.

"Maybe."

Zeke put his hand gently on Ben's arm. "She's got a pretty serious boy friend, a lawyer, mainly environmental stuff. And he picks a banjo real good. Guess you didn't know. Sorry."

Ben tried not to betray much emotion. After a moment, he looked straight at Zeke.

"An environmental lawyer, huh? What's *he* saved lately?" Ben said, studying the wide floorboards. "Well, I'm gonna ask her if she wants to eat some really wild trout."

He jammed his hands in his pockets and walked across the room to one of the windows. From the corner of his eye he noticed a flash of movement. Suddenly, at the edge of the lawn near the woods, he saw a hawk pounce on the ground with its wings spread wide. It glanced around with a bobbing head. After a moment it flapped its great wings and lifted off the grass. Beneath its body, the talons clutched a snake writhing helplessly as the hawk flew away through the trees.

"Things happen so fast," he said, softly.

"What?" Zeke said. "What's happening?"

Ben shrugged and turned around.

"It's just that one day I'm piss poor, then maybe really rich, then piss poor again. But poor in a whole different way. With a sister to take care of."

Zeke lit his pipe and filled the air with cherry-sweet aroma.

"You took a big gamble to save this place," he said. "We both did. Should make you feel good. Who else could have done what you did?" Ben heard the gurgle of Zeke's pipe as he puffed deeply. "Yeh, you're gonna be some hero around here to a lot of folks," Zeke said. "I better go tell mama we can still live in a place where moss grows on the back of everything. And I better give some more flies to the sheriff. That's why he's in the parking lot."

For a moment the house was quiet after Zeke left. Ben could hear a crow cawing outside, then a squirrel's chatter. Then there was silence again. Looking across the large room full of books and musty furniture, Ben wondered what to do next.

He heard footsteps in the hallway and feared Watt was returning to renege on the grand bargain. Instead, Reggie appeared in the doorway, wearing a blouse and skirt tightly clinched at her waist. She saw Ben and enormous happiness brightened her face as she crossed the room to hug him.

"Oh, Ben, we're going to be so happy here," she said, tightly clinging to him. "Watt told me. You're my hero. Everything's ahead of us. The best stuff. You'll see."

Reggie began coughing, but continued clinging to Ben. When the spasm subsided, she looked at him with tears in her eyes. "A family again. Just think!"

Ben patted her back. Through the window he saw the edge of the great forest that would endure because he returned to Mossback. He pondered what version of the story he would tell Katherine.

"Yeh, the best stuff," he said.

ACKNOWLEDGMENTS

A first novel is seldom the author's work alone. In my case, several fine readers demonstrated a better path for telling my story, and first among many was my wife Paulette Webb, a wise and sensitive editor. I am also enormously grateful to Katie Baer, S. W. "Trip" Farnsworth III, Stuart Ferguson, Paul Schwartz and Michael Paul for pointing out their versions of a better path. Tom Rash and Marni Graff were invaluable with their close edits that saved me untold embarrassment. I deeply appreciate Maureen LaVake's and Frank and Patti Phelps's constant encouragement. Finally, thanks to all my fellow writers at Wildacres Writers Workshop for their helpful comments about early versions of this story, and, in particular, to Ron Rash, a poet, novelist and teacher who inspires a passion for storytelling.

Photo by Paulette Webb

Michael Cavender is a North Carolina writer who directed the Highlands-Cashiers Land Trust, North Carolina's
oldest land conservation trust. He was also a newspaper
reporter and fly-fishing guide on the rivers and streams
of the southern Blue Ridge Mountains. A graduate of
the University of Tennessee, he lives near Chapel Hill,
North Carolina, where he is working on his next novel.

Made in the USA
Middletown, DE
09 February 2024

49407380R00196